Palma Christi

PALMA CHRISTI

A La Llorona Files
Supernatural Crime Novel

Elizabeth Walker McIlhaney

SUNSTONE
PRESS

SANTA FE

Sunstone books may be purchased for educational, business, or sales promotional use.
For information please write: Special Markets Department, Sunstone Press,
P.O. Box 2321, Santa Fe, New Mexico 87504-2321.

Body typeface › Californian FB
Printed on acid-free paper
∞
eBook 978-1-61139-562-4

Library of Congress Cataloging-in-Publication Data

Names: McIlhaney, Elizabeth Walker, 1951- author.
Title: Palma Christi : a La Llorona files supernatural crime novel / by
   Elizabeth Walker McIlhaney.
Description: Santa Fe, New Mexico : Sunstone Press, [2018] |
Identifiers: LCCN 2018037047 (print) | LCCN 2018042825 (ebook) | ISBN
   9781611395624 | ISBN 9781632932389 (softcover : alk. paper)
Subjects: | GSAFD: Suspense fiction.
Classification: LCC PS3613.C53365 (ebook) | LCC PS3613.C53365 P35 2018
   (print) | DDC 813/.6--dc23
LC record available at https://lccn.loc.gov/2018037047

WWW.SUNSTONEPRESS.COM
SUNSTONE PRESS / POST OFFICE BOX 2321 / SANTA FE, NM 87504-2321 /USA
(505) 988-4418 / ORDERS ONLY (800) 243-5644 / FAX (505) 988-1025

Dedication

TO SAM CARL McILHANEY, who introduced this "baby sister" to Elvis, Sherlock Holmes, Ibsen and Bob Wills, then took me to London, Versailles, Toledo and Sunday dinner in Scotland, while providing me with a special lens for viewing our family's beloved New Mexico as it nestles within the entire history of the Western World, always reminding me that Texas, with its frogs, arrowheads and catfish, refuses to let go of us completely.

Special thanks to GARY MICHAEL (MIKE) CORDOVA of Albuquerque, a direct descendent of a soldier who came to New Mexico with Spanish Conquistador Juan de Onate y Salazar, for his help with the Spanish, Indian, Arabic, Latin and English, and to JERRY BROWN JR. of Houston, Texas, and GARY for their feedback on the original manuscript.

PROLOGUE

FATHER MARQUEZ GAZED DOWN ON THE FROSTY JEMEZ RIVER, watching the gentle October snow that was early this year.

He was feeling *her* tonight. Would she never leave him alone? He was old now, in his eighth decade. Why wouldn't she just leave him alone, let him gently fade away into death, releasing her hold on him?

The moon was full tonight, but no one would know it, not with the snowy cloud cover. The first flakes always deceived, just like *she* did...but did she? After all these years, decades even, surely he knew the truth about her?

Sadly, he had to admit, no, not even now. Fooling him into believing she was gone for good, only to return once he believed the absence was permanent. Fooled once, fooled twice...he recalled the U.S. president who stumbled over that old adage in a speech, a better stand-up comic than a president. She had fooled this old priest countless times, and he had no excuse, no adage. He wasn't a president nor a comic, only a priest who had suffered an entire lifetime at the hands of a ghost witch, thus making him a crazy priest.

He shivered as he felt her vibe roaring through the canyon like the wind, but silent: a whistling in the distance that wasn't the wind. No breeze on the skin. Not the wind, not a whistle, but the moaning, groaning, forlorn grieving, centuries-old-wailing that Hispanic Catholics recognized anywhere in the world, he eventually had learned. As a boy, he thought she belonged only to New Mexicans. And he still wasn't sure he was wrong about that, despite the claims by so many in other countries to have known her first.

His beloved New Mexico, the mysterious and magical land loved and nurtured by so many Indian tribes for centuries by the time Spanish explorers arrived by accident in 1527, after their ship ended up at what became Galveston, Texas, instead of on the Florida coast as planned. Did she come with them or was she already here, waiting for them, knowing they would see her, hear her? Fear her.

The raven-haired apparition, La Llorona.

Two in the morning, the moon not much more than a sliver, providing little light. It was time.

Getting it there was going to be a challenge, but it would be done. Like it had been last time, silently, without detection. Safely for all.

Dragging it up the stairs required great strength, as did lifting it into the trunk.

The drive didn't take long. A week night, the streets were quiet, the darkness from the moon's invisibility as well as a cloud cover hinting at snow, protective.

The big old car was parked easily next to the bridge, lights cut before it slowed. The old gray hooded jacket justified by the chill in the air. Passersby from any distance would assume just another guy in a hoodie, stepping out of his car to enjoy the river area at night. Or something more sinister. No one would dare linger nor come close to find out.

But at the moment, no passersby could be seen nor heard. Silence all around. No cars nearby, no voices, no TVs or radios from nearby homes, no cell phone sounds, no security cameras, no public lighting—nothing to distract nor interfere. Nor observe. The lifeless form thus lifted from the trunk, dragged to the edge and pushed from the bridge to the stagnant pond below.

The shallow waters were beginning to calm as the car drove into the night before its lights appeared in the distance.

1

MRS. SHAW WAS CLOSING HER LIVING ROOM CURTAINS WHEN she saw him. Switching off the lamp, drapes fully drawn, she carefully peeked through the folds to watch. A tall person was wandering through the shrubs in the front yard across the street.

That's silly, she whispered to herself, censoring her own thoughts. People don't *wander* through shrubs.

The tall figure, outlined in the dusty autumn twilight, seemed to be dressed all in black, but maybe her eyes were playing tricks on her in the shadows. She watched as he stopped, standing at the front door as though waiting for someone to open the door for him. But only for a moment. Then he moved so quickly, he was across the driveway, around the corner of the garage and disappearing behind the back of the house in what seemed like an instant.

Only then did she realize there were no lights at the Cervantes home. Strange on a week night, when she knew both Ester and Rudy had to work the next day, and usually at this hour in their carefully organized household, they were getting the kids ready for bed. A strict and devout Catholic couple, they didn't go out much at night except to the occasional funeral rosary when one of their family members or friends died. But she knew they hadn't come home, since her living room during the day, with curtains open, allowed her to see all the comings and goings of the family. If she didn't see them, she heard them from almost every room of her house, not because the Cervantes themselves were so noisy, but because the many relatives who visited regularly from all over northern and central New Mexico were. Recently a niece had married a man from Mexico, so relatives from that country showed up regularly now, too. It was hard not to hear the noisy extended family, which is why she often had considered moving from this home since her husband died two years ago. But her husband's presence was so imbedded in their home, she couldn't bring herself to move. Not yet anyway.

So why were there no lights, and even more strangely for that family, no signs of noise? She realized her curiosity was turning into fear. That strange person she had seen in front of the house was not a member of the family, he was too tall. And too skulking. And why does someone appear to be *wandering* through shrubbery so thick it is impassable to all but the tiniest of rodents?

Abruptly she realized the person must have climbed out of the house through the window behind the shrubs where she first saw him—that was why he appeared to be moving over the shrubs. He was sliding out the window and over the shrubs to the ground. Concentrating on closing her drapes, she barely noticed him at first, which is why he seemed to be almost floating over the shrubs when she did focus on him, like a big black ghost. Now she realized he wasn't floating at all, just getting out of a window and on the ground as fast as he could.

She grabbed the phone and called 911.

"Sorry, ma'am, we didn't find anything. No one is home, and nothing seems out of place. All the doors and windows are locked, so we can't go in without a search warrant or until someone comes home. Maybe the guy was trying to break in, and something scared him away." Manny Rodriguez sounded like he said this same thing to people every night. He probably did, given the burglary rate these days, Mrs. Shaw thought to herself.

"Thank you officer, I appreciate the fast response, my friends tell me that is rare." She hadn't shared her perceptions of the floating ghost on top of the shrubs, knowing it would cause her story to be less credible to the police.

Rodriguez smiled wryly at her words that were both damning and flattering. "You say he was tall and dressed all in black?"

"Well, it was getting dark, so it was hard to be sure, but it seemed to be a man dressed in a long cloak or cape. But what was strange is I thought I saw something like a veil or bandana, also black, floating in front of his face. I guess it could have been long hair, but it seemed to cover the entire face. That could have been shadows, as I only got a fleeting glimpse before he disappeared around the side of the garage."

"And you are sure it was a man? Not a woman? We don't see many men in capes or cloaks these days, that sort of went out with the Zorro era," Rodriguez said, maintaining a respectfully straight face as he spoke. "These days only women wearing long dresses would fit that description, although when committing burglaries, even that would be a questionable choice of clothing. You are sure it wasn't a long dress?"

Taking his words as seriously as he seemed to be, Mrs. Shaw gasped, then seeming to ponder for a moment what he was implying, said, "You know, I guess it could have been a woman. I hadn't thought of that, since he—she—was so tall. And you don't think of women jumping out of windows or breaking into houses, but these days I understand it isn't so unusual. Yes, I guess it could have been a long dress, I just wasn't thinking of that, assumed I was watching a man. As my late husband would have said, 'That's what you get for assuming.'"

"Well, thank you, Mrs. Shaw. I guess that is about all we can do for now. You say it isn't normal for the house to be empty on a night like this?"

"No officer, not at all. I have watched this family's habits for many years now and I know them well. This is most unusual. If the parents go to a funeral rosary, they get someone to stay with little Johnny. Often that is me, or relatives who don't feel the need to attend the rosary. They seem to be related to half of Santa Fe," she laughed. "All the kids rarely are gone at night, ever. We'd probably have a safer city if most people raised their children the way the Cervantes do, with family elders hovering over them in clusters more often than not."

"Here's my card and on the back, I have written my cell phone number. Randy Johnson, my partner here, and I, are on duty until tomorrow morning, so call us if you see anyone come home, would you?"

Johnson smiled and nodded politely to her at the mention of his name. He had remained leaning on the car, within earshot, keeping an eye on their surroundings.

"Certainly, officer. I doubt I will be able to go to sleep until someone does, so I surely will call," she said as the officers turned to leave. Driving slowly down the dark street, they carefully scanned the quiet middle class neighborhood in this town where people have lived longer, continuously, than in any other in the United States, the town the Spanish named La Villa Real de la Santa Fe de San Francisco de Asis.

"Estos pendejos curas," Santa Fe Police Captain Joseph Anaya yelled as he threw down the morning newspaper, too angry to read anymore. "Another priest arrested on charges of molestation thirty years ago. This time in Belen. When is this going to be finished once and for all, me entiendes?"

"Well, let's hope all these old charges coming to light will mean the current priests will learn to keep their noses clean, or should I say their robes?" Johnson sneered as he sipped his morning coffee, recovering from what had been a long, but relatively uneventful night patrolling the streets of the old city, the only event of note a possible attempted break-in by either a man in a long cape playing Zorro, or a very tall woman in a long dress. Maybe it was a woman playing Zorro. Anaya's angry outburst now had him wondering if it was a priest in his robes. What a thought. Did priests commit burglaries as well as molest kids in this state? His evangelical Protestant Oklahoma roots hadn't prepared him for being a cop in this old Southwestern city, but he was enjoying his unexpected education.

"I can't stand for it to go on any longer like this," Anaya said, hands over his face, elbows on his desk. He looked up, directing his weary brown eyes with the wayward salt and pepper eyebrows to Johnson's bright blue ones. "You aren't from around here, you don't know what it's like for those of us whose ancestors helped found this place, to see what was once the most revered institution in the state, our Catholic Church, smeared like this—and we're into the third decade of this caca. In the 1990s, when the media reports began in our state, we figured it would be a few bad priests and that would be the end of it. Little did we know it was the start of a pinche world-wide expose' that would reveal a bunch of mala leches hiding out in the Church for only God knows how long. Forgive me, Lord, no puns intended," he laughed wryly, looking reverently for a moment at the ceiling and crossing himself.

"The scandal here in tiny Santa Fe exposed almost two dozen. In 1680, when the Pueblo Indians revolted against the Spaniards, kicking them out of here, they killed just about as many priests. Maybe priestly perversions led to that revolt.

"We had about one in three bad priests at the height of our scandal here 20 years ago, but now we are an example of how to stop the Church's disease, thanks to standards set by Archbishop Michael Sheehan, who was brought in after the archbishop before him had to resign for having sex with several under-age women. Sheehan stepped up to a horrendously difficult challenge and dealt with it. He didn't try to deny nor hide the truth. And he taught his staff how to hire good men for the priesthood, not perverts.

"Santa Fe's full name translated into English, Johnson, is The Royal City of the Holy Faith of Saint Francis of Assisi. The same saint whose name our Pope Francis chose. Maybe that is a good omen for our city and its future. I hope so. He is the first pope to take the name of the blessed saint. Maybe it is no coincidence that he was named pope after our city was past the worst of its scandals, proving the Church can move out of denial and lies, can get rid of predators, and not recruit more. If Santa Fe can do it, as bad as our situation was, before most of the rest of the world even realized the Church had a problem, then any city can. Maybe it was God's way of rewarding Santa Fe, to appoint a pope who after all these centuries of popes, finally chose our patron saint's name."

"What all was he saying in there?" Johnson asked his partner once they had escaped Anaya's lengthy outburst."What is 'pin da ho's'? And what did he mean about a cure? What's caw caw?"

Rodriguez laughed out loud. "In plain Oklahoma English? He said those bad priests are assholes. And no, he didn't call them whores. He said that instead of being caring, healing priests, they are worthless good-for-nothings. And caca is Spanish slang for shit."

"Got it," Johnson lied, nodding and feeling linguistically challenged at the moment.

"Romero. Take the call holding on three," Anaya yelled from inside his office. "It's the Santa Fe River drowning."

"Detective Connie Romero here," she said, putting down the coffee she had hoped to finish before the frenzy of the morning shifts began. It was stale anyway. She'd been up for hours, down at the river where the little boy, Anthony Armijo, had been found, working with the forensics team. She already was exhausted, due to the emotional stress of a dead child whom no one believed drowned in that river. Only the autopsy would tell them for sure, but no one was expecting any water in the lungs in the report. The boy died, or was killed, then placed there. Now they just had to prove it. That could take years. Santa Fe didn't have homicides of this nature, but no one was expecting a fast closure to this case. It was her first child's death as a homicide detective, assuming it was a homicide. How could it not be, given the circumstances?

"Hola, this is Mary Tafoya. I'm calling about the drowning in the news this morning, sabes, el nino, that little boy?"

"Si," she said gently, hearing the timidity in the woman's voice and not wanting to scare her away. "Can you help us? Did you see something?"

"No, no, I didn't, pero they found my son in almost that same place—hizo 30 anos, and they never found the killer?" She spoke with the locals' blend of Spanish and English, thus ending most of her sentences with question marks. "The police said he didn't drown, that he was murdered? Was that pobrito murdered this time?"

"We don't have an official statement from the coroner yet, but we are treating it as foul play so far. How do you know the location is similar?"

"Because I went there, it was easy to find, sabes, you know, where it was roped off? The DeFouri bridge at Alameda, with the only pool in the river anywhere near after the rains, she said, still speaking softly, as though she were permanently melancholy. "How could anyone do this so close to the Santuario de Guadalupe? It's even the oldest one in the United States, but the Blessed Virgin could not protect us from such an evil force."

There probably is no connection, given the time frame—three decades, but as the New Agers around here say, there are no coincidences, Connie thought to herself. "We need to look into this, Mrs. Tafoya. What was your son's name and when was he found exactly?"

"Danny Tafoya. Daniel Secundino Tafoya. Tenia solo eight years," she said as she choked up.

"Give me your phone number and address, Mrs. Tafoya, and I promise we will follow up on this. Nineteen eighty-seven?"

She gave an address in the part of town known as The Barrio, with houses now worth in the millions for those who chose to sell. Many of the old Spanish families refused, choosing to live simply among their wealthy neighbors, usually Anglos who moved there from other states, even other countries.

Connie headed to Anaya's office, coffee cup in hand, to give him the info on the cold case. She knew he already was yelling this morning. Wait 'til he heard what she had to tell him. Obviously he was going to have a bad day, given how it was starting. They all were.

It was nine in the morning, Thursday, and Rodriguez was finally on his way home to get some sleep when his cell phone rang. "Rodriguez," he barked, not recognizing the caller ID number.

"This is Mrs. Shaw, and I thought you should know that no one returned to the Cervantes house last night. A few moments ago, Mr. Cervantes returned home with the two girls. But his wife and their son aren't with them. Should I go tell him what I saw last night?"

"No," Rodriguez told her, realizing from her worried tone that she probably stayed up all night just to watch their house. "You try to get some sleep. I'll go tell him myself, I'm not far from there now."

He swung onto Siringo Road and headed west, arriving at the Cervantes house in less than five minutes. He was stepping out of his car when a man came out the front door, staring at him oddly, obviously wondering why he was there.

"Mr. Cervantes? I'm Officer Manny Rodriguez. Are you aware that someone might have tried to break into your home last night, sir?"

A look of shock and dismay appeared on the deeply lined face, old beyond its years from too many decades in the bright New Mexico sunshine. "No, sir, I was not. How do you know this?"

Rodriguez gave him the short version, and invited himself in to check the house. Cervantes explained the family had been at the hospital with their son, who was suffering from food poisoning, apparently. His wife still was there. The girls had been at their grandmother's house all night, he explained to the officer. The boy was okay, but it had been a tough night for the whole family.

They walked through the tidy home, and everything appeared in order to both men. They went outside and walked around the entire house, looking for footprints and other signs of unwanted visitors. Other than some twigs that might have been broken when the Zorro wanna-be may have tried to get close to the window of the son's room—the only window in the front of the house except for the picture windows in the living room, there was very little to be found. And birds or the wind could just as easily have broken the twigs. There were no footprints or even deep impressions in the grass in the front, nor on the side where he apparently went over the back fence into an alley. The driveway was extremely clean concrete, leaving no clues. The house and yard were immaculate, making it easy to detect footprints and other signs of intrusion, but there were none to be found.

"Do you have any reason to suspect someone of wanting to break into your home, Mr. Cervantes?"

"En ninguna manera. Doesn't this sort of thing happen a lot in Santa Fe these days? So it wouldn't be so strange, would it, since we all were gone?

"No, you're right, it isn't strange, given what is happening regularly now all over town, except for one thing—it happened at dusk. It wasn't even completely dark yet," Rodriguez explained. "That is why your neighbor, Mrs. Shaw, was able to get a good look at him, or her, since we aren't sure it was a man. She described a Zorro costume, but it could have been a woman in a long dress, although either one seems unlikely. Anyone who breaks into a house with intent to steal something, anything for that matter, doesn't do so at dusk, and they don't dress like Zorro. They don't wear long dresses either. They do it in the middle of the night or very carefully in broad daylight, but never in the front yard. This is not a normal scenario, which is why it is puzzling to us. Tell me, sir, how old are your children?"

"My girls are eleven and thirteen, and my boy is eight. Why?"

"No reason, just trying to cover all the bases. I don't mean to worry you. Where do you work?"

"I'm in charge of the stables and riding programs at the Double Z Resort outside Tesuque. And my wife works at the Santa Fe National Bank on the Plaza."

Rodriguez had pulled out a notepad and was jotting down notes. "What are your phone numbers?"

Cervantes rattled off the numbers for his wife and him. "I will thank Mrs. Shaw, es muy simpatica," he said, obviously perplexed over everything he had learned since the cop car pulled into his driveway. "Thank you sir, and if we notice anything strange, should we call you or the station, or just dial nine-one-one?"

"Always dial that number immediately if you notice anything strange," Rodriguez said, handing Cervantes his card. "My cell phone number is written on the back. Feel free to also call me. This case interests me—the Zorro description, but long hair, or a veil or scarf, instead of a mask. The time, and the fact you guys rarely are gone—Mrs. Shaw told us that. It is as though the person knew all of you were gone, and wouldn't return while he was checking out the house, perhaps trying to break in. My shift is normally ten at night to eight in the morning, but it was longer last night as I was covering for someone who was sick. That's why my partner and I got the call in the first place, and why I am just now getting off work. But call me during the day if anything strange happens. Don't worry about waking me up, everybody else does already," he said with a dry laugh.

"'ueno, Officer," Cervantes said, turning to go inside. "I must get my girls to school, they are late."

Refilled coffee cup in hand, Connie headed downstairs to the basement where the old case files were kept. That long ago, it wouldn't be on the computer. She went to the unsolved homicides for 1987. Sure enough, there it was, in early December. Danny Tafoya, apparently killed somewhere else, moved to the river and placed in the water to make it appear he drowned. There was a lot of water in the river then, and the pool where he was found was deeper than the river in general, so it was easy to make the death appear to be a drowning. The killer either was stupid and had hoped the Santa Fe police department was, and wouldn't order an autopsy, or he was arrogant. Probably both.

She kept reading. The detective in charge of the case retired years ago, moving back to his native village of Mora in northern New Mexico. With several suspects, and no arrests, the case still was open, although the file obviously had been collecting dust all these years. The boys were found within a few feet of each other, she realized, and were the same age. She didn't need instinct, just common cop sense, to know she needed to proceed as though the cases were related. It would be easy to drive up there and talk to him. She always enjoyed the drive to Las Vegas, and the beauty of the Mora Valley beyond it was stunning.

She made the call to Mora.

"Detective Justino Hernandez? This is Detective Connie Romero in Santa Fe. How is retirement treating you?" she asked with a smile.

"Si, si," Hernandez laughed, "retirement is great. What do you need? I know it's something, or you wouldn't be calling an old guy like me, all the way up here in Mora," he said, still laughing. New Mexico's Hispanic men rarely began a conversation without humor, and the older they were, the stronger that trait. They liked to flirt too.

"Andale," Romero laughed back at him. "I hear you. I need you to help me with a cold case you had about thirty years ago. Remember that little boy, Danny Tafoya, found drowned in the Santa Fe River east of the Santuario? Except he wasn't drowned, he was murdered and his body moved there?"

"Claro, true that, how could I forget? That poor little boy. And his mother. That poor lady, I thought she was going to kill herself. It was her only son. She already had lost her husband and an older son in a car wreck. She couldn't understand why God would allow her remaining son to be taken from her like that. But neither could I. Ijo, it was sad. We worked hard together, trying to piece together what might have happened, which seemed to make her feel better. But we never could figure out who did it, not well enough to make an arrest. The nun at the funeral home spent hours with her, counseling and comforting her. Without that nun, I think that woman would have gone crazy. She used to cry and moan that La Llorona took her kids. She never blamed the ghost witch for taking her husband, just her kids. I don't think she missed him much. Her kids were her whole life.

"I never told anyone this, it seemed too impossible at the time, but I thought then a priest might have done it. And now, with all the bad priests they've found here in New Mexico since then, I am even more convinced a priest did it, one in particular. But even to have looked in that direction then probably would have gotten me fired, or at least removed from the case, so I never talked about it."

The more the old man told her, the more certain Romero was that she needed to see him in person. He would remember more than he would in this phone call. And he liked to talk, useful under the circumstances. Give him some time to remember things between now and when she got there. "I want to come see you. I need to clear it with Anaya. How about tomorrow afternoon?"

"'ueno, that would be good. I have much to tell you that never got written down in the reports. Call me on those cell phones you guys use now, when you are just outside Mora, and I'll tell you how to get to my house. It's easy to find. Try to get here a little after noon, and we'll have a bowl of green chile stew for lunch. My wife and I eat it every day, keeps us young."

Connie immediately made another call. "Dolly, hi, how are you?"

"Connie. Got something for us again?"

"Yes I do. Two in one this time, a new case and a really cold one. Can you drive to Mora with me tomorrow?"

"I think so. Let me make a couple of calls and get back with you in a few minutes."

Delilah Iola "Dolly" McIntyre and Connie had worked on several cases over the years that resulted in a strong working relationship as well as what they both considered a special friendship. The nature of the cases they worked had served to help them forge the strong bonds personally and professionally.

Like Connie, Dolly was from an old New Mexico family, but the similarities stopped there. Connie's had been in New Mexico since the late sixteenth century, Dolly's since the late nineteenth century, giving Connie a three hundred-year head start in the local cultural heritage department.

Dolly was on a special task force coordinated through the state attorney general's office that brought special skills and experience to unusual cases throughout the state. It started out as a secret group in the 1950s, but over the decades, such secrets and the requisite off-the-books funding necessary to keep them alive, became blazing media fodder with headlines that were headaches for the Old Guard that ran the state for the first half of the 20th century. Eventually, once the hoopla had died down and faded in most people's short media-driven memories, a New Mexico governor and Dolly's father had set up a trust to fund the task force, using their own money in the form of political donations to the Democratic party to fund it into perpetuity, something no one could possibly get away with today. But no one had tried to dismantle it either, the fund had become too essential in solving crimes. No politician would dare touch it, especially since taxpayer money wasn't involved, and now it was set up as a non-profit foundation. Although members of the task force had to be approved by each governor, the attorney general was the one who chose them, enabling it to be bi-partisan into perpetuity, despite its funding origins. The legally foolproof arrangement kept it out of the total control of governors, away from the influence of legislators, and under the permanent supervision of the attorney general's office.

Contrary to conventional wisdom, Dolly wasn't on the task force because of family ties. The attorney general who invited her to join was the son of the governor who had set up the non-profit arrangement with her father all those years ago. Everyone assumed he still was repaying political favors to her family for the support her father and oldest brother had given his father when he was a state legislator, speaker of the state house, and eventually, governor for several terms spanning three decades. President Bill Clinton even spoke at his funeral in a tiny town east of Albuquerque—not by invitation from anyone, but because he knew and loved the old governor when they were both governors, and wanted to share his memories with vivid stories at the funeral service, which he did eloquently as usual.

But any political favors owed family to family had been repaid long ago. Dolly was chosen officially because of her background as a print journalist. Years ago, she had worked closely as a reporter with the New Mexico Foundation for Open Government, which brought her to the attention of the AG at that time, now a U.S. senator. The reputation she forged then as a reporter gave the current AG the formal reasons he needed to appoint her, but he chose her specifically because of the combination of those skills combined with other, lesser known ones she possessed.

Dolly's and the current AG's families were two of the oldest Southern Baptist families in the state, getting their start in ranching, farming and other business endeavors when the state was a fledgling territory, having been part of Mexico until 1847. It didn't become a state until 1912, her mother having been born in the Four Corners area in 1910. Dolly joked that if their families had been Hindu, her younger sister and the AG would have been the bride and groom in an arranged marriage, given they were the same age.

One day not long after he took office as the new AG, his office called her to set up an appointment with him, saying only that he wanted to meet with her to "discuss some things." She had no idea why he would want to see her. She assumed it had something to do with her work with the former AG-now-senator, or her many calls years ago to the AG's non-profit division when she was trying to expose some non-profits in northern New Mexico that were operating outside the law, at which time she learned the laws were good but enforcement was nil due to funding and staffing deficits.

So when he sat down with her in his office almost a decade ago and said he had been told by people whose opinions he trusted of her psychic abilities, her "intuitive gifts," to be specific, she was dumbfounded. Years later she learned that one of his sources had been a long-time member of the Sikh community near Espanola, a PhD professor who had been one of Dolly's teachers when she took a few classes in Dr. Elisabeth Kubler-Ross's program at a northern New Mexico community college in the early 1990s, when the famed Swiss psychiatrist still taught classes in the program. Later in her life, illness prevented that, causing Dolly to feel fortunate she attended when she did.

An adult convert to the Sikh spiritual path, the middle-aged Anglo professor, a petite, fragile and gentle American-born woman from Indiana, who always wore the simple, all-white Sikh fashions, complete with white turban, used textbooks written by Harvard professors to get her students to listen to their intuition while teaching them about the mind-body connection. Dolly had loved her class.

"Connie, hi, I can do it. When do we leave?"

"Meet me here at the station at nine. We are meeting with a retired detective and he said his wife will have green chile stew ready for us if we get there in time for lunch. I will give you all the details on the way. I'll drive an unmarked, unless you'd prefer to drive us over those Mora roads. You decide.

"'ueno." Dolly smiled as she used the Spanish word she had heard her father, and so many people since, use with just about every phone call they made or took, for as far back as she could remember, a generic New Mexico greeting for ending conversations. She remembered asking him why he ended his phone conversations with "wano?"

He explained that it meant *good* in Spanish, spelling it for her and explaining the *b* at the beginning is silent, which is why it sounds like everyone is saying wano as though they had a Texas drawl. He also explained that even though it meant *good*, that in actual day-to-day conversations, it was a catch-all greeting meaning things are well, I am well, it is all good. So by using it instead of hello and good-bye, it also communicated a positive response at the beginning or end of conversations, enhancing camaraderie. New Mexico Anglos probably used it more than any other Spanish word in the local Spanglish vernacular, which frequently combined English and Spanish. New Mexico was the only one of the 50 states to have two official languages, and until after World War II, most of the official business in the state was done in Spanish, not English. Most native New Mexicans had Spanish, English and Native American terms in their vocabulary, whether or not they realized it.

She hadn't been to Mora in a long time. The Mora Valley possibly was one of the most beautiful in the state, certainly some people felt that way about it. But its history was a long and sometimes violent one. What kind of homicide case would require an SFPD detective and her to have to go there?

She would do the driving. She knew Connie would be relieved.

2

CONNIE CLIMBED INTO THE PASSENGER SEAT OF DOLLY'S CREAM-colored Escalade, having conceded driving rights when Dolly reminded her of the recent rain and snow storms in the Mora area that would have left the notorious rutted roads more difficult to navigate than ever.

"At least you didn't bring that ancient Toyota." Connie teased. Dolly had a noisy 1987 Toyota Tercel wagon that she still drove regularly in the Albuquerque metro area. With occasional exceptions, she only used the quiet Escalade for work assignments that took her out of the metroplex.

A recent TV hit series filmed in New Mexico resurrected the old Toyota's celebrity status when one of the main characters, a criminal, drove an almost identical version of the old car. For years it could be seen nearly everywhere in the state, especially in the Santa Fe and Los Alamos areas, where it took on a cult-car status. When her Toyota was only a few years old, an auto dealer in Albuquerque told her if she put an ad in the newspaper, it would sell the next morning by eight, adding a story about an owner in Las Cruces who was driving one with 600,000 miles on it. Some twenty-five years after that conversation, Dolly's barely had 200,000 miles and ran great.

"You know that's my dog car, and they couldn't come today. Police business is too risky for them, plus this behemoth will handle the muddy Mora roads and driveways well," Dolly quipped.

"And how *are* your babies?"

"Lovely of course," Dolly laughed. She had two Chow Chow dogs she had raised from earliest puppy-hood, a miniature horse and three cats. The dogs, Alexander and Cleopatra, Alex and Cleo for short, lived mostly in the house, and Aristophanes The Horse, Ari for short, mostly on the back sun porch when all three weren't in the fenced yard, or in the house with her. The cats, Harold, Hugo and Lolita, used their own special door, coming and going as they pleased.

"And how are *your* babies?"

Laughing, Connie said, "Fine, fine. Now that they think they are grown, they treat me like I'm their baby. As long as I go along with that, we are great. As to your question, no drama right now. That's the good news. Hopefully there won't be any bad news any time soon."

Connie and Dolly had met a couple of decades earlier, when Dolly was running a support and discussion group at a local funeral home for people who felt they had experienced visitations or signs of afterlife from people who had died, or who had had their own near-death experiences. Dolly had been a recent graduate of the Elisabeth Kubler-Ross program that had been offered in the 1980s and early 1990s at the community college in El Rito, near Abiqiui, and Connie had been a novice member of the Santa Fe police force and a single mother who needed to process some of her supernatural experiences relating to the death of her beloved grandmother.

After her beloved grandparent passed, Connie had a series of experiences that upset and confused her until joining Dolly's little group. There she learned to recognize the messages her grandmother was sending her from the Other Side for what they were, communications meant to bring comfort, not fear nor worry. And she learned her experiences were quite normal, experienced by many the world over, and probably by many more who didn't recognize them for what they were. A grief counselor at another funeral home in Santa Fe with whom Dolly had attended the Elisabeth Kubler-Ross program was so well versed in these things, she knew to prepare her clients for the communications ahead of time. She told Dolly she received many kinds of thanks over the years by doing this, and heard many amazing stories. But ironically, the details were quite consistently similar for just about everyone. Once Connie began reading the books that documented experiences similar and some even identical to her own, her entire philosophy of life changed radically, she later told Dolly. "And for the better," she emphasized.

The experiences with her grandmother after death, and the stories others shared of their loved ones who had died and continued to communicate with them gave her a faith she never had been able to acquire when a young and devout Catholic. Her grandmother did more for her faith than the Church ever had, she told Dolly. Now she was able to believe that Jesus really did come back and show himself to his disciples after his supposed death. She still felt he probably did die, at least for a while, but she also could believe now that he didn't stay dead, and that he could have the power to let his followers know that. Until her own experiences with her dear abuelita, she never could believe he lived after dying on the cross, no matter what the priests and nuns told her. Her Catholic faith stopped at the Cross, her new-found faith was infinite because she was convinced her grandmother was alive, just not in her body here on earth. Whether she had the same body or not was irrelevant, Connie told Dolly. "Once you feel the spirit, the presence, of a loved one who has died, you *know* they live even if you don't know where."

About fifteen years apart in age, the two women made a deep connection with each other almost immediately, continuing the friendship outside the group when a corporate take-over of the funeral home led to Dolly leaving the company.

Much had happened in their lives since they met, both personally and professionally. By the time Dolly got her appointment from the AG, Connie had become the city's primary homicide detective, a first for a woman. Divorced from a husband whom she had married while still in high school, in tandem with her first pregnancy, Connie had spent most of her adult life getting an education, moving up the career ladder of the police force, and coming out as a lesbian, more or less in that order.

When she and Dolly met, Connie wasn't out yet, and it was Dolly's recognition and awareness, she told Dolly later, that helped her get the courage to finally come out. But her timing was due to the death of her grandmother, whom she knew wouldn't have understood, and who had helped make it possible for her to get her education and choose the career she did, by being her live-in nanny for Connie's three children. Connie could not have done any of it without her abuelita. In return, she never would have made her suffer by coming out before her death. Connie had seen no need to force new values on her devout conservative Catholic abuelita that late in her long life.

Dolly had spent her life trying to stand up for human rights of all kinds, and Connie's situation was no exception. When Connie finally revealed to Dolly that she had a woman lover, Dolly wasn't even surprised, said she had thought that might be the case for quite a while. Connie had kept the relationship a secret from everyone, including her children, until her grandmother passed. Her children were teenagers, two of them already in college, by the time she told them.

They barely blinked, Connie told Dolly later. "Whatever, Mom, you're cool, no matter what you do, 'cause you're a cop. Who cares who you sleep with? We just want you to be happy and not mourn so much for Nana, she wouldn't have wanted that."

"Does this mean I've raised great kids?" Connie asked Dolly, who replied, "of course" reflexively. Connie did have great kids. The cop and the old grandma had done a great job with those three, no one would argue otherwise.

Their father hadn't been involved except to pay the legally required child support, which fortunately he had done, and his absence probably had been more of a blessing to the family than a loss. He lived in another part of the state and left them alone. He didn't know about Connie coming out, as far as anyone knew, not that it mattered, Connie told Dolly.

As the women sped up the highway to Las Vegas, they caught up on all the news, personal and professional. Dolly didn't have one special man in her life at the time, although there actually were several important ones, always making her personal life complicated. But having no one special wasn't a normal state for her, and it never lasted long when it did happen. As Connie said, "I am holding my breath, since I will be able to breathe again so quickly, based on your record. You never can keep the men away for long, nor can you stay away from them for long. You think holing up down in Albuquerque's South Valley in that miniature casita alongside the Rio Grande with two big dogs, a tiny horse and some cats will hide you from the male of the species? You? I think not. I know not," she laughed. "And don't try to tell me it is because you are a woman of a certain age either."

"Isn't miniature casita redundant use of two languages? Just like adding the word, river, to Rio Grande is?"

"I was attempting to avoid the word hovel," Connie laughed. They'd had this conversation before. Connie was a native Spanish speaker, which meant she was fluent in New Mexico's homegrown version of Spanish, which was unlike any other in the world, but she had no formal Spanish education. Dolly was raised around people, including her father and some of his employees, who spoke Spanish in various amounts, and she also studied the language in school a bit. Yet no linguist by nature, she was not even close to fluent.

"You know I prefer historic adobe," Dolly said, as Connie snorted. "My family works hard for generations to avoid living in a place like that, and here you choose it, when you could live anywhere you want."

"You don't have to live with me, just ride in my car, so at least enjoy it, and let's see what this old geezer cop has to tell us," Dolly laughed. "Catch me up on the case so far."

"Well, you've seen the news stories, right?" Dolly nodded. Connie knew the former journalist would have done her research already. "The ones in both the Santa Fe and Albuquerque papers have been accurate, as much as we told them. A few details were kept back, to help us identify the killer hopefully, and screen out the usual crank calls and other weirdos who will want to confess, but that isn't important to you and me right now. I've talked to the boy's parents, and forensics has been all over the crime scene of course. You and I are going to interview a retired detective who handled a case just too similar to this one about three decades ago. I feel we need to hear what he has to tell us in order to have a foundation perhaps for what just happened. I think it important we start with him rather than finish with him. He may save us some time by pointing us in directions we might not have known to look. After we talk to him, I hope we have a better idea of what your role needs to be. Both were altar boys, so my team and I have to interview all of the altar servers and their parents. I'll be busy with the routine aspects of the investigation, so as usual I'm expecting you to come up with the creative approaches."

"Sounds like a good plan. And we couldn't have a nicer day for this drive. We're too late for the peak colors of fall up there, but some will be left. That area is gorgeous any time of year though. There will be snow on the mountain peaks already."

"And bad roads," Connie laughed. "Your car won't be clean by the time you get home tonight but New Mexico beauty always wins out, right? We all have dirty cars here. It means we've gotten rain or snow or both. Clean cars mean too much drought. A woman politician in California said sometime back when their drought was big news yet again that when her car was so dirty the door handle was sticky to the touch, that was when she knew it was time to wash it and not before. Dirty cars are now a sign of water ecology. Did you know that?"

"No I did not, but it makes sense."

Once the women began entering the vast Mora Valley, resplendent in its famous beauty as always, Connie called Hernandez for directions as he had instructed her to do. As expected, the mountain peaks were snow-capped, while a few autumn colors lingered in spots here and there throughout the valley and up the lower sides of the mountains.

They drove a few more miles along state highway 518, but before they came to the town of Mora, they turned onto the narrow paved road at the sign he described, and drove the required 2.6 miles before calling him again for final directions. This time he talked them through the twists and correct turns on rutted dirt roads, forks in the roads, and finally, several unevenly connected erstwhile driveways, until they saw an old mustachio'd Hispanic man in what appeared to be an equally old sweat-stained brownish felt hat that probably was a pork pie back in the day, wearing a buttoned and starched white shirt underneath his old blue denim overalls. Standing with a big smile in front of an even older adobe house, he was beckoning them to pull up in front of it. The sun reflected brightly off the pitched tin roof, a long porch spanning the front and side of the old home's traditional L-shape. The spotless windows glistened from their Chimayo-blue window frames, accented with indoor window boxes of bright red geraniums. The outside window boxes contained only dirt, waiting for spring. Hollyhocks, dormant until next summer, were everywhere.

Removing his hat once they were inside, directing them to the well-used round table in the cozy kitchen, Hernandez revealed a head of thick salt and pepper hair cut with a style that made one think of what Elvis might look like if still alive, full head of hair intact.

Dolly asked him if he could direct her to a restroom, and excused herself from the room, wandering down the long hall as directed until she came upon a beautifully kept old fashioned bathroom, with a glistening white claw-footed tub and a huge window, framed by white lace curtains, low enough one could step through in case of a fire, or a beckoning lover, which looked out onto hollyhocks so thick that even flowerless, no one could possibly see inside easily. She could hear Connie talking about children and grandchildren with the elderly couple, knowing they would feel sorry for Dolly when they learned, and they would ask, that she had neither. She would take her time in the restroom.

She found herself smiling as she stood at the window, gazing out the traditional New Mexico adobe house window at the northern New Mexico autumn blue sky, and thought about the jubilant Detective Hernandez. As a native New Mexican, Dolly knew he wasn't unlike the majority of the Hispanic men in northern New Mexico and southern Colorado, descended from a dozen or more generations of Sephardic Jewish, Moorish and Spanish ancestors in this area, who took a full head of hair for granted at any age, often with only a smattering of gray even in their ninth decade, or tenth. When watching news on television, she would notice Middle Eastern men often seemed like doubles of these New Mexico Hispanics, but once they spoke, or yelled in groups with arms raised, fists shaking in anger or holding firearms, all similarities ended.

No one in the world had the accent of New Mexico Hispanics when speaking English, nor did anyone in the world speak their exact version of Spanish. No surprise there, given that the first Europeans who came to New Mexico, in the early 1500s, were from Spain. Many small towns in northern New Mexico still spoke a dialect that resembled the Spanish heard in Spain in the 16th and 17th centuries. She recalled reading a book on the subject she happened upon at the library some 40 years ago when living in San Antonio, Texas, written by a University of New Mexico doctoral candidate. That book likened the phenomenon to finding a village in the United States where everyone spoke the Old English of the Middle Ages.

Adding to the complexity of the New Mexican Middle Eastern and Mediterranean cultures, many Christian Arabs came to New Mexico, especially in the last 150 years or so, many of whom were Lebanese and Syrian, often becoming prominent families in their communities. Today, unless one knew the history of a surname or a family, it often was difficult to discern those old Arab families and individuals from the New Mexico Hispanic population, based on physical appearances alone, especially since so many of the families had intermarried through the generations. She recalled some of the most well known of the Lebanese and Syrian names, many familiar to her from a young age— Maloof, Abousleman, Bellamah, Hindi, Sahd and Faris. Many of the original settlers had been Maronites in their old countries, an ancient Christian sect, but most practiced Catholicism in New Mexico, which led to the intermarrying through the years with the locals.

Catholicism became the prominent religion of the area once the Spanish missionaries began arriving in the 1500s, bringing their religion to the area and claiming it as the New Kingdom of St. Francis for Spain almost 100 years before the Puritans brought their extremist Protestantism that got them kicked out of England to Plymouth, Massachusetts.

In recent decades, more and more information had been found proving many of the early settlers from Spain were Sephardic Jews who came to New Mexico to escape the persecution of the Inquisition. Spain expelled its Jews and Moors by 1492 unless they converted to Catholicism. Many Jews pretended to do so, then immigrated to America when that became an option, continuing to appear as Christians publicly, only practicing their Judaic faith secretly. They became known as Crypto-Jews, and many old New Mexico Hispanic families were among them.

Because Moors were persona non grata in Spain by 1500, they apparently never came to New Mexico with the Spanish, although by the time the Spanish arrived in the New World, many Moors and Spaniards had intermarried throughout the generations. How could they not, given the Moors, originally of Arab and Berber descent from Northern Africa, ruled Spain for about 800 of the most progressive and innovative years in its history? The Moor-dominated city of Cordova was the most progressive city in the known world during that era.

Thus the modern New Mexico Hispanic could easily be descended from Spaniards, Arabs, Berbers and Jews who resided in Spain, Lebanese and Syrians who settled in New Mexico, and Native Americans in New Mexico, especially the Pueblo Indians, with whom the Spanish developed close relationships upon their arrival.

Given all the Arab blood among New Mexico Hispanics, Dolly always found it ironic that Islam did not come to New Mexico in any formal manner until late in the last century, when the first formal Muslim community in the entire United States was founded in 1979 near Abiquiu, the beautiful area made famous by artist Georgia O'Keeffe.

New Mexico only had about 200 Muslims per 100,000 people now, according to recent census info she had read, since she liked to read census reports about her state. Given the New Mexico population of only about two and a half million these days, that meant only about 4,000 were Muslims, a relatively small number for a state renowned worldwide for its religious tolerance and diversity.

Freshening her lip gloss, straightening her always-wayward hair, finding the liquid hand soap a brand with which she wasn't familiar, but immediately loved because of its aroma, she pulled her mind out of New Mexico history and culture, ready for the task at hand. She never would get used to talking about murders, especially murdered children, for hours on end, as interviews of this type often required. She had to steel herself every time.

When she returned to the homey kitchen, finished with her historical reverie and fully focused on the present once again, Hernandez introduced her to his wife. She was as jolly as he was, and obviously quite a looker in her day, for she still was what one would call a handsome woman, Dolly thought to herself, careful with hair and makeup, but not so much with the clothes. She wore a faded dress of an undetermined color covered by a full apron that probably had been with her for decades. Dolly still had one her own mother had worn, which she kept when her mother passed away, so she knew all about the value of old aprons. They made the food better. Good cooks grew attached to their aprons, and didn't discard them easily, especially if they grew up in times and places that required them to be frugal. Growing up in New Mexico had required most people to be frugal for centuries, whether Anglo with roots in the Deep South like her mother or a multi-generational New Mexico Hispanic like Mrs. Hernandez.

Connie excused herself for the restroom down the hall, while Dolly asked the elderly couple about the history of their large, meandering home. They took great delight in her question and launched into a brief version of its history until Connie returned to the table.

As soon as she was seated, Hernandez, not needing any prompting, jumped into his story while his wife finished placing their green chile stew and tortillas on the table, apparently not interested in any more small talk. She politely disappeared into another part of the rambling old house, most of which had been built by his great grandfather. Other family members had added a few rooms now and then, always adobe.

Accepting the couple's invitation to begin eating, the two women indulged in the delicious meal, declining the offer of beer or whiskey, choosing the freshly brewed, aromatic coffee. The detective sipped his beer but rarely touched his food, obviously eager to talk. "I have quite a story to tell you, so eat slowly and when you finish, there is a lot more," he laughed. He talked to them as though he had been waiting years, decades actually, to find someone who would listen to his theories about the old case.

"I always had a hunch about a priest, who knew the murdered boy well, but I never could find enough proof, or any proof, for that matter, so didn't dare mention my suspicions to anyone. That would have been defiling God and the Church in those days. This case you are working on now sounds just like that one. I checked around since your call yesterday, Detective Romero, and sure enough, that priest, who is old now, like me, still is active in that parish. He hasn't retired yet. Father Sanchez. I'm sure you know of him.

"Connie nodded. "But I confess, I quit being an active Catholic not long after my abuelita died almost twenty years ago. So I don't interact personally with any priests."

"Not unusual for cops, you know," Hernandez said to her. "The job makes it difficult to keep the faith." She nodded again.

"I grew up here in the Mora Valley and that priest did too," he continued. "I was a few years ahead of him in school. He didn't have a father and in those days, that wasn't normal. Single mothers are more the norm than not these days, even around here, but in those days, during and after World War II, a single mother in this town who wasn't a widow was so unusual, rumors and gossip surrounded any who lived in these northern New Mexico villages. Children born out of wedlock were always raised in the grandparents' homes, usually as the child of the grandparents, or they were farmed out to married siblings of the wayward mother. No girl would dare raise her illegitimate child openly, outside of her parents' home.

"No one seemed to know anything about this boy's mother, since she didn't grow up around here, and no one was sure where she was from, although her name, Rufina Sanchez, her looks and her fluent local Spanish told us she was one of us, probably from one of the villages around Taos or Santa Fe. She never talked about her husband, but did wear a wedding band. She was a devout Catholic, which stopped some of the gossip that would have flown around her otherwise. She went to Mass every single morning, taking her son before school, even when he was a teen. None of us kids had to attend church with our mothers every day except her son, even though several mothers did attend daily. We felt sorry for him because of that. Having to go once a week was bad enough. Every day sounded like torture to us.

"Even though the mother's behavior stopped any nasty gossip about her, it didn't help her son. Poor boy. He had problems from an early age. We didn't know it in those days, of course, we just made fun of him. But once I became a cop, and took some courses at Santa Fe Community College over the years, whenever I could fit one into my schedule, which was often, thanks to a police chief for many years who encouraged us to get more education, I was able to understand many things from my childhood that otherwise I wouldn't have thought about. When I found myself dealing with this priest again during that boy's murder investigation, my college courses in psychology, plus what I learned on the beat, gave me a lot of insight into him and his behavior when we were boys. Unfortunately it wasn't a good thing, because that is what made me start feeling that he was involved with the murder, or he was the murderer. If he wasn't, then to this day, I would swear before God that he knew more than he ever told the cops. My gut instincts told me he withheld information that could have helped us solve the murder. Either he was protecting himself or someone else. Investigating anyone in the Church in those days was unthinkable."

"Would it have been a situation where someone confessed to him, so he felt he couldn't tell?" Dolly asked him.

"No, no, that's not what I'm talking about. We ran into that situation regularly in Santa Fe, since everyone went to confession in those days, especially my early years as a cop. The priests knew more about most crimes in that town than the cops ever did, even when we did manage to send the guy to jail. These days, it isn't the same, with all the Anglos and New Agers moving into Santa Fe in the last few decades from out of the state, and many of the locals losing their faith and no longer attending Mass, much less making confession. Priests who are friends of mine say it isn't the same world in Santa Fe, things have changed so much.

"No, that is why this situation was different. This priest knew something and it wasn't about the confessional. He could have told me that if it were. The priests were good with us cops, generally, helping us with our cases while keeping their parishioners' secrets. It was easy to know when a priest was protecting the confessional, or just not being forthcoming with us, which was rare. That is why he stood out so much during that investigation. He never tried to make us think he was protecting a confession."

"When you ran into him again with this case, what caused you to remember what he was like as a child?" Connie asked.

"There was a lot of talk about La Llorona around that little boy's murder," Hernandez said, his eyes glazing as he looked back into the past. "A boy found murdered, drowned, in the Santa Fe River, every New Mexico Hispanic knew that had the stamp of La Llorona all over it. But I never bought it. From the beginning, I felt the boy was murdered somewhere else and put there to make it look like a drowning. The coroner's office confirmed that when they said he hadn't drowned. The river had a lot of water in those days, not like now with this drought, which is just like the drought in the 1950s when half the time the river was only a trickle. Sometimes it was dry.

"That priest took a special interest in the case. Since I knew how strange he was as a child, I had my suspicions from the start. He had everyone else fooled though, even the mother. They all thought he was such a caring man, someone who had taken a special interest in her boy after he lost his father and brother in an auto accident when he was four. He spent a lot of time with the boy, became sort of a second father to him, everyone said. That wasn't unusual with the altar boys, but it was unusual for a priest to take a special interest in a boy before he was old enough to be an altar boy, yet this priest did. No one thought anything of it because of the tragedy that had descended upon the family. The priest got more respect than ever in the community because of his attention to the poor child. His alibi was solid for the apparent time of death, but given how the body had been moved to the river, it was hard to determine accurately, the coroner had said.

"Before we got the coroner's report, the boy's mother mentioned to me that she couldn't understand how her boy had drowned, since he had been swimming since he was a toddler and was an excellent swimmer. She mentioned that to me when I was doing the follow up investigation in order to formally close the case. She never thought to mention it earlier, she said.

"She wasn't in her right mind, was in such shock she couldn't be expected to remember everything," I realized. "But I was surprised she hadn't mentioned that fact to anyone. Because she did to me, I talked to his swim teacher at the Fort Marcy pool, who confirmed what a good swimmer he was. I didn't close the case. I changed it to a murder. It never has been closed, but you are probably the only cop on the force now who knows that or cares. Everyone who worked it is long gone."

"But what about the priest when he was a boy?" Dolly asked again, trying to get the old man back on track, growing a bit frustrated as he seemed to want to tell them everything but the answer to that question, which was making her grow even more curious about the priest's childhood.

"He used to dress up and pretend he was La Llorona." Hernandez exclaimed with a rough laugh. They both stared at him in amazement. "You don't believe me, do you?"

Both women said almost in unison, "Yes, we do."

"But we are shocked," Connie said.

"Wouldn't that be like allowing your child to dress up regularly like The Devil Himself?" Dolly asked. "Good Catholics would discourage such behavior in their children, not encourage it."

"Ask some of my neighbors, they remember too," he continued, getting up to grab another beer from the frig, obviously relaxing more as he realized they were taking him seriously. "I talked to them about it," he said, sitting back down and taking a swig. "They said his mother knew about it. I personally think she did encourage it. She certainly did not discourage it, let me say that. She was a strange one, that one."

His eyes glazed a bit and he stared into space, his hands around the cold beer bottle, reminiscing. "Her son was only four or five years old when my friends at school who lived next door to him told me they saw him dressed up in woman's clothes. Through the years, kids talked about it behind his back, often sneaking to his house at night and peeking into the windows, hoping to catch a glimpse. But they didn't need to do that.

"When he was in first grade, I was in fifth, he came to the Halloween party at our school dressed like La Llorona. I remember how proud his mother seemed, but my mother let me know that if I ever tried that, I would be in big trouble. Or that La Llorona herself would get me. I think that's how most kids and their parents felt, that to do that was tempting the witch herself. We were all too afraid of her, too sure she existed, to dare try to make fun of her by dressing up and pretending to be her. We felt that was like asking for the Devil himself to appear. I think the parents were more fearful than we kids were, because they equated La Llorona with losing their children. Most of them would have felt that if they let us dress up like her, they would lose us. But not that boy's mother. That caused a lot of the parents to wonder again who she was and what her family roots were, but we never found out. Any Hispanic from northern New Mexico would never show such irreverence toward the Llorona, we all thought, no matter how well she seemed to fit into our culture otherwise.

"That first time, since it was a costume party and we kids just figured since he was weird all the time, he wouldn't be normal if his costume wasn't weird, we forgot about it. For a while. Then the neighbor kids told us they saw him dressing up like that every day after school, when his mother was at work. When he was younger, before he started school, she didn't leave him at home alone. We don't know where she took him, so when he dressed up in her clothes, she always was there, the neighborhood kids told us. We all thought it was so strange that his mother would let him do that. But when the kids said he was home alone after school every day, dressing up in her clothes before she got home, so she didn't know about it, well we knew then that he was a freak. We thought she might have encouraged him before, but now we knew he really was strange. He was doing it on his own. Usually he tried to look like La Llorona, they said, but he never dressed the same way every time. It got so that every morning at school, a bunch of us guys would gather around the neighbor kids to see what he had worn the day before. We started teasing him, calling him the La Llorona Kid, making fun of his dresses. He had no friends, but after the neighbors started talking about him, kids went out of their way to avoid him.

"I went through eighth grade at that school, the little schoolhouse here in Mora that they don't use any more," he said as his wife brought him another beer, not realizing he already had a new one. The two women shook their heads when she offered them more coffee.

Connie's phone signaled her that she had a text message. Excusing herself from the table, she went into the next room to check it. The others soon could hear her talking, and Dolly realized she must be speaking to the medical examiner's office in Albuquerque, and quietly told Hernandez, who nodded in understanding of the importance of the call, and continued enjoying his beer.

Connie knew the minute she saw the text to call Dr. Bryant that he might not have good news for her, since he couldn't possibly be finished with the little boy's autopsy yet, given the horrendous backlog that always existed.

She dialed the number he had given her and got right through to Dr. Bryant. The two of them had a long relationship developed by many cases through the years.

"Bryant," he said with a voice sounding of fatigue.

"Detective Romero returning your call, had to drive up to Mora today, I'm still here, interviewing a retired detective in relation to this case possibly."

"Wish my job called for trips like that," Bryant laughed. "Got some complications with the little boy found in your river up there."

"Figured as much when I saw your text," she said. "Is this going to be a slow one?"

"Appears so. He didn't drown, there was no water in his lungs nor other signs of drowning. And he wasn't strangled. It looks like he died elsewhere and his body was placed there later. It's the cause of death that isn't obvious, so we are doing a full toxicology workup, and that is what is going to take a while. The lab isn't backed up for two years anymore, but it still takes a few months usually. I am going to try to pull some strings to speed this one up, may be able to do that since it's a child, I'll let you know as soon as I know something."

"Thanks, Doc. And could you ask your office staff there to look up an old autopsy report for me? A woman called the office the other day and told me about her son, who was found in the same place about thirty years ago. He wasn't drowned either. We never found who did it. I'd like you to take a look at that report. That's why I am here now, because of that old case, they may be connected." She gave him the data he would need to find the old file.

"Thanks, I'll look it over carefully and give you a call."

Glancing through the old cold case file while waiting for Dolly to arrive that morning, she had seen that the department had worked it actively for almost a decade. One suspect's name jumped out at her, Father Marquez. He had been interviewed many times, by several members of the department over the years, including Hernandez. It was obvious everyone suspected him, but nothing came of the suspicions. This file would make for good reading material at home in the evenings, she had realized, as she glanced through some of the lengthy interviews, most of them handwritten long before the days when everyone had computers at their desks. By hearing Hernandez' take on the old case, she would be reading with a lot more insight than if she had tried to get through everything before she met with him. Years of experience had taught her that interviews should lead the way, paperwork should follow, not vice versa, when it came to cold cases.

Connie returned to the table, and Hernandez continued what he had been saying when her phone interrupted them. "The stories about the boy continued until I left to go to the high school in Las Vegas. I went and lived with my aunt and uncle during the week so I could attend the school, and living in that big town—it was big compared to Mora—made me decide I wanted to be a cop. But I wanted to go to a bigger town, and so after high school, I went to Santa Fe to become a cop. I went home to Mora every weekend until I graduated from high school, but I didn't see those neighbor kids much after we left eighth grade. Most of them didn't go on to high school, but worked on their parents' farms or joined the military, or just took off for the big towns—Santa Fe, Albuquerque, Denver. I forgot all about that boy until I ran into him as a priest when the child was found in the Santa Fe River. I wasn't surprised he was a priest. It made sense to me. He had been a lonely boy, so wasn't used to having friends, nor girlfriends, probably. And he loved to wear dresses. I was glad he found a profession where he fit in," the old man laughed, but not unkindly, Dolly observed. "Until I started realizing he might have killed the boy."

"Does the mother live here now?" Connie asked.

"No. Years ago, her son moved her away and no one seems to know where he took her. I wasn't here then and didn't hear any of the details. My parents were old and didn't care, no one paid much attention to her. When she allowed her boy to dress as the Llorona, all the adults in the village pulled away from her. Until then they had been cordial although no one ever seemed close to her. She worked as a cook on one of the big Anglo-owned ranches near Cleveland, so she was gone long hours most days. Everyone thought it strange she didn't live on the ranch, but figured she wanted her boy in school here, and she spent so much time at the church here. The one in Cleveland didn't have daily Mass. The one here doesn't offer it now, the doors aren't even open during the week for people to pray and light candles, too many vandals.

"I didn't have any clues that led to that priest, then, it just was a gut feeling about him, since he made a point of being so involved with the case, and it had such a strong Llorona connection in the community, something which I knew as a boy he would have found fascinating. My gut feeling I learned to trust as a cop made me realize he might have created the entire crime to look like the witch did it. And I never lost that feeling, just never could prove anything enough to even name him as a possible suspect. But in those days, no one suspected priests of anything anyway. He was totally immune of suspicion, and he knew it. I never let him know of mine, for I knew it might cost me my job if I couldn't prove anything."

"I'm not so good about attending mass these days," Connie said. "But if you're a cop long enough, you meet most of the priests, and hear gossip about at least some of them, as you know. That is why I am surprised you didn't know he was in Santa Fe until that boy's death."

"But he wasn't," Hernandez said after a loud beer belch. "He had been in California until about a year before the boy's death, when he had finally been assigned to Santa Fe. He told me he had been trying for years to get back to New Mexico, and finally was allowed to take that position. He wanted to come to Las Vegas, but when they offered Santa Fe, he didn't refuse, knowing it might be his only chance to get back to his home state."

3

THEY ALL SAT IN SILENCE FOR A FEW MOMENTS, EACH LOST IN thought about what he had just told them. Both women were a bit dazed, in shock from his revelations. He finally paid some attention to his stew, and began eating rapidly, even though by now it had to be cold, Dolly thought to herself.

Mrs. Hernandez entered the room, smiling at them, obviously aware of the mood in the room. Either she had been listening or already knew the story, probably both, Dolly surmised. She offered more coffee, more stew, more tortillas. After filling the women's cups, she brought out a plate of homemade biscochitos.

Grabbing one, Dolly bit in. "Delicious," she exclaimed. She tried to avoid sugar and wheat and lard, but these could be an incredible cookie when made by New Mexico women with their old family recipes. She would never pass up such a rare treat. Even the Late Great Nutrition Guru, Adelle Davis, taught that lard had health benefits, she reminded herself.

Connie also helped herself while Mrs. Hernandez cleared the rest of the dishes from the table.

"What do you think about the many so-called sightings of La Llorona that have been reported throughout the years around Santa Fe?" Dolly asked the old detective.

He was silent a few moments, pensively staring at his beer bottle. Dolly began to wonder if he was too inebriated to give her a real answer when he said, "I believe all of them, all the ghost stories, including La Llorona's."

Again, both women were stunned. "You do?" Connie almost shouted.

"Of course I do," he said, smiling at them, seeming to enjoy their shock and awe. "Why would I have been so concerned about a priest who dressed up like her as a boy if I didn't believe in her existence?" he asked them. They both just stared at him.

Finally Dolly said, "But you were a cop. They aren't supposed to believe in spirits and ghosts, are they?"

He and Connie laughed out loud in tandem. "No of course not," he said, "but that doesn't mean we don't. Right, Connie?"

Having put her on the spot, Connie looked embarrassed, like she had been caught stealing from a cookie jar, not the plate in front of them. "Well, I have to admit, I don't *not* believe she exists, I just don't consider myself a believer in her, does that make sense?"

"In other words, what you really are saying is that you don't want to admit to anyone you think she probably is real?" he laughed.

"Yeah, that's about right," she admitted, a wisp of a sheepish expression passing quickly across her face.

Dolly just sat there, munching her cookie, the third one, not believing this conversation was happening. It was more surprising to her than the news about how the priest acted when young.

"So you didn't have a single clue that might have helped build a case back then?" Dolly asked Hernandez. "Even one might help Connie here look in the La Llorona priest's direction now with some success, assuming there is a connection. Was poisoning considered? The mother in your case called us, you know, and she says the body this time is even in the same place. We're still waiting on the coroner's report."

Connie didn't say anything about her phone call, wanting to see how the old detective answered Dolly's question.

"We didn't have the technology back then," he said. "The coroner's office wasn't as efficient as it is now. A lot of murders went unsolved that, today, would be, with DNA, toxicology testing. To my knowledge, the coroner did all the testing they could in those days, for poisons and such. It should be in his report if not ours. I remember strangling was considered when it was learned the boy didn't drown, but the coroner ruled that out, too."

"But even if they had done more tests then, that won't get us any closer to finding the murderer now, will it?" Connie exclaimed in anger and frustration.

"What do you know about cross-dressers and transgender people, besides what you told us about your childhood experiences with your school chum? Did you realize they are all over Santa Fe now, openly, relatively speaking? And by that I mean, cross-dressers by definition often keep their practice private, even hidden, while transvestites tend to be publicly flamboyant. Lately, transgender has become a more accurate description of someone who once would have been considered a transvestite, and the term transvestite has taken on a rather derogatory meaning. Most transvestites really do want to be the opposite sex, and may endure the sex change, while most cross-dressers do not want to be the opposite sex and are quite comfortable in the gender God gave them.

"Being in the police department makes us an expert these days, it seems. Ever since they started doing all those sex change operations up in Trinidad, transgender people spend time in Santa Fe in tandem with their Trinidad appointments. A lot of them choose to stay in New Mexico, not necessarily Santa Fe though. The change itself once took years, but now it can be done much faster, depending on the person's budget and psychological perspective. Some do better making the change quickly, others find a slower transition more comfortable. Did you know that? And they attract others to the area, such as seriously committed crossdressers, who, like I said, generally aren't transgender and thus don't want a sex change."

Hernandez almost doubled over with laughter. "No, I didn't know about the population explosion in Santa Fe , but I am not surprised. We get them in Las Vegas too, those Trinidad people. You know they call it the sex change capital of the world, don't you? At least they did before I retired, when that sort of thing still was a big secret. Today everything gets on the nightly news, it seems. No one has any secrets except politicians, and theirs don't last long. And what is it about Colorado? The first state to be famous for a sex change clinic starting in the 1960s, and now the first to sell marijuana to the general public? It used to be such a quiet, normal state.

"I didn't study cross-dressing in any of my college classes. I just knew that an isolated boy with no friends being raised without a father by a religious fanatic mother, a boy who liked to dress up as a woman, not to mention as La Llorona, couldn't possibly grow up to be a balanced human being as an adult. When he returned to Santa Fe, I couldn't help but feel sorry for him, knowing what I did. Until I realized he might be a murderer. Then, I confess, my compassion flew out the window."

"A lot of people, especially non-Catholics, don't think there is anything balanced about becoming a priest," Dolly said. "There are those who think the priesthood attracts the not-quite-normal man."

"And they probably are right, now," Hernandez said. "For centuries, I don't think that was true, but in my lifetime, the priesthood, the kind of men who choose it, aren't the same. I doubt anyone would argue that. The world has changed too much. Priests should be allowed to marry. But you aren't here to debate Catholic doctrine."

"Well, back to why we are here. We've had so many problems in Santa Fe," Connie said, "domestic incidents, hotel incidents, street incidents, you name it, because the Old Santa Fe Trail has turned into the 'Trinidad express.' The department has given us special workshops, to protect us, they said, so we wouldn't get ourselves killed, or the department sued, due to our ignorance on the subject. We had about one a year for several years, each one with supposedly the most-up-to-date information on the subject. But now that the transgender movement is fully established and the media has gotten on board, everything is changing so fast, it is hard to keep up. But so far, I'd say every Santa Fe cop who has been on the beat at least ten years is now an expert who can determine very quickly, without asking, if he or she is dealing with a woman, or a man who appears to be a woman, a woman who appears to be a man, or someone who is in transition. It also helps if the cop just asks," she laughed.

Hernandez almost doubled over in laughter again. "Glad I retired when I did, I don't think I could take a very tolerant attitude. In my day, we just had to deal with natives—Indians, Spanish and Anglos. And a few Anglo Texans, but they've always been around, never gave us any problems. And they brought money to the town, so everyone liked them generally. They always stood out, still do. All they have to do is open their mouth and we know they are from Texas, right?"

The women nodded. "And you notice Dolly here retains a bit of her Texas twang from the decades she spent there," Connie teased. "She's bi—half Texan and half New Mexican. Truly, I am not joking. Her father was born in Texas and her mother in New Mexico, and she has lived decades in both states."

Hernandez, listening, took another swig. "We won't send her packing," he laughed.

"Crossdressers don't usually become murderers," Connie said, getting the conversation back on track. "There is strong speculation among some who study these things and write about them, that any man who becomes a priest among the religions in which they have to wear dresses—your Catholics, Episcopalians, even

Buddhists, those types—may have a tendency to that sort of thing, or may have had in their childhood. Cross-dressers often start the behavior in childhood, and then literally seem to grow out of it. Others do not, and some come to it later in life. A connection to pedophilia or murder hasn't been made by experts, at least not the ones who taught us. Cross-dressers generally are considered quite harmless to others.

"Meanwhile, the Trinidad express has slowed some over the years, since so many doctors now do sex changes throughout the nation. Plus, Santa Fe has gotten so expensive. Paying for all that medical care and an extended stay in Santa Fe requires big bucks."

"They're going to Las Vegas and surrounding communities now, occasionally we even hear of one or two here in Mora," Hernandez said. "We never heard about them in this general area until the last decade or so. It isn't expensive like Santa Fe is, and they can be very private in the nice old hotels and beds and breakfasts while they go through their medical procedures. Because of the location of the state mental hospital, we have a high proportion of out-patients and former patients in the entire Las Vegas area, so I guess the sex-change folks feel that for less money, our crazies are preferable to the combo of eccentric artists and economic elites known as one-percenters that now dominate Santa Fe culture."

"Well, you see what I am saying, don't you?" Connie asked. "Sanchez probably is a bona fide cross-dresser. He started in childhood, and perhaps he outgrew it, or perhaps becoming a priest is how he continues his practice. But we wouldn't call him a transvestite, and even pedophile priests generally aren't murderers. There have been a couple of cases where priests murdered under-age girls they had seduced, but among the priests who like the little boys, there seem to have been no cases of murder reported anywhere in the world. If they have been, they've been kept off the internet so far. The pedophile priest has an entirely different profile than the secular pedophile, who often is a serial sexual predator and murderer. Just look at the vast numbers of children who disappear each year in this country alone.

"Sanchez fits the profile of a child who was a misfit," Connie said, "and who chose a profession in which he could be a fit, while keeping, even practicing, his secrets. Maybe he still wears women's underwear. I am sure no one cares. His profile fits a cross-dresser who had a difficult childhood, and not all cross-dressers have unhappy childhoods. Maybe he didn't, but his was strange—no father, only child, his mother didn't discourage and may have encouraged the dressing up, it started before he began going to school and it continued until puberty or beyond. That doesn't make him a murderer. It makes him a good candidate for the priesthood. Studies show these men—they can be women too, but you don't run into those as much, as least we haven't in Santa Fe—usually are heterosexual, and often they aren't very interested in sex, or if they are, it isn't part of their cross-dressing rituals—perfect profile for a celibate priest. I suspect the priesthood is full of these types. They wouldn't have much use for the pedophile priests either, much less murderers. Was there any sign of sexual abuse in your case?"

"We didn't know," Hernandez said. "No one who knew the boy said anything that would indicate any. The coroner didn't find anything, but I doubt he looked as closely as they do today, given how the technology has changed in 30 years, along with their methodology. You told your coroner to check?"

"Oh, yes. Any murdered child is routinely checked for signs of abuse of any kind during the autopsy these days," Connie said.

"Now that you have told me what experts say about cross-dressers—we ran into them every so often when I was a cop, at least one or two a year, but we received no training," he laughed, "I am questioning my own suspicions, because it doesn't make sense that he would be a cross-dresser, murderer and possibly pedophile, all in one. But my gut still tells me either he was involved with the murder or knows who did it. I can't shake that, no matter how much you tell me. But just because a guy cross-dresses, does that mean he might want to have a sex change, wish he were a woman?"

"Actually, no," Connie said. "That is why this all gets so complicated. Sometimes it seems that half the people in Santa Fe dress daily in what would be considered costumes in any other city in America. And women are part of all this too—they cross-dress, have gender identity issues and are having sex-change procedures. Some may be pedophiles, although few are murderers. Most are not criminals, but simply people who just want to be free to express who they feel they really are. Santa Fe provides that safe atmosphere. Both men and women of all types can blend into the Santa Fe environment easily.

"Given more art is sold in Santa Fe than in just about any other city in the United States, only surpassed some years, but not all, by New York, Chicago or

Los Angeles, and rarely all three at once, I must add, since Santa Fe usually comes in at number two or three largest art market in any given year, it makes sense that many of the residents often would dress the part of eccentric New Mexican artist. Add in the fact that Santa Fe has more writers per capita than any city in the entire country, a group also known for its eccentricity, and, well, it becomes obvious why unusual people with unusual habits would feel it was a good choice, a place where they could blend with everyone else. They couldn't do that easily in say, Topeka.

"As for cross-dressers and transvestites, they aren't even the same thing, by definition. They are two categories, according to the experts. And the folks who want the actual sex changes, whether they actually get them done or not—it is all about the money and many who want the change can't afford it—aren't usually into crossdressing or being a transvestite. They just want to be the gender they are not. Each of these categories has its own culture. But in a tourist town like Santa Fe, they all tend to meet in the same places—bars, clubs, hotels—and sort each other out. It doesn't always go smoothly, which is why we get called in often enough that our bosses give us workshops on the subjects." Connie was laughing as she spoke, shaking her head in wonder at the kind of life she led, compared to the one her parents led in Santa Fe.

"The true male cross-dresser is the most benign of the bunch because he usually is a male heterosexual who may not be very interested in sex. That isn't true of the other two groups, who may be highly sexual, but not necessarily homosexual. Some are bi. Cross-dressers are not very aggressive, they have a strong female nature, that is why they like to dress up as women, but otherwise they often are pillars of their community, which is why the priesthood is an ideal place for them to find a career—gentle men who get to wear dresses all the time and aren't expected to have sex. If your Sanchez is a true cross-dresser and from what you tell me about his childhood, I'd say he is, he wants to be perfect except for that, which isn't a problem since he gets to wear dresses all day every day, so you probably won't find any serious sins in his confessions."

"I trust my gut and my gut still tells me he knows something," Hernandez said. "About both murders, since they were both being trained to be his altar boys. That simply cannot be a coincidence. If that feeling goes away, I'll call you. I have a lot to think about now. Being a cop in Santa Fe used to be so simple, we often got calls from people saying they just saw La Llorona, and we always answered those.

But we never saw her. Now you get calls from people saying they thought they picked up a woman and it is a partial man? Ese, you can have your job. I'm happy to be here in my old farmhouse with mi esposa."

Finally Connie shared her news from the medical examiner's office with them, about the fake drowning, and the promise that Bryant would check on the old case details.

Hernandez sipped his beer while she talked, then said, "This doesn't surprise me. Little Danny wasn't drowned, but that was about all the autopsy revealed. With today's toxicology testing, you not only might get to the bottom of what killed your boy this time, but what killed mine as well. I know they won't be able to do more tests from the old case, but if they do find poison this time, they could dig the other boy up and test his remains, just in case. If the two cases have enough similarities, you ought to be able to get approval for that, if the mother gives permission. And if she already is calling you, I expect she might. I don't know how any one person could live through the tragedies she did, yet you say she called you immediately. She always was a sharp one, and I see that hasn't changed. I hope you can help her find closure this time around, I really do. We all need it, but no one as much as she."

"I agree," Connie said, while Dolly nodded. "And you can be sure we'll keep you up to speed on everything," Connie added. "You may remember something or think of something you had forgotten, or that hadn't been obvious before. You never know with cases like this, they can take so many twists and turns before they are finally solved, assuming they even get solved.

"Before I forget, were there any other staff members at the cathedral then whom you considered possible persons of interest at first? Or possibly helpful now? Anyone we need to interview?

"Sister Rosalie, a nun who would be quite old now, but to my knowledge still lives on the cathedral grounds and works there, and her brother, Father Marquez, a retired priest who lives in Jemez Springs last I heard. I haven't seen anything in the papers about them dying, nor moving again, so you should be able to find them easily enough."

"And your take on them?" Dolly asked.

"Ah yes, my take," he sighed heavily. "Back then they weren't suspects but then neither was the other priest except in my mind. Like I said, in those days, no one, and I mean no one, would look at priests and nuns as suspects, period. It didn't happen. So when I say anything, you must keep that in mind. These are my ideas, not those of other cops nor anyone else for that matter, at least not anyone who was talking back then. I interviewed all three of them several times, as did some other cops, but we were trying to get more information about the families of the altar boys at the time, possible relatives who provided transportation, things like that, than we were trying to figure out if the priests or nun did it. And of course, the nun wasn't even considered for a moment, not even by me, I admit. Nuns don't kill little boys. Priests don't either, but I know there always can be a first time for anything. I know that now. Back then it was truly outside-the-box thinking, to use the popular Anglo saying. Back then my suspicions were just plain weird, 'loco' the other cops said behind my back, I heard them laughing about my ideas, so I shut up and learned to keep them to myself."

"But wasn't it strange that a nun lived with the priests?" Dolly asked.

"Yes and no. She was Father Marquez's sister, that is why, along with the fact that she was old enough to be Father Sanchez's mother. So she is really old now. Frankly I'm surprised she still lives there, but I am assuming she does. Had quite the green thumb back then, don't know about now. Even had her own greenhouse with a lot of tropical plants that don't grow here. She especially adored her Palma Christi plants, which she brought in from all over the world, so she had all different types, and thus all kinds of flowers when they bloomed. She showed them to me a few times, they were beautiful, I must say. She told me they were named for the healing and bloodied hands of Christ, and she felt the Lord wanted her to cultivate as many as she could in the arid Santa Fe climate, where they cannot grow naturally. She provided a lot of flowers for the cathedral, both Palma Christi blossoms and from her other flowering plants. Quiet as a mouse. You never knew she was around if you didn't know about her."

"I've heard about her," Connie said. "She is still there. I know some of the regular church-goers mention her presence, discuss it. No one seems to dislike her, but they don't especially like her either, mainly because she keeps to herself so much, no one knows her. I think that lifestyle suits her because she seems to be such a natural introvert. Spends a lot of time praying I'm told, in the cathedral. People see her at all hours when they light candles and pray. She cooks and cleans for the priests there even now, I hear. Does a decent job too, although it would surprise me if some volunteers or other staff members don't also help her by now, given her age, she must be getting up there. I'll check on that, since we have to interview everyone connected to the cathedral and the rectory. We start our interviews tomorrow, but I wanted to talk to you first, felt you could provide us with background, even if the two crimes aren't related. They were altar boys in training at the same church, working with the same priest. And yes, we now have a foundation from which to work more effectively, I feel. I am so grateful you agreed to meet with us."

"Of course, I wouldn't think of saying no. I am as anxious as you are to see this case solved and if it helps solve my old one, well that would be a miracle. I would be grateful to you, am grateful you wanted to hear what I had to say, let me talk all afternoon," he laughed.

"I sure couldn't do that back then. When I couldn't find a clue, much less proof, that Father Sanchez was involved," Hernandez continued, "I realized I was correct to keep my thoughts to myself. But I never quit looking. All those years I worked for the department, I kept my eye on him and what went on at that church. Came up with nothing. Until now. But whether you can prove anything this time, much less connect it to last time? You may need a few miracles before it's all over. I hope you get some. I didn't. I still feel so badly for that first little boy's mother, and now another mother suffering. Even as a retired cop, hearing of these things brings me great pain. Makes me drink too much. Ask my wife." He sighed, took a swig of beer, then belched loudly.

"Why do you think Father Marquez retired to Jemez Springs?" Dolly asked. "Was he known to have problems of the kind they used to treat up there, or does he just like it there or what? That strikes me as bizarre, given the reputation it has as a place priests went to be cured of pedophilia in the days experts claimed that was possible."

"Well, you know that treatment center closed years ago," Connie said as Hernandez swigged some more beer.

"Yes, that's my point. Why there? Memories from when he had to be treated perhaps? It is beautiful there. I've always wanted to live there myself."

"He had no history of treatment," Hernandez said, "but given the secrecy around that place, you never know. I did check him out quietly as best I could when that first murder happened, and came up with nothing. Being from a Catholic family myself, it was easy to learn the local gossip discreetly. His reputation was flawless and apparently well deserved. But then so was that of Father Sanchez as well. And both were well liked.

"I think I remember someone saying he planned to retire someday to Jemez Springs and help run a retreat center the Catholics have there now, open to the public. A rustic spiritual spa you could say, along the Jemez River," he laughed. "Beats those upscale things people spend thousands on now, if you ask me.

"Something else I just remembered about him too, interesting, now that I think about it, given the La Llorona connection to Father Sanchez as a boy. Local gossip used to say that Father Marquez had some sort of gift, above and beyond your average priest. Some of the women used to claim he was psychic and if you caught him on a good day for a counseling session, he almost went into a trance and told you things, that later turned out to be true apparently, according to the rumors. But he wouldn't do it for everyone, no one could figure out how to get him to do it, but many went to him for counseling who wouldn't have ordinarily, in hopes that he would tell them things, predict their future. When asked about it, I heard he always denied everything, just claimed he was a good counselor and sincerely committed to helping people with their problems.

"According to one rumor I heard, La Llorona could be heard around the rectory some nights, some said people even claimed to see her on the grounds. It isn't too far from the Santa Fe River, and people thought it might be connected to him and his so-called gifts. But I never took any of that seriously at the time. Good little Catholic ladies are so easily misled, in my opinion. That was true when I was young, and I doubt it has changed much even today. He probably was a very good judge of people, which made him a great counselor, but no psychic, and certainly no working relationship with La Llorona herself." He laughed loudly at the absurdity of it all, and drank some more beer.

After some small talk as Mrs. Hernandez returned to the kitchen, the women graciously took their leave, thanking the couple profusely for the delicious meal.

As they bid each other good-bye, all four of them realized a special bonding had taken place that day, and a friendship had been established. Hugs ensuing all around, the women got in their car and drove away. The sun had passed its peak in the sky for the day and was starting its journey of descent. The mountains surrounding the Mora Valley meant sunrise came late and sunset early, regardless of the season, and were especially dramatic now that the year was well into autumn.

"So what do you know about La Llorona?" Dolly asked as they began the two-hour drive back to Santa Fe.

"Actually quite a bit just from what we cops hear around Santa Fe. You add what we might know from family legends and local lore simply because we grew up in the area and the stories just pile up."

"So tell me what you know. Is two hours enough time?"

Connie laughed. "More than enough. Frankly, the books people have written through the decades compiling the locals' stories are just as good as anything I can tell you. The stories about her appearances get sort of boring after a while because they are all pretty much the same."

" So you're saying if you've heard one, you've heard them all?" Dolly asked.

"That's exactly what I am saying. Maybe that is why La Llorona isn't more famous outside of Hispanic culture. Once we outgrow our childhood fear of her, we realize there isn't much substance to any of it."

"So you don't believe any of the stories?"

"Well, I hesitate to put myself in the category of non-believer, but I don't really fall into the believer one either. What is that, sitting on the fence? Sort of like the alien thing. You know cops even have stories about their experiences with UFOs. Everyone in this state has an opinion if not an experience, or at least a sighting, it seems. But I don't want to be in either category, non-believer nor believer. I guess if I had an experience in either realm, with the aliens or the ghost witches, I would become less detached. I do think most of these people are telling the truth when they give us their stories. But remember, we have a lot of crazy people in this state too. I know for a fact there is such a thing as herd mentality, mob mentality, we deal with it all the time with demonstrators. So when one person thinks she experiences a ghost, or La Llorona, it can be easy for others to think they do too. And men report sightings almost as often as women do.

"Evangelical preachers and politicians can get large crowds of people to think all kinds of things that aren't necessarily factual. That doesn't mean they aren't true, there is a difference. I know Catholics have all kinds of stories about experiences with saints and angels, even Jesus Himself. I suspect Baptists do too? And I know the New Agers have amazing stories, often mixed in with all kinds of weird outer space theories."

"Protestants in general, evangelical or not, have tons of stories about what they like to call miracles, that involve angels or Jesus, usually. I think in the case of miracles, such as healings, the truth is in the results. If a person is healed miraculously and thinks Jesus did it, well, who is to say He didn't? As for the New Agers, they seem to believe in anything and everything when it comes to the supernatural, don't you think? Just read a public bulletin board in Santa Fe."

They laughed in unison, then Dolly said, "Then let me tell you what I know about La Llorona, in case you feel my perceptions have any blanks to be filled. I first heard the legend of the colonial Spaniard woman who drowned her two children in the river when her vengeful grief drove her crazy after she learned of her husband's dalliance with another woman when I was in grade school at Mission Avenue Elementary. The old school still is in use, you know, just off north Edith in Albuquerque's North Valley. It was fairly new when I began first grade in the mid 1950s. The main reason I know that is because my sister who is ten years older than I am had to go to an elementary school much further from our home. All four of my much-older siblings were bussed long distances to school because my family lived so far out in the country in those decades. By the time I came along, the city had moved closer to us.

"Of course it was the Hispanic girls in my classes who told me about the wailing ghost who walks the ditch banks, searching for her children. And they didn't just tell me. They expressed the story to me, shall we say, vividly," Dolly giggled, "with a scary, humorless passion and an obvious deep belief that caused me to be terrified in spite of the skepticism I felt I should have for such things. I wasn't exposed to children my own age before I started first grade except once a week for maybe an hour or two at our family's Baptist church downtown, a smaller one, not the big First Baptist. My parents began going there in the 1930s and by the time I was born, one of my uncles was the preacher.

"So you can see how spending all day with about 35 mostly Hispanic Catholic children in the same over-crowded classroom and on school playgrounds September to May every year for six years was a big deal for me.

"I never had engaged socially with Hispanic nor Catholic children until I met them in school, as I don't recall any Hispanics at my Baptist church in downtown Albuquerque when young, but later there were a couple of families. Unlike today, Hispanic Protestants were rare here. Many of our neighbors were Hispanic, but there was no effort made by my parents to involve me with their children, nor for that matter with Anglos who lived in the area either. My family tended to keep its children quite insular, for many reasons, a big one being that we lived on a dairy farm and neighbors weren't close in the suburban sense of that word. My parents were too busy to arrange play time for me with people they didn't know well, and any would require driving time to and fro.

"So you can see how my exposure to Hispanic girls my age with this wild story would make a huge impression on me. I spent an hour a week in Sunday School learning religious stories until I could read well enough on my own to read the Bible and various church publications and Bible story books for youngsters. But I didn't make a single friend my age at church who taught me anything about my culture or religion in all those years. Only adults did that, and it was all the basic Baptist line, what parents in my family and Sunday School teachers had taught their children for generations. Then I spent all day every school year with those girls for six years who loved to tell me about their Catholic religion and Hispanic legends. I didn't know any Baptist children that excited or passionate about our stories. The adults weren't either, now that I think about it. But I gather a lot of nuns approached how they taught religion to their students with about the same fervor, or lack of it, as my Baptist teachers. A lot of emphasis on being good, and what that involved, the reason we had rules, and what happened if we broke them. The difference was that Baptists didn't have a lot of options for fun in our lives, while it seemed to me Catholics did.

"And we didn't really have rituals, not like the Catholics did. No special jewelry either. They all got to wear crosses, even earrings that were crosses, or lockets with paintings of Jesus or Mary or other saints. We didn't even have any saints, much less ghosts or witches.

"'If she sees you, she'll get you. Never let her see you,' those girls used to warn me. I loved to hear the stories, but never took them too seriously. Their old Catholic culture that resembled culture in Spain four hundred years ago far more than it did Cold War era Baby Boomer culture in America in the 1950s, always seemed so alien to me. The fact that I usually was the only Southern Baptist Anglo in my class during all six years I attended Mission never made me feel different so much as it made me feel superior. That was my mother's doing. She taught me that most of those Catholics really weren't Christians, because only Baptists and a few other Protestant groups were the true Christians. That's why it was hard for me to take the stories completely seriously, but at the same time, I couldn't shake them completely. They did scare me, or at least the way the girls told me the stories scared me, with all their eeeh's and ooooh's." She laughed. "I loved to hear the Catholic ghost stories, for Baptists just simply didn't have anything nearly as fascinating, much less scary. I probably hadn't thought about La Llorona since sixth grade until today. So I gather you have current news of her?" Dolly giggled again.

"Actually this lapsed Catholic Mekskin lesbian does," Connie giggled back. "She was seen regularly in Santa Fe's old PERA building before they closed it a few years ago. By employees, not crazy people who might have wandered in off the streets, although God knows we've always had plenty of those in Santa Fe."

The PERA building, Dolly's thoughts raced. A huge hulking monstrosity built in her lifetime, it was where the bulk of the business of the state of New Mexico was carried out by the various government agencies and their employees for half a century.

"Even seen by cops," Connie was saying. "Plus there are those stories by several employees in the old PERA building when the PERA was in it -- not just reports by our usual local crazies and hysterics. I don't think any such reports have come out of the new Public Employees Retirement Association building, proving the location of the old one was connected to all the strange goings on reported there since it was built in the middle of the last century. Other ghosts were seen and heard too, not just La Llorona, you know.

"And New Mexico historian Marc Simmons has written that even today, she is seen regularly in Santa Fe, dressed all in black," Connie continued.

"But the girls told me in grade school she wandered the ditch banks dressed all in white. Are there two of them, or just two versions of the same ghost story?" Dolly asked.

"Sometimes she is seen in white and sometimes in black."

"But why the PERA building, of all places? That seems so unghostly, to say the least. And I don't recall any ditches near it, although it isn't too far from the

Santa Fe River. Nothing in downtown Santa Fe is far from the river of course. What was her PERA style, black or white?"

"Supposedly, she was seen regularly throughout the building, always dressed in black. It seems the place is built on top of an old Indian burial ground. Every few years someone around here writes another book about her, collected stories of local experiences. I've read some of them."

"Maybe she floats around the PERA building regularly to remind everyone of the tragedy of modern-day governmental bureaucracy," Dolly giggled. "You know what they say about how things get done here, that New Mexico is not part of the U.S. of A., but is actually a Third World Country. That building still is being used, isn't it? By state employees? Have you heard any new stories since they took it over?"

"Not that I recall, but that doesn't mean there haven't been sightings. It can take years for some of these stories to surface. People keep quiet out of fear. And La Llorona sightings go through phases here in Santa Fe," Connie said. "Active ones and dormant ones. About 1969-1971 there were a lot of sightings, for example. And in the 1940s and 1950s. Although you also have to wonder about who is claiming to have seen her during the so-called active phases, since so much is up to the interpretation of the viewer. They could be seeing other ghosts and just assume it's La Llorona, or hallucinating because they are on drugs, or off their meds.

"When I was young," Connie continued, "many of us were taught to view her appearances as an omen, a warning, perhaps to help us save our children from impending tragedy. Everyone knows she tends to show up right before tragedy descends on a family. No one argues that. What does get argued is what it means, a warning to help parents prevent tragedy, or a premonition of an impending death? Those who believe it is the latter also believe she has a hand in making the death happen. The two interpretations of her appearances probably are the reason she is seen all in white or all in black."

"And so we are back in the sacred city," Dolly said as she turned off the interstate and headed toward the police station.

"You know I've got a lot of work to do on this case now that I have the old background from Hernandez. I know a lot more about Father Sanchez now. I agree with Hernandez on this. I just don't believe there isn't a connection, now to both murders, and I plan to find it. I'll have some of the other cops help me with interviews, since we've got to talk to all the altar boys with their parents and if we can get permission, alone as well, so we'll be working in teams. It's going to take a while, and with everyone so frightened and all the emotions running high because of the horror of the crime, it's going to be a tough week or two ahead.

"Why don't you try to talk to the two priests and the nun by yourself, and let me know what you think? Then we'll decide where we go from there. Call me when you have the interviews set up, and I'll let you know if we find out anything significant as soon as we do, if..."

"Two priests and a nun. It's gonna be an interesting week," Dolly said quietly, lost in her thoughts as she headed to police headquarters to drop Connie off before heading home to Albuquerque.

4

MRS. SHAW LOCKED HER FRONT DOOR AND STEPPED ONTO the walkway carrying a covered dish, her standard New Mexico-style casserole with green chile, which meant she substituted chicken for tuna. The morning was sunny, but she could feel cool fall air as she walked across the street. Mrs. Cervantes answered her knock.

"I saw you come home earlier with your boy, and thought you might need some prepared food since you've had to be at the hospital with him," Mrs. Shaw said.

"Oh, that is so kind of you, gracias. Won't you come in?" Mrs. Cervantes held the door open for her.

Stepping inside the door, and closing it behind her, she followed Mrs. Cervantes into the kitchen and set the dish on the counter. "You can put it in the fridge until you need it, and just warm it up in the oven or the microwave. How is Johnny?"

"He's sleeping right now, those doctors gave him so many drugs, it scares me, but they do help him sleep," Mrs. Cervantes said, looking worried and frustrated. "Sit down."

"Tell me all about it if you aren't too tired." Mrs. Shaw said as they took their chairs at the table. She had lived across the street from the Cervantes long enough that she and Mrs. Cervantes had an easy camaraderie, and were used to gossiping in great detail about neighborhood goings-on over the years. Mrs. Shaw knew she would want to talk about what happened, would need to. Despite her huge family, Mrs. Shaw knew that Mrs. Cervantes always welcomed the chance to tell her all about anything that upset her, simply because Mrs. Shaw was a good listener and didn't judge, unlike many of Mrs. Cervantes' relatives, who were full of judgment and ridicule and weren't always the most sympathetic listeners.

"The doctors say he got food poisoning, but we can't figure out how. No one else in the family got sick, not even the people who came to see us and ate something here in the last week, we checked with all of them. And Johnny didn't eat anything the rest of us didn't eat, I am sure of that, at least not at home. No one else at his school got sick, we checked with the school and so did the hospital. The only other place he goes is to church, to the activities Father Sanchez has for the boys his age, for the ones he is preparing to be altar boys. We haven't been able to talk to Johnny yet to see if he ate anything there. I told the hospital he might have, that they usually have some kind of refreshment, but I don't know if they checked to see if any of the other boys got sick. I forgot to ask them and they didn't tell me like they told me about the school when they checked. Johnny almost died, they said." Suddenly she was in tears, remembering how harrowing the last few days had been for her and her son.

Mrs. Shaw stood up and put her arm around the weeping woman, quietly comforting her. Mrs. Shaw was not a Catholic. She had been raised Episcopalian, but hadn't attended church regularly in years. She didn't trust any Catholic priest these days with children and never felt good about the Cervantes allowing their son to go into the altar boy instructional program. She knew it was a family tradition going back centuries, so she had kept her opinion to herself. But given what Mrs. Cervantes just told her, she had her suspicions about that priest, whether he intentionally poisoned the child or accidentally, it didn't matter. If it was an accident, it proved he and his staff weren't careful about hygiene and food preservation, and if it wasn't, well... Her thoughts trailed off as Mrs. Cervantes, face stained with tears, got up to get a tissue and pour herself a cup of coffee. "You want one too?" Mrs. Shaw nodded and got the cream out of the fridge. The women sat in silence for a few moments, savoring their coffee and pondering the situation.

Mrs. Shaw finally broke the silence. "Were the police called in?"

"Not that I know of. The doctors said something about doing tests, but not all the results were back when we left the hospital today. They seemed to think Johnny just ate something bad that we didn't know about, they didn't seem to think somebody poisoned him, I asked them. But I don't think they took me very seriously. I think the tests were mostly to see if Johnny has some disease, they seemed to think it was more about something wrong with him than something he ate, but he never gets sick like this. I told them that. He doesn't get sick at all, except the usual cold or occasional flu when it goes around. But he doesn't have stomach problems, ever. I think he's had stomach flu just once in his life, when he was in kindergarten."

She abruptly changed the subject. "When we were at the hospital, I saw in the newspaper that one of the boys in Johnny's church group was found dead in the Santa Fe River. Anthony and Johnny were good friends. Johnny almost died and little Tony did. God isn't taking care of that group. I must talk to Father Sanchez as soon as possible about all of this. He must be so upset about his two boys, with everything happening at the same time."

Mrs. Shaw stayed another half hour while the women chatted about the events of the last few days, including the prowler Mrs. Shaw had seen, sipping their coffee.

"It sounds to me like you saw La Llorona," Mrs. Cervantes said after Mrs. Shaw repeated her story of the entire incident in great detail. "She often shows up when tragedy strikes a home, especially when there is a death or danger of death. What was that policeman's name who talked to you and to my husband? I need to call him and tell him, the Santa Fe police know all about La Llorona, they get calls about her, some have seen her. I don't know why my husband didn't think of her, but he probably was too exhausted and worried about Johnny when he talked to the policeman the other morning."

Later, as Mrs. Shaw strolled home in the bright mid-day sun glowing from the crystal clear blue skies of late fall, she pondered everything Mrs. Cervantes had shared with her, but wrote off her La Llorona theory as just a superstition held by many New Mexico Catholic Hispanics. She felt the prowler was aware there was no one home, so tried to break in, happened all the time in Santa Fe these days. And her suspicions about the priest were stronger than ever, now that she knew the dead boy found in the river and Johnny had been in the same group at church and were good friends. That didn't sound like coincidence to her. She would have to find her newspapers from the last few days in the recycling basket and read those stories carefully about the little boy. She had ignored them earlier. Now she planned to follow that story very carefully.

Dolly reveled in being back home. Hovel, she thought to herself, smiling. Let Connie and anyone else think what they wanted, she loved her little home, hidden away next to the Bosque, the forested area through which the Rio Grande meandered as it flowed from top to bottom in the state, giving geological definition to the state's eastern and western halves as it paralleled the Continental Divide.

The Bosque in the Albuquerque area contained the largest cottonwood forest in the world. The gigantic old trees had fascinated her since she was a small child. There weren't any in her yard as a child, only one behind it on the ditch bank. But a relative who lived nearby had several in her yard, and that was how she was introduced to the smell of the huge cottonwood leaves in the fall, as they piled up before the adults burned them, creating the distinctive New Mexico late autumn aroma. Whenever she came across the earthy smell of the piles, before they were burned, she found it so fragrant, it seemed like a spiritual incense worthy of any great religion. Except Baptists of course. They didn't do incense, at least not for worship, adding that to the long list of things they avoided that she had begun keeping in her head from a young age. But the aroma only was noticeable if there was a big pile of leaves. Pick up a leaf by itself and it was just a big beautiful leaf, no special aroma. Something about the piles created the chemistry of that aroma. Too bad it couldn't be sold as incense or perfume, the way pinon aroma was.

Cottonwood leaf piles, before as well as while burning, and roasting green chile, were unique New Mexico smells that made it difficult to leave the state once one arrived, whether by birth as she had or during other stages of life, like so many had for centuries. It was where people fell in love with a place and never got over it, whether they got to stay or had to leave. She had left for many years, but was able to return, and never once regretted the return. She considered her present living situation a little paradise. Hovel indeed. Like living on a beach in Hawaii with palm trees in your sand shack's yard. Some places defied conventional standards of living and her state was one of them.

An irrigation ditch ran next to her back yard, which was fenced to contain her little horse and two dogs. The back porch ran the length of the house, and that is where all three spent a lot of their time, plus her kitties, especially when she was gone. When home, the dogs often were inside with her, and sometimes even the pony was, the cats lounging among all of them. She never had housetrained the little gelding, but knew he could be, so she had planned on it when she got him. But it never became necessary. She wondered if the information about his previous owners was incomplete, for he acted like someone had taught him proper house horse behavior. Regardless of the why or how of it, he instinctively knew how to do his business out in the yard, and not on the porch nor in the house. Maybe he followed the lead of the dogs, she often wondered, who had chosen a specific part of the yard to be their doggie outhouse. Maybe that was a Chow thing. Other breeds she had owned and of which she had known through friends and family didn't seem to do that, but all the Chows she ever owned had, as long as they were in their own yard. Outside the yard they marked their territories and left their droppings anywhere, like all dogs. That was a big plus about Chows, the way they created an area of their yard as their bathroom, regardless of how often their human owner cleaned it for them.

All six of her pets, adorable to her and adored by her, took walks with her on the ditch bank. She had to keep the dogs on leashes, it was the law, although not too strictly enforced in that area unless a problem arose. But her dogs would chase anything and everything, so she was an avid enforcer. Considered by experts to be one of the oldest dog breeds in the world, some said Chows were among a handful of remaining ancient breeds. In their original Chinese homeland, they were used as hunting dogs, as well as guard dogs, and even as sources of food. Modern times and centuries of breeding hadn't changed those hunting and guarding genes. No one seemed to care anymore whether Chows themselves made delicious meals, fortunately. Her dogs loved to chase and catch, and usually, eat, what they caught. With raccoons, porcupines and skunks as well as bunnies in abundance where she lived, hunting critters in that area was risky business for a dog of any breed.

The nearest twenty-four-hour animal hospital where porcupine quills could be removed was about forty-five minutes away. An experience years ago on a ranch outside Sapello, near Las Tusas, north of Las Vegas, taught her the importance of not letting dogs run loose in porcupine land. Her Chow in that incident had to be driven on first the rutted, difficult roads of the ranch, late one afternoon in early fall, then another thirty minutes or so to Las Vegas, for the nearest vet who would remove them. Fortunately he was an old-timey doc with lots of experience, and was willing to work late into the night, for literally dozens of quills had to be removed painstakingly by hand while her dog was knocked out with anesthesia. It was traumatic for everyone involved. Her dog drooled for months afterward during her sleep as a result of damage from the quills around and in her mouth and on her tongue. Her drool eventually even left a stain on the hardwood floor where she liked to sleep, right by the front door where she could be on guard and had a top to bottom window from which to watch the world when she was awake.

When it came to leashes and chasing things, a pony was another matter entirely. He didn't run anywhere if she was near, but stayed right next to her whenever he could. She described him as having dependency issues, a welcome contrast to her highly independent and emotionally autonomous Chows, who loved her greatly but didn't necessarily need her except for the comforts of life, and they weren't even sure about that consistently, moody little critters that they were, albeit adorable.

Thus the dogs would be on leashes when they all took their walks, while little Ari himself would be bridled, the reins secured over his neck. He followed, unattached to, and right behind, her, as well as the dogs, who pulled her as though she were an Alaskan sled most of the time, keeping her arm muscles in shape as she held them to a tolerable pace.

They took a lot of nighttime walks during warm weather, and sometimes even when it was cold. She loved the silence, the stars, the coolness, especially when days had been hot, and the welcome humidity created by the ditch in the dry high desert climate was so refreshing, the water swishing quietly. Frogs, ducks and various types of birds populated the relatively lush area, along with bunnies and the coyotes who ate them as often as they could. At night, some of these creatures could be seen or heard, emitting surprised-critter sounds when the strange group came near them.

She realized from now on, these walks would remind her of the La Llorona stories with which her elementary school friends had regaled her half a century earlier. She tried not to, even now, just like then, something about La Llorona scared her even when her mind didn't want to be frightened, didn't believe she should be frightened. It was just a Catholic Hispanic fable, nothing more, but the chills that went up and down her spine sometimes when she thought about the tales those girls told her contradicted any rational attitude she might have on the subject. To this day, she could feel their passion and belief as they told her the stories they learned from their mothers, aunts and grandmothers, even great-grandmothers. Walking along ditch banks became terrifying for her after she began hearing those stories, even though she only did that in broad daylight. She sometimes walked home from school with friends to their houses along a ditch bank that was quite deserted much of the way. It was much scarier to her than the one behind her home, the banks on which she had walked and played during much of her childhood. It felt safe and witch-less to her, based on all those years of experience proving it was.

Walking along a New Mexico ditch bank at night was a great way to remind oneself of the La Llorona tales, that was true, she had to admit. Even now, her Hispanic neighbors would encourage her not to take these walks at night, for many reasons, not just because of possible ghosts along the way. Anglo neighbors would tell her the same thing, ghosts or no ghosts. Crime in the metroplex was a huge problem, or so everyone assumed, given the never-ending local news stories about all the robberies, shootings, stabbings. She knew it was extraordinarily rare for any of those crimes to happen along a ditch bank next to the Bosque in the South Valley. The most that might happen was she would find a dead body someone had dumped, as that did happen occasionally along the ditches, maybe once every few years. She'd take her chances. Maybe La Llorona would protect her, she joked with herself and her little compadres.

Chows supposedly were used to ward off evil spirits from the temples in ancient China. If ghosts were afoot, evil or benign, she trusted her dogs to warn her appropriately. So far, no ghosts. No dead bodies. No witches.

Dolly called the cathedral office first thing the next morning after the trip to Mora, identified herself and her professional status with the state, and asked if Father Marquez was still there, knowing he wasn't, thus not surprised when told that. She was looking for nuanced reactions to her questions. "How long ago did he leave?" she asked the receptionist. "I'm not sure, it was several years before I came to work here. Just a minute, I'll find out." She put Dolly on hold, and she seemed to stay that way forever.

"He left in nineteen ninety-seven," she said upon her return at last. "Is there someone else who could help you perhaps? Did you know him?"

Dolly found the woman's questions a bit off, something in the tone of her voice. "Where did he go? I really would like to talk to him about a cold case I am working from many years ago. And no, I don't know him."

The woman hesitated before answering. "He lives in Jemez Springs, he's retired," she said.

"Can you give me his phone number?"

"I can't do that without permission. Perhaps you should talk to Father Sanchez. He's here. But may I suggest you make an appointment and come see him in person, perhaps tomorrow?"

Now she really was clamming up, for both priests. They needed to see who she was and find out what she wanted first. Definitely a problem here. "Sure, I need to talk to him anyway about another matter, so that will work out just fine. What time can he see me tomorrow?"

After setting an eleven o'clock interview with Father Sanchez the next day, Dolly did several online searches for Father Robert Marquez, using every kind of identifying word and phrase imaginable, but found nothing. The fact he left the diocese before everyone's business could be found online was part of the problem, convenient for him if he needed to spend his last years in Jemez Springs. Only priests with severe problems got to retire there—pedophiles, alcoholics, the mentally ill. "Got" to retire was not an exaggeration. The town, nestled on the edge of the Jemez Mountains a few miles beyond Jemez Pueblo, was one of the most beautiful in New Mexico, perhaps in the United States, certainly in the Southwest.

So why was he really there? The answer to that question might provide important insights into both cases. And where was he the day, and night, of each death?

An excuse to make the gorgeous drive to Jemez Springs would be a welcome treat, even if the results ended up being less than joyful.

Dolly arrived punctually for her appointment at the office of Father Sanchez . The old man moved slowly as he rose from his desk when she entered the room after her soft knock and his invitation to enter. She knew that Detective Hernandez was a few years older, but one never would have known it. Chavez seemed decades older than Hernandez. Where the old detective was filled with jocularity and vigor, the priest appeared heavily burdened and aged, fragile almost.

"Sit down, sit down," he said, waving toward a chair. "I know you are here about our little altar boy found in the river," he said with resignation in his voice. He sounded tired and looked worn out.

"Yes and no. I actually am here about the Danny Sanchez case three decades ago," she said, wanting to catch the old man off guard by bringing up the case immediately, to see how he reacted. She wasn't disappointed.

Father Sanchez' face turned to stone for a brief second. She was sure some of the color left it too, even though the lights in the office were so dim, it was hard to be sure. The room had windows, but the blinds kept the bright Santa Fe sun at bay. He recovered from his apparent shock so quickly, she almost wasn't sure she perceived it. But years of experience had taught her that the subtle, subliminal responses people gave when interviewed not only were real, but also the most honest.

"Danny Tafoya. What about him? That case never has been solved, has it? But that was almost 30 years ago. Has it been reopened?" She noticed the priest was speaking quickly, as though he suddenly had lots of energy, the words almost tumbling over each other in his haste. Interesting, she thought to herself. The subject actually energizes the old man.

"The case never closed." She watched his reaction closely as she spoke. "Any murder case not solved remains open, no statute of limitations. You know that from hearing confessions your entire life, surely." She was choosing words on purpose now, trying to get reactions from him. But his face remained bland, through an act of will, it seemed, not a result of boredom. He probably expected her to to be good at reading faces and body language, so was trying on purpose to remain inscrutable.

"The boy was found this week in almost the exact same place as Danny was found, ironically not far from the Santuario de Guadalupe. Both were made to look like a drowning, but turns out neither was. Yet we don't know exactly what killed them. The old case is being reviewed again because of questions this new one has raised about the cause of death." The old man's right eyelid began twitching.

"Excuse me, can I get you something? Some water perhaps?" He rose to go to the little refrigerator on the other side of the room. Trying to get control of himself, she observed.

"Water would be fine, thanks. I've looked at Danny's file and I know you were interviewed by the police. Did you know you were a suspect?" Nothing like being truthfully blunt to get a reaction.

"Is Perrier okay?"

"Sure." She could hear him opening bottles.

"Lemon?"

"Plain is fine."

Father Sanchez handed her a small glass bottle of the old fashioned bubbling French water, which she happened to love, and slowly seated himself again behind his desk. But his moves were slow this time because they were so deliberate, not because he was old, something she had seen a thousand times in interviews when she asked questions people didn't like.

"Yes, I knew," he said, looking directly at her now. "They never told me, but it was obvious by the questions they asked and the interrogations that went on for years with that one detective, Hernandez was his name as I recall." She nodded in agreement. "It was not a time of my life I like to be reminded of."

"Do you have any idea why he wouldn't give up with you?"

"Yes. I think he sensed I knew something, and I did. But then, I know a lot that I cannot share with anyone but God. I told them that over and over, but it didn't seem to do any good. Finally, though, they quit coming back. I never knew if it was because they finally believed me or had information that turned their attention elsewhere."

"So you are saying you did know something and the sanctity of the confessional swore you to eternal secrecy?" she asked. Hernandez said he never claimed it was a confessional issue.

"Yes, that is exactly what I am saying."

She knew from the old man's demeanor the conversation was about to end. "And what about the death this week? What can you tell me? Or do you also know things about it that you cannot share?"

"No, this time I have heard nothing. But there is someone you might like to speak with who may be more help than I can be. His name is Father Marquez. He is retired from this diocese and lives in Jemez Springs where he still does counseling. Here is his phone number and address. I had just arrived here when the Danny Sanchez murder happened. Father Marquez had been here many years then and the police knew him well, many were his parishioners. I always felt they singled me out only because I was new in town, an easy target. They only interviewed Father Marquez once to my knowledge, but he actually knew far more than I did about the situation, things that didn't come from the confessional. He shared what he knew with me but I doubt he told the police much of anything. Now that he no longer is working here and there is a similar murder, he may be willing to say more to you than he did to the investigators back then. I don't know. But I encourage you to visit him.

"Don't try to talk to him over the phone. You need to see him in person, or you won't get any information from him," he added, like it was an afterthought.

She was more puzzled than ever, now that the old man was directing her to Father Marquez, almost eagerly it seemed. Was this a ploy just to get rid of her, a time-consuming dead-end? Or was he really trying to help her, and the case? She'd find out just as soon as she could make the trip to Jemez Springs. Obviously he didn't know Hernandez had visited with Marquez many times. Why not?

"I know you spent a lot of extra time with the boy that was found murdered. I also know you don't have a reputation for pedophilia. Your record is spotless in this town, officially and through the gossip channels. You've been here long enough now that if you had problems, someone would have figured it out, don't you agree?"

"I do, and you are right. I am not a pedophile. I grew up without a father, raised by a single mother who worked long hours to take care of us. Detective Hernandez grew up in the same town, and by now probably has told you a lot about me, how I used to dress up like La Llorona. The fantasies of a lonely young boy with too much time on his hands, and a fascination with ghosts, I fear.

"Hernandez has told people I am a cross dresser, but I am not, and was not when young. I just had a strange obsession with La Llorona. As a Santa Fe priest for several decades now, I have learned a lot in the confessional about the torture sexual deviation of any kind can bring people. And I have a keen awareness of the many definitions and conditions, what is normal and what isn't, medically speaking. As well as what the Church teaches of course.

"I myself think my youthful obsession with La Llorona was strange, and I know any expert would say it was. But I always have provided full disclosure to the people who trained me and hired me over my lifetime, and so far, no one has had a problem with it. I apparently outgrew it, like young people outgrow a lot of interests and propensities that cause society to label them as strange. Some youngsters wet the bed, some walk in their sleep, many have nightmares and fear monsters in their closets. I was fascinated by, and afraid of, La Llorona. Dressing up like her was my way of facing my fear of her and the strange stories I heard about her all my young life.

"I even hear them now here in Santa Fe, you know of them, everyone does. Even cops claim to see her here. So was I drawn to an actual evil spirit, which many claim she is, or was I simply a boy with a strange obsession? Even shrinks and priests are torn on that one, given the number of supposedly sane people who claim to encounter her, people who claim they are fully functioning stable adults leading normal lives.

"And none of this connects me to those murdered boys, God rest their souls. I am in deep mourning for this one now, and never have quit mourning the death of Danny all those years ago. I still say prayers for him daily."

"Thank you, Father," Dolly said as he got to his feet. "I appreciate you being so candid with me. You have been most helpful. Oh, one more thing. Why did you not tell the police what you just now told me, all those years ago, about Father Marquez knowing more than you did?"

"I probably would have lost this assignment. I grew up in Mora and it took many years for me to get an assignment in my home state. It was too precious for me to lose. Father Marquez was my supervisor and I felt it was his choice to tell them what he knew, not mine. I didn't want to risk bringing his wrath down upon me."

"And what about the wrath of God?"

He got up, opened the door and bid her good day.

She thanked him for his time and left the premises, pondering their conversation. Why did Father Sanchez fear the old priest's wrath? Had he witnessed it or been a victim of it, or was that just a figure of speech he used? And was it significant that he had said this time he had heard nothing, instead of this time he knew nothing? Mere semantics, or a significant clue to the truth?

Sister Rosalie had the appearance of a woman many years older than she was. Did all priests and nuns age quickly? The cloistered lifestyle had not helped this nun age well, and that was an understatement, Dolly thought to herself as she sat down to visit with the elderly nun in her office at the rectory. The fact she *had* an office was a surprise—definitely an unusual situation, just as Detective Hermandez had described.

"Now, my dear, why is it you want to speak with me?" the woman asked, smoothing the sleeves of her habit. The fact she wore one was unusual. You didn't have to be Catholic to know habits weren't fashionable among most nuns these days.

Wanting to jolt the woman into being more spontaneous, knowing otherwise this would be a canned, time-wasting interview, Dolly asked her whether she believed La Llorona existed.

The old woman visibly paled for a fleeting moment, regaining her composure quickly. She obviously was experienced in maintaining a face not easily read. Did that come from a lifetime of spiritual devotion or a lifetime of faking? Dolly found herself wondering which it was as she waited for the woman to answer her question. She had succeeded in catching the woman off guard.

"Do you mean that witch associated with local myths?" The disdain in her voice clarified her stance on the subject.

"Yes," Dolly replied. "Several people with whom I've spoken about the cases with the two murdered boys seem to think there is some kind of connection, either in reality or, if you aren't a believer in such things, then in the mind perhaps of the killer or even those connected to the victims. I know some of the people in the police department claim to have seen the witch. And cops aren't known for being unrealistic generally. Quite the contrary."

"Things of this nature are put here to test our faith," the old nun explained. "God allows the Devil to toy with our mind and emotions only to remind us that He is our Lord. Such illusions have nothing to do with the evil in humans that causes them to murder children. Anyone who thinks a fantasy witch has something to do with the crimes committed against those boys has lost touch with the Lord God. And if you believe them, it only will slow your ability to find who killed them. Obviously the killer from thirty some years ago still hasn't been caught, so rumors and gossip about a make-belief witch certainly didn't help solve that crime. And they won't help solve this recent one either. I would encourage you and your fellow policemen and women to pray more instead of wasting time on idle rumors."

Acting chastised, Dolly asked the old woman if she had any idea who might have committed either murder. The woman replied immediately with an emphatic, "No.

"I obviously can be of no use to you, as you can see. Spend your time among the unfaithful. That is where you will find killers." The old woman rose and, habit skirts swishing, walked out of the room, not bothering to let Dolly out.

Dead in the water. This case was going nowhere for her. She knew she was being stonewalled by everyone. The old priest and the even-older nun knew a lot more than they were telling her, but to continue trying to pry that information out of them was a waste of time.

She pondered what to do next as she drove through the narrow streets of central Santa Fe, noticing how few tourists were walking them, but then she knew that was normal until ski season, which hadn't begun yet this year.

Someone needed to get a break in the case, or this second murder was bound to go cold too. Just like the first one. Hopefully she would find some answers in Jemez Springs.

5

FATHER MARQUEZ STOOD ON THE BALCONY OF HIS SECOND floor apartment, gazing on the Jemez River below, watching the snow falling silently in the darkening mountains. The moon was only a sliver, but no one would know it, not with this cloud cover indicating the impending snow storm that was introducing itself just now with the gentle snowfall. The November storm was welcome, bringing much-needed moisture to the old forest.

But it wasn't the snow that drew the old priest outdoors to his balcony. It was something else, something he knew from long experience never to speak of. Something that began when he was a mere boy, and had been a normal part of his life ever since. He knew it wasn't normal for others. And he knew if he ever said a word, it could have ruined his career as a priest, and therefore his life. Now that he was retired, he still knew he could never speak of it, for then his reputation would be ruined and he didn't want to die without respect.

He could hear the wailing in the distance, it was just beginning, gently, in rhythm with the snowflakes as they fell silently. If anyone else heard it, they would assume it was the wind in the canyon, but he learned long ago how to differentiate between mere wind and *her*, La Llorona. He had been hearing—and seeing her— since he was a child. As he got older, he quit questioning her arrival. But it had been a long time since her last appearance, far longer than usual. Ten years maybe? She used to visit him at least every year, sometimes more often. He had hoped she had forgotten about him, that with his retirement, she would have no further need of him. Yet here she was again. He didn't have to ask himself what it meant, he knew all too well. Another child had died. But where? He knew there had been no deaths in his community—a small town like Jemez Springs couldn't contain news like that for more than a few minutes. If nothing had happened here, why was she appearing? And why did no one else see her? Or did they keep as quiet about it as he always had? Perhaps he should start a support group and see who showed up. A group where people who had seen La Llorona could come to share their experiences, their fears. He laughed. Only in modern-day America could such a thought even enter his mind. But with recovery groups for everything from Amway to Southern Baptists—and yes, even Catholicism—it wasn't such a far-fetched idea. Except for one thing. Alive, yes, but no saint this. She was an apparition, a ghost who had no intention of allowing the worldwide legend around her to die. She thrived on being terrifying.

He had read all the books and stories about her that had been written during his lifetime. Santa Fe cops and other government employees reported encounters with her. But the sightings that got written down usually made her out to be a benign, even helpful character, more like an angel than a ghost, much less an evil ghost. He often wondered if there were two La Lloronas, and the evil twin was the one who visited him, while the one who got reported so much was the good angel twin.

Through the years, what he had come to suspect was that La Llorona had been running a public relations campaign for herself for centuries. She knew how to appear angelic and helpful to humans often enough that her more fearsome and evil nature became less believable. This gave her more power to do her evil deeds, or to influence humans to do them for her, which is how he suspected she worked.

But she never tried to fool him. Perhaps she knew what a coward he was, and that he would never tell what he knew. But even if he had, it wouldn't— couldn't—stop her, so what was the point? He often wondered if some evil deed he had done in a past life had caused him to be cursed with her presence and his knowledge of her evil throughout this life. It was enough to make him believe in reincarnation. He knew from his academic studies and the confessional that a lot of Catholics did. He still wasn't sold on the concept, even though he knew it was the Catholic Church that took all references to it out of the scriptures when putting the Christian Bible together. It had been part of the Jewish belief system until then, and thus apparently the early Christians'. He knew that such historically documented information, kept in the Vatican libraries, should convince him of its veracity, but he felt more comfortable with the concept of getting through just this one life, not hundreds, or worse, thousands. Maybe God was guiding those early Catholics when they decided to tell the people we only live one life, not many. Keeping it simple. Even God had the right to change his message from time to time.

Whatever La Llorona's reasons, she had been showing herself to him since he was a boy, and always, after one of her appearances, he would learn later, if he didn't know already, of the death of a child. Unnatural deaths. Always. If a child died from an illness, she did not appear. Homicide or suspicious accidents— tragedy drew her out. But why did she always seek *him* out? *Why?*

He had prayed and done penance much of his life, trying to get an answer, but none ever came. Where was the sin? With his parents, with his past lives, with a curse someone placed on him at a young age? He had explored many religions and spiritual beliefs and philosophies throughout his life, trying to find some answers. In the process, he had become an expert on ghosts, those spirits that supposedly get stuck and can't move on to the next world. He knew the difference between those ghosts who need to be freed, to be given permission to leave the earth plane, and spirits that were assumed to be visitors from the Other Side, the spirits the mediums could see and with whom they claimed to chat. Television and movies made those spirits, and the mediums who claimed to communicate with them, normal household concepts these days. Would he have suffered as much if he had had that kind of knowledge as a child? He would never know. He had it now and it never gave him peace. After many years with no appearances, he had begun to believe he was free of her oppression. Until now. He hoped for a second it really was the wind, but one look at the snowfall told him there was no breeze, much less wind. It was her, his little era of peace, gone.

Sometimes he wondered if New Mexico was particularly cursed by her presence. Its residents seemed to experience so many more sightings through the centuries than those in other states and countries. He had felt so drawn by the Holy Spirit to the Jemez Mountains his entire life, and until he retired, he had resisted the Lord's call. He had wanted nothing to do with the controversial Catholic activities in Jemez Springs. But upon retirement, he knew he had to go, he couldn't resist the lifelong call. Finally, it was time to say yes. Now that he was here, he had to ask himself if it had been God or La Llorona beckoning him. He still didn't know why.

He was a New Mexico teenager when two events quietly took place in two locations less than 30 miles apart in the vast ancient mountains that would change the world forever. The first atom bomb was created by the Americans during

World War II, and right after the war ended, a center for priests who needed help with their personal problems opened right here where he lived now.

Some of the most brilliant scientists in the world secretly developed the atom bomb in Los Alamos, the town the United States government built on the northeastern edge of the Jemez Mountains, and a brilliant Catholic priest began an equally secretive endeavor in Jemez Springs that turned out to have as explosive an impact on the world as that bomb. The two towns were 30 miles apart as the crow flies, a couple of leisurely hours on paved highways by car today, and many more hours apart back in those days when only dirt roads connected them, and then only during good weather in the warm months.

Beginning in 1942, the United-States-government-created community of Los Alamos was built to birth, nurture and develop the Manhattan Project, nestled in the grandeur of classic New Mexico beauty on the edge of the vast and ancient Jemez Mountains, which themselves were created by the largest volcanic eruption in known history on this continent. Rock fragments traced to the eruption had been found as far away as Oklahoma.

The first atom bomb produced in Los Alamos was tested officially in July 1945 near Alamogordo, in the southern part of the state, with very few aware of the event at the time. The success of that test immediately led to the use by the United States of its new weapon to destroy Hiroshima and Nagasaki, leading to the end of World War II. An hour or so before that first bomb was dropped on Japan, a Hiroshima college professor announced for the first time, to an exclusive group in that city, that the Japanese were developing an atomic bomb.

In contrast, it took almost fifty years for the world to even begin to fully realize the magnitude of the destruction released on the world by the other Jemez project. Both projects began with the best of intentions on the part of their creators. The first to save and protect the free Western Christian world, and the second to save and protect specifically the Catholic world. Some might argue the goals were identical.

During the years the bomb was being developed in Los Alamos, an American priest serving in Quebec, Canada, was seeing a need and developing a vision for a healing center to help priests who had overwhelming problems with alcohol and attractions to women that sabotaged their ability to serve their communities and their Lord. After making queries throughout the United States and Canada for support, the archbishop in Santa Fe at the time, filling the position Archbishop Jean-Baptiste Lamy once held, gave him his only positive response.

It was in 1947 that the priest's vision was birthed in reality with the building and opening of the Congregation of the Servants of the Paraclete on land purchased in Jemez Springs, connected directly through mountain dirt roads to Los Alamos that were impassable much of the winter. Driving on two-lane paved highways required at least half a day, if the weather was good, of driving around the mountains and through Santa Fe. The two projects just as well have been continents apart. But it didn't matter, since the goals of both were maximum privacy and secrecy, easily achieved in their respective locations.

Famed author Willa Cather wrote a novel about Lamy that made him famous outside New Mexico—*Death Comes for the Archbishop*. She never lived in New Mexico, and wrote the book as a result of French influences in her life, not Spanish. Born a Baptist, she spent most of her life an Episcopalian. After making New Mexico Catholicism famous with her novel, she died in April of the year the bishop-approved center opened in Jemez Springs.

Catholic priests and monks who had problems with alcohol and womanizing were sent to the Jemez Springs center by church authorities who hoped for miracles of modern medicine and faith, and who believed in the vision of its founding priest. But almost immediately after opening, the center began receiving priests from throughout America who had a far more sinister problem, a sexual affinity for children and teens, conveniently found among the altar boys more often than not, but young girls certainly were not immune from the predators, in those days before girls were allowed to be altar servers.

No one outside the church, and very few within the vast Catholic church domain, knew about this for a long, long time because of a massive cover-up. Not even the residents of the tiny Jemez Springs village new about the pedophiles being brought into their midst. The founder of the center was apparently a good man with good intentions, who sincerely wanted to help the troubled priests.

But after only a few months of dealing with the pedophiles, he wrote the appropriate superiors and explained to them that these men could not be healed and should be removed from their vocations as priests. And that they no longer should be sent to the retreat center, where its resources were wasted on them.

His words were sent to deaf ears. Despite the immense secrecy within which the center always remained enshrouded, bits and pieces of his battle in this regard came to light over the years. He died in 1969, but it wasn't until his papers were released to the public in 2009 that so many of the details became available. They left no doubt about his personal integrity, high ideals and lofty goals, nor about how others in positions of power within the Catholic hierarchy rode roughshod over his requests, ignoring his insights while building a bureaucracy of evil within the Church that hasn't been rectified to this day. Sexual abuse of children has a way of wreaking its havoc upon many subsequent generations after the original victimization, psychologically and spiritually, if not also physically, therapists now understood.

By the 1960s the old priest was trying to buy an island to house the pedophiles for the Church, so convinced was he of their inability to change or to be productive members of society, and by then, of the total inability of the church to deal with them through methods that served the best interests of parishioners. His death in 1969 stopped that project, since his superiors and replacement had no interest in it, still heavily ensconced at the time in an international bureaucracy of secrets and lies where pedophile priests were concerned.

He was unable to stop the influx of the pedophiles into his center, and thus forced to deal with their treatment and subsequent release. Alcoholism and uncontrollable attractions to adult women paled in comparison to the insidious pedophilia problems the center was finding itself forced to treat. The men were being released if and when they apparently were healed of their affliction, and sent back into parishes as the priests they were, with no one the wiser as to where they had been. They always were the new priest in town, usually the new priest in the state. Where they were assigned, the fact they were allowed to remain priests at all—these decisions were out of the hands of the good man who founded the center. In his own way, he too was a victim of the bureaucracy of the Catholic church that had taken on a wayward life of its own, one without the Light of the Christ. Few if any today would argue that. Few if any then realized it.

Unfortunately, New Mexico parishes suffered the most from this process, because the priests were sent to every place possible throughout the state, from the tiniest remote mountain villages to the largest urban areas. When no more positions were available, more were released into other parts of the nation, like a silent plague. Some eventually ended up in Europe even, fleeing, hiding, from the problems they created in the United States.

Thus the Jemez Mountains became the birthplace for a set of Evil Twins conceived with good intentions. One born within the secular confines of government, in efforts to save the Western World, synonymous to most people on earth with the Christian World, the other within the world's oldest, largest and most famous Christian institution. These twin phenomena would determine the course of world history for decades, probably even centuries. Maybe even until the end of the world. Certainly until the end of the world as it was known then and now.

His reverie about the past exhausting him, Father Marquez went inside his apartment, welcoming sleep, albeit troubled as it was recently.

It was a perfect day for a drive to Jemez Springs, the beautiful landscapes in sharp contrast to Dolly's thoughts of the destructive forces birthed in the Jemez half a century ago. Taking longer than ever to completely pass the ever-growing Rio Rancho as she drove along state highway 550, which could take her almost to Farmington, her mother's birthplace, Dolly soon reached San Ysidro and turned onto N.M. State Highway Four, which wound alongside the Jemez River most of the way to Jemez Springs.

Dolly arrived in the center of this special state, renowned even then for its natural beauty and famous artists, soon after three of the most important world events of the twentieth century. At the time of her birth in the middle of the century, no one but a handful of people held the secrets of those profound events.

Born in a Catholic hospital in downtown Albuquerque on a winter night so unusually snowy for the fairly temperate climate, the schools were shut down for days, the nuns helped Dolly's forty-year-old devout Southern Baptist mother get her here after a grueling forty-eight hours of labor, unusual considering Dolly was her fifth child. The old doctor who had delivered most of Dolly's older siblings preferred to avoid caesarians, even though her mother had requested one before going into labor, and once the labor seemed never-ending and without results, she requested one again. Both times he refused, saying he didn't really believe in them if the mother and baby were healthy, and in this case it was his medical opinion that they were. He felt natural birth was best, surgery a radical option to be used only in a crisis. An older woman's fear of having a child at her age was not a crisis to him, especially in the case of a healthy, seemingly youthful mother like Dolly's had been, often mistaken for someone a decade, or even two, younger than her real age. Despite his rational approach, the fact remained that no woman in that era chose to have children in her forties.

The pregnancy was an embarrassment to Dolly's mother, since none of her peers were having children at that age. Dolly's older brother, twelve years her senior, confided to her decades later, that it was to him as well. No mother with a house full of teenagers got pregnant, he said, not among his peers. At least the good old doctor who was confident he knew best allowed anesthesia during the actual birth when the time finally arrived. Dolly always regretted her inability to know what she was thinking and feeling during all that. She hated the idea of having started her life fully drugged, but knew that just about every baby of her generation did. No wonder the Baby Boomers became known for their drug culture in the 1960s and beyond. The doctors started them on drugs at birth.

Having a working knowledge of both Vedic and Western astrology, Dolly knew that both the ancient system out of India and the traditional system used in the Western world, indicated that her Saturn in the first house conjunct her Western Libra rising sign meant a likelihood of a difficult birth. And the underlying meaning of that reluctance to be born on her part was a soul who didn't want to come back into this world, a been there, done that, attitude toward life from the get-go. If there was such a thing as an old soul, she was one. And her mother's experience was factual, so even if astrology was bogus, it still got it right when it came to her mother's and her experience of the birth—a too-long and therefore exhausting labor for both. Reluctant baby, reluctant mother. What a bad start, some might say. But then some might say the same about the creation of the nuclear age with the development of that first atomic bomb, birthed just five and a half years before she was, a couple of hours away by fast car and paved roads today. Back then it was almost impossible to even find Los Alamos.

Right on the heels of the series of nuclear tests in the central part of the state, the now-internationally-famous Roswell UFO crash happened, near the village of Corona, south of Roswell, in July 1947. As if the Roswell crash and the atom bomb weren't enough world-famous events for one New Mexico decade, a Catholic priest with good intentions secretly founded a healing center for priests in Jemez Springs. But by the time she was born, he was beginning to realize the pedophile priests being sent to the center were proving to be unfixable in any traditional sense of that concept.

All three events were shrouded in secrecy for decades, but once the facts began slowly leaking, and eventually quickly pouring, out of the state, New Mexico was on the international map in a way that no one could possibly have predicted when the territory became a state in 1912. By the time World War II was over, the entire world knew about New Mexico.

Some felt it was Divine Justice the Bomb was created there, since so many New Mexico soldiers suffered at the hands of the Japanese in the Pacific during the war, especially in the prison camps and during the horrid Bataan March. New Mexico Hispanics and Native Americans as well as Anglos fought, suffered and died by the hundreds in the Philippines in particular. Movies have been made, and books written, about the cruel prison camp conditions to which the men were subjected. The fact any lived to return home was miraculous. A major Albuquerque hospital was even named Bataan after the war.

Dolly passed through Jemez Pueblo, in her opinion the New Mexico pueblo with the most idyllic setting of all. She knew that many felt that way about Taos Pueblo, which certainly was the most famous of all the pueblos, but that didn't change her feelings about the ancient Jemez village. The view of the mountains and foothills, flat mesas and red bluffs, while driving toward the pueblo, was one of the most stunning in the state, any time of year, with too many shades of blues, purples, pinks, reds, oranges, browns, taupes for even a seasoned artist to name, plus greenery and wild flowers in summer, a panoply of high desert and mountain foothill color in autumn, snow in winter. She often wondered if there were enough official shades in the art world to label every single one this view could offer. She doubted it.

This spectacular panorama was all that was visible while driving the twenty miles or so from the tiny village of San Ysidro, with its two hundred or so residents, founded in 1699 by a Spaniard, to Jemez Pueblo, founded hundreds of years ago, maybe a thousand years or more, with almost two thousand residents, some full-time, some not. Once the highway began nearing the pueblo community, the valley spread out as far as the eye could see. Cultivated fields of green in summer turned to varied shades of orange and gold in autumn, tilled red and brown dirt in spring, and various shades of snow-covered white in winter. Maybe the Bible scholars were wrong, and this actually was where Eden had been. It certainly could be an Original Paradise, complete with resplendent apple orchards and great rattlesnake specimens, more abundant some years than others, depending on climate conditions. The inhabitants still hunted deer and rabbits regularly. She had been the fortunate recipient of some of the pueblo venison one year from a neighbor who was a member of the pueblo. She had made venison stew with it, using juniper berries from her own bushes. It was delicious.

Her father used to comment as he drove this section of the highway to Jemez that he wished he was an artist just so he could paint that view with its many colors and shadows, which changed with the seasons and the weather, and hourly as the sun rose, soared, then set. His mother and both of his sisters were artists who could and did paint scenes of that type, but he never tried painting himself. Dolly was not sure he had the family gift, since when she was quite young, she asked him to draw a picture of God for her and it was really bad. As a child, she excelled at drawing and could tell he did not after that request made early in her life. But she didn't tell him it was a bad God drawing, since he had tried, and apparently taken her request quite seriously, putting down his newspapers, which he read for hours every evening, to spend a goodly amount of time trying to draw God for her.

He may not have been an artist in skill, but he was one at heart. She always understood his deep appreciation for natural beauty, such as this beautiful area, for no matter how much she traveled, this remained one of her favorite in the world so far. If there was a creator God, as monotheists claimed, this had to be some of that great entity's most award-winning works in the entire universe.

As she drove through some of the most beautiful scenery in New Mexico, perhaps in the entire United States, she turned her thoughts from world history to her phone conversation with Father Marquez. He hadn't seemed surprised to hear from her at all, in fact it was as though he was expecting her call. But maybe he was just lonely and made everyone who called him feel that way. She had done some research on him, and learned he apparently chose to retire to Jemez Springs, he wasn't sent there by the Church to recover from anything, like most of the priests in Jemez Springs were. He also wasn't totally retired. He did some counseling at the Catholic retreat center where he also resided, and where she planned to spend the night. Given his credentials, that didn't surprise her. He had two masters degrees and a double PhD, yet remained in Santa Fe all those decades. He probably could have served anywhere, with credentials like that, or taught at one of the many Catholic universities. And contrary to what Detective Hernandez had said, he apparently held no administrative position at the center.

Father Marquez had suggested they meet at one thirty in the lobby of the retreat center, nestled next to the Jemez River, on the north side of the village. As she walked into the peaceful center, she saw Father Marquez standing across the room with his back to her, looking out the plate glass windows at the river below. He turned when he heard her walking toward him.

"You must be Dolly McIntyre?" he asked with a pleasant smile as he held out his hand to her.

"Yes, I am. Father Marquez, I presume?" as she gave him her hand, which he shook firmly.

He motioned to a corner of the huge, sunny room where a couch and comfortable easy chairs were arranged in front of a roaring fireplace. "The sun belies how cold it is this time of year," he chuckled as they sat down in two chairs, both of them facing the welcoming fire. "Would you like something to drink, some tea or coffee, water?"

"No, no, I'm fine, thank you," Dolly replied, pulling her notebook and her phone out of her tote bag. "Do you mind if I record our conversation?"

A look of dismay passed briefly over his face before he replied, "No that's fine, although I may ask you to turn it off for some things we discuss—if we can have that ground rule, then I don't mind."

Obviously he was expecting them to cover some sensitive matters, she thought to herself. "Let's begin with me explaining to you exactly why I am here and how that came to be, so you will have the context for my visit before I start recording or writing, how does that sound?" she asked, attempting to put him at ease. If he wasn't comfortable with her, he wouldn't tell her as much as he could.

He assented, and she spent the next twenty minutes filling him in on everything she knew, starting with the thirty-year-old cold case, and Father Sanchez' suggestion that she contact him. He listened carefully, asking astute questions from time to time. She didn't leave anything out. She knew that the more details she shared with him, the more likely he was to open up to her willingly, or at the very least, reveal things to her even unconsciously with facial expressions and body language.

She watched him carefully as she spoke, but he revealed nothing to her the way most people do when confronted with the gory details and unanswered questions of unsolved murder cases. Either he was an excellent actor, or he truly had no strong reactions to anything she said. He seemed tired, and resigned. Perhaps nothing surprised him anymore. She often had thought that priests probably had more of an inside track than any other profession into people's true lives because of the confessional. Only those who could afford contemporary counselors with their various titles and credentials—psychiatrists, psychologists, social workers— chose to go to them generally, but all Catholics went to the confessional at some point in their lives, although not as regularly or in the numbers they once did. Although it wasn't unheard of for a person to lie to their secular counselor, few who went into the confessional booth had the courage to defy God, Jesus Christ the Son, the Holy Spirit, the Church, the Pope, all the Saints, and the Priest on the other side of the screen, all in one fell swoop, by lying. People either confessed their sins or they didn't bring them up. Not confessing a sin wasn't nearly as serious as lying about one. You didn't need to be raised Catholic to know that. If only priests could write tell-all books once they retired.

When she finished, Father Marquez sat quietly for a few moments, hands in prayer mode, obviously deep in thought. She looked out the vast windows, taking in the beauty of the mountain autumn day, waiting for him to speak.

"The police suspected both Father Sanchez and myself when Danny Tafoya was murdered," he said at last, still staring into space, almost as though he were in a trance. "You probably know that. They never actually told us that, but it was obvious after they kept coming back to us for more interviews. We told them the same things over and over, the truth. So our stories never changed. I assume Father Sanchez once again is a suspect?" He finally looked over at her as she nodded.

"Everyone is at first, you know that. But by now, unlike when Danny was murdered and he was the new priest in town, he has earned a stellar reputation, which I assume you also know. He isn't so much a popular well-loved priest as he is an upright one that everyone seems to trust. Apparently he is taken seriously and respected. The SFPD always knows the inside gossip about the priests in that town, and you know that too.

"They knew there were things we couldn't tell them because of the confessional, we told them that of course, but they kept trying to get more information out of us. Being a relatively young priest at the time, it was extremely disturbing to Father Sanchez, the entire ordeal. He took his vocation so seriously. To move back to his home state only to be suspected of a child's murder was almost too much for him. I don't know that he ever has recovered completely. I know I never did, and by the time it happened, there wasn't much I hadn't experienced as a priest, or so I thought at the time. In those days, priests were above suspicion automatically, unlike today, when they all too often actually are lawbreakers, and innocent or not, always suspects in any crime of this magnitude and circumstance.

"Today, the police would have made us official suspects, but they didn't dare in those days unless they had a solid case against us, or one of us, and they didn't. There was none to be had." He looked at her then, expectantly.

"Yes, I met with the detective who handled that case and he told me the same thing you are telling me." He nodded as she spoke, once again staring straight ahead, seemingly lost in his memories of the past. Was she going to end up confirming his long-held suspicions without getting any new information out of him? Would this trip end up being useful to him but a wild goose chase for her? Trepidation was beginning to engulf her.

"Father Sanchez sent you to me because he thinks I know some things he did not. He told me so when he called to tell me you might be contacting me at his suggestion. He never had shared his opinion with me before, but I wasn't surprised. He was and is a very observant person, so it doesn't surprise me that he could tell I knew more than I let on at the time, the confessional notwithstanding. I had hoped by moving here, I was permanently removed from my old life in Santa Fe. But your presence here today proves to me I am not," he said, looking directly at her once again.

His stare was so intense, she almost winced. She wasn't even a Catholic and he was making her feel guilty, for just showing up in his life. She remained silent, waiting for him to continue.

"We were taught as priests to protect our own always. As a result, the Church has gotten itself into a great deal of trouble in recent years and that trouble continues. While we continue to protect our own. What most people do not realize is that many of those appearing to be protectors were coming from a point of naivete, not evil. Today many priests come into the vocation at an older age than they once did, many have been married and raised children, had secular careers. But that is only a recent phenomenon. In my day and for centuries before, young men went into the priesthood as teens generally, or as young men in their twenties. For many the Church was the only life they ever knew outside of their family of origin. Before sex and the ways of sex were a daily part of the public information system, priests learned most of what they knew as teens growing up around other young men, and later, from what they heard in the confessional. They were not trained to recognize, much less understand, sexual perversion. Priests who got involved with women were not unknown, of course, and that possibility was addressed in our training. But anything outside of normal male and female relationships and the temptations that could arise from such were nonexistent in our training and our psyche. The Church has been blamed for protecting the monsters who have hidden in the priesthood, but the reality is that few within the Church had any idea they were protecting sexual predators and perverts until it was too late, for they didn't know how to recognize such people, and the situation that could and did arise all too often. How many pedophiles have you known in your life, personally, not through your work with the police?" he asked, again looking directly at her.

Caught off guard at his question, she could only stare back at him for a moment before answering. "Three that I can recall, and even then, it took me years to realize it, due to my naivete. It was when I lived in Texas. They were gay men who preferred under-age boys to adult men. Well-respected men, I might add—in publishing, writing and film, one a Harvard graduate.

"That is what I mean. Given the statistics in this country, you probably have known even more. Everyone has. But you haven't lived your life in a religious order where people take vows to be as pure and good as possible for the rest of their lives, to live as examples for ordinary people. How could a priest be expected to recognize sexual perverts among his comrades and peers along his life path if ordinary people who aren't expecting everyone around them to be shining examples of moral virtue usually can't either?

"Today, this issue is being addressed in training, fortunately, but that doesn't make up for the broken lives and hearts scattered throughout the world. It isn't just the victims of the bad priests, nor the bad priests themselves, who have been broken. The priests, and nuns, who worked with those wayward men, and who knew their victims and the families, also have been broken by these situations. The days when people who choose the Church for their vocation can live naively removed from the raw realities of the human condition are gone. Perhaps this horror has come to pass to force the professionals in the Church to become more real, more like Jesus the man who walked among men and women, rather than using their vocation to escape the realities of life on earth. It was a much-needed change and it is sad that sexual perversion was the means to that end, but God works in ways we cannot always understand. Now, not only the Church but all of society is aware of pedophilia, and once awareness exists, healing can begin, which of course includes prevention.

Realizing she was being stonewalled, albeit in a most genteel and intellectual and actually quite interesting manner, she tried a new tactic just to move the conversation somewhere besides where it was stalemated.

"Who was involved with the altar servers in addition to the priest or priests who worked with them, anyone?" she asked. "Perhaps nuns or older, more experienced servers? Some of the local brothers?"

"Actually, very few people ever are involved with altar boys besides the priest or priests whom they assist during services. Obviously it now is common knowledge this is why so many of the perversions have happened so easily. No one ever thought a priest needed to be chaperoned."

Was he joking or serious? She didn't smile since he didn't, waiting to see if he would say more or once again, avoid answering the question directly.

"There is one nun who does help with the boys, which is highly unusual. I know she was questioned at the time of the murder 30 years ago, and that you are questioning her now. Sister Rosalie is my actual sister, by that I mean we had the same parents, and because of that, she was allowed to fill a different role in relation to us priests at the basilica than a nun normally would. Many of her duties are usually carried out by the priests themselves, or brothers or hired staff members. Once I left, she remained in her position simply because there seemed to be no need for her to leave. She manages the rectory and certain aspects of the basilica. She is an extremely capable woman. And I don't say that just because she is my sister, but simply because it is true. She manages the building and grounds maintenance as well as the people who work and live in them. And she is an excellent cook. She oversees the hired staff members as well as the volunteer groups who do most of the cleaning and tend the yards."

"And what was her relationship with the altar servers, if any? Dolly queried.

"Mostly provider of homemade goodies, since she loves to bake. Being an altar boy in our parish was extra special because of her services. It wasn't only the food, though. Over the years, she formed close relationships with some of the servers, and served as a second mother and sometimes a counselor to them, especially some who were not given enough attention nor nurturing at home."

"So what does she think about the murders? Surely you have discussed these with her?"

"Actually, I haven't spoken at length with her about either, because in both cases, the boys were ones to whom she felt close, and it was too upsetting for her. This second situation has been especially hard for her, since I don't think she ever really recovered completely from the first death in the 1980s. I do know that she is a strong believer in the legend of La Llorona, and she thinks she is somehow connected to the deaths, but how I don't know. "

"La Llorona, the ghost?" Dolly asked, obviously stunned, given her recent encounter with the elderly nun.

"Yes."

"A nun who believes in ghosts. Interesting."

"But not unusual. We Catholics believe in miracles performed by the Saints, and we believe in Evil, which can take many forms. La Llorona may be one of them, no one knows for sure, but the stories have been told for centuries and Hispanics throughout the world claim to have seen her, including your cop cronies in Santa Fe. So this isn't an ordinary ghost story, nor is it unusual that she believes in La Llorona's existence, even as a nun. She and I were raised in Hispanic culture, in the Estancia Valley, but our mother was German. Her family came to New Mexico when she was a little girl. She was a Catholic so it was easy for her to fit into the local Hispanic culture in that respect. My sister and I were hearing the La Llorona stories from our classmates at a very young age. My sister always took them quite seriously.

"Several times I tried to discuss Danny's death, and she simply couldn't handle it, so I gave up. Sometimes family members are the least useful in these situations, and ours was especially vulnerable, given we worked together so closely for so many decades. She also lives in the rectory, has her own quarters. Once I retired, she wouldn't have been allowed to stay except that her age puts her in a category now that as a female, she simply could not be tempting to any young, middle-aged, nor even older, priest. Biology has worked in her favor in this instance, ensuring her a home there until she no longer can work. Given the state of her health and her basic constitution, that could be many years from now."

"So you don't have any idea whether she suspects anyone specifically, in either murder?"

Dolly knew what he was going to say before she asked the question, sensing he was stonewalling her yet again.

"I think you should talk to her yourself," was all he said, with no emotion showing in his demeanor whatsoever.

She sensed him shut himself off from her and knew this interview was finished. Now was the time to tell him she wasn't leaving the retreat center yet. She thanked him for his time, and told him she was going to spend one night at the center. She noticed an almost imperceptible flinch. He didn't like that. She hadn't expected him to.

"Do you have a reservation?"

"Yes, I made one online, but I need to check in at the registration desk."

He pointed her in the right direction. "Enjoy your stay."

For an old man, he certainly left the room quickly.

6

AFTER CHECKING INTO THE CENTER, DOLLY WENT TO SEE HER room. It was austere, almost quaint in its simplicity. If the building had been really old, it would have been quaint. Inexpensive mid-twentieth-century architecture did not lend itself readily to the use of the word quaint in her opinion. Locking her door, she went out a side door to the parking lot. The crisp autumn day could not have been prettier. She decided to get something to eat, since she hadn't signed up for meals at the center, only morning coffee. She loved any excuse to eat at the Jemez Springs restaurants, especially the two mainstays that were across the street from each other. Today Mexican food for a late lunch it would be. And it was.

Arriving back at the center, she took her suitcase with her to her room and changed clothes, then wandered out back to the path that led down to the Jemez River, to an area complete with seating for the guests, but invisible from the windows of the center. The bench-sitters were guaranteed privacy.

As she listened to the water rolling past her, breathing deeply of the fresh mountain air, her eyes taking in the cliffs that soared above the deep river canyon, she found herself thinking about her childhood and the wonderful experiences her parents gave her in these mountains and the Sandias, the mountain range next to Albuquerque. The ranges weren't that far apart, but geologically they could have been on different continents, they were so different.

The Jemez range was created by a gigantic volcanic eruption about a million years ago. Actually there were two eruptions some half a million years apart, apparently, give or take a few thousand years. She always found scientific timelines fascinating. The massive forest that covered the mountains grew out of the rich dirt formed on top of the volcanic ash and rock. Hot springs as well as cool ones could be found throughout the range. The cool springs provided drinkable water, while the hot springs reminded humans that a volcano still existed below and, scientists predicted, would erupt again in the future. They said it probably wouldn't happen again for ten thousand years, give or take a few centuries or even a millennium, but experts often got it wrong when it came to volcanic eruptions, an imperfect science at best.

The Sandia Mountains were formed by the Rio Grande, much like the Colorado River formed the Grand Canyon in Arizona. Other factors were involved with the Sandias. An earthquake fault line ran along the Rio Grande from southern Colorado all the way to Chihuahua, Mexico. The last Albuquerque earthquakes the scientists counted, as opposed to mere tremors, were in 1906, two that year. Occasionally tremors were strong enough that everyone felt them.

She recalled her experiences her freshman year of college, when tremors were strong enough to wake people up in the middle of the night and shake the furniture. She just happened to be home on a break from college, so got to experience them firsthand. No one she knew then seemed to know they were living in an earthquake zone, so it created quite a media storm at the time and a lot of fear among many, at least trepidation, which was her reaction. Modern science, better media coverage of the subject and of course, the internet, meant that most people now knew Albuquerque was in an earthquake zone. Even so, the climate and beauty of the area caused few if any to suffer anxiety over the possibilities, so unless tremors were experienced, it was a fairly dormant subject. The state tourism industry certainly wanted everyone to forget, or at least keep their mouth shut, given tourism was a major player in the New Mexico economy.

Her parents rarely took bona fide vacations when she was growing up, due to their work schedules, especially her father's. What they did instead was make short trips to both the Jemez and the Sandias, for lunch, or an early supper cookout, during the hot Albuquerque summers when the cool mountain temperatures were a welcome respite. Few homes were air conditioned in those days. Her family had one big swamp cooler in a brick room off the kitchen that only ran a few hours during the hottest of summer days. The rest of the time, and in the rest of the mostly adobe house, open windows and lots of fans, coupled with the many and massive shade trees and lawn surrounding their home, kept them cool enough for comfort. Albuquerque summers were cooler then anyway, especially in the rural area where her family lived. The asphalt and concrete that half a century of non-stop development brought to the area since after World War II had not helped the climate.

Those Sandia mountain excursions always included a cookout in the campsite picnic areas provided by the National Park Service, and wading in the now non-existent streams. She remembered when they all dried up, during the drought that battered the state the first few years of her life. Before she started school, they went most frequently each summer to the Sandias for their cookouts and wading sprees. Even her mother waded. As most good Southern Baptist women of her generation, born in the Victorian era of the Western World, she didn't wear pants in the middle of the twentieth century. She would take off her shoes and lift her skirt a bit in the deep areas. Her father just sat around, smoked cigars and relaxed. Her brothers, who didn't always come along depending on their summer work schedules, and her older sister, often hiked the areas. Even with the dirt roads, the family could get to a campground in the Sandias in about an hour, always less than two no matter how far up into the mountains they drove, so they often went for a supper cookout during the long summer evenings. The kids galavanted around while their mom cooked and their dad helped her, usually by starting the fire and keeping it going properly, and keeping an eye on Dolly, since she was such an active and adventurous little tyke, but not old enough to hike with her older siblings.

Trips to the Jemez were rare during those years when the Sandias had lots of water. By the time she started school when she was six and a half, and all of those had dried up, a few more each year until there were none, the family took fewer and fewer trips to the Sandias. Instead they went more frequently to the Jemez. The drives each way were twice as long or more, but the streams were filled with fish and her father liked to fish, something he never did in the Sandias.

Rental cabins were available deep in the Jemez, near Fenton Lake, in a tiny community of mostly summer homes about halfway between Jemez Springs and Los Alamos, and when she was two, her family actually spent about a week in one. Located between the lake and the fish hatchery, it was on the road to the old dude ranch that was used by the famous Chicago prohibition gangster, Al Capone, as a hideout from the law. She had heard several versions of the stories from people in the area while she was growing up. Some said the ranch, only a few miles into the woods past the fish hatchery at the end of a rutted dirt road, was built by him, a believable story given the isolation it would have had in the 1930s. It was incredibly isolated even when she was young, the road to it from the hatchery barely passable at times even in summer. And the rock toll-booth-like entryway that she was told once housed Capone's armed guards certainly provided evidence of an actual fortress in days gone by. Media stories in later years claimed the place already was a dude ranch, which Capone and his gang utilized after enjoying the hot springs baths in Jemez Springs while trying to hide out from the various branches of law enforcement, and perhaps even rival gangsters. All she knew was that old-timers who lived in the area year-round for decades always said he built the place and then it became a dude ranch, once he no longer had any need for it. Probably old land deeds could reveal the truth, not that it mattered. No one disputed the fact Capone stayed there and used its extraordinary isolation to hide.

Capone was in the area in the 1920s and 1930s. In 1971, David Bowie, the famed British rock star, came to the area to film portions of the film, "The Man Who Fell to Earth," at Fenton Lake. Other parts of the movie were filmed throughout the state. The sanitized, heavily edited and censored version that was released initially was quite different than the original, extremely long, uncut version now available to anyone anywhere for purchase or rent, and occasionally even shown at movie theaters, given the cult classic status the movie quickly achieved.

That week in the early 1950s when Dolly's family stayed at the rental cabin less than two miles from Fenton Lake, her father didn't stay with the rest of them the entire time, but instead went back to Albuquerque a couple of times, and her oldest brother went with him, since they both had work responsibilities. Her other teenaged brother stayed behind with their mother and his sisters. Their father would have insisted. Even though the area wasn't nearly as isolated as it would have been during Capone's era, it was isolated by any definition of that word in the 1950s, still was in many respects, although the paved road through the community where the cabins had been made a big difference now. There still was no paved road to the ranch, whose buildings had been demolished a few decades ago. Now it was traversed only by hikers, fishermen, hunters and forest rangers.

The interior of both the Sandias and the Jemez was accessed only by one-lane dirt roads when she was a child, so even though paved two-lane highways provided access to the edge of each mountain range, the going was slow on the narrow old highways, and even slower once the dirt roads began. She used to love the stories her parents told, when she and her siblings complained about the slow, bumpy, mountain dirt roads, about how things were when they were young. Her father drove from Lubbock, Texas, to Farmington, in the Four Corners area of New Mexico, the two years he courted their mother before they married in 1928, on roads just like the mountain roads, but often worse, depending on climate conditions, such as mud, and no government crews doing regular maintenance. She and her younger sister would exclaim with various forms of *eeeuuww*, asking why he even bothered, why not just write to each other? Their parents would reply that they did that too, regularly, laughing at the memories. Then they would describe the cars in those days. It all sounded quite awful to the youngsters. Visiting the mountains and driving those difficult roads a few times during hot months, when getting out of the stifling high desert dry heat in Albuquerque was a treat, made for fun times. Playtime in the creeks and forests, while eating the campfire food her parents cooked, often lasted hours before dusk, when her parents would load them up and head home.

For some reason she didn't fully understand to this day, she always was frightened after dark as they drove home through the mountains. The forest frightened her when the sun went down. Her parents told her that she was like her grandmother, since her dad's mother loved to paint—and sell—mountain scenes, but was afraid to be in the mountains after dark and thus rarely participated in family outings if the return home before dusk wasn't guaranteed. Dolly hadn't felt that way past childhood, she apparently outgrew the fear. Her grandmother never did, but then her grandmother didn't experience any mountains until she was in her 30s, spending her life only in Texas before that. Texans could brag about their hills and mounds, but they did not have mountains, no matter what they might try to tell you. Her parents set them straight about that from a very young age, making it clear they lived in New Mexico and not Texas by choice. They were taught to feel sorry for those poor Texans who had to live most of their lives hot and mountain-less, a few with mere mounds but many with only flat plains, replete with only the kind of torture humidity, mosquitoes and chiggers can provide, when not suffering through tornadoes and nor'westers or nor'easters, as their father called the winter storms that could hit parts of Texas without warning, lowering temperatures by fifty degrees in no time. Air conditioning was not available during the years their parents lived in Texas, so the stories they told were of a time when technology for controlling climate in one's home, office and automobile didn't exist. She felt lucky and blessed they hadn't subjected their children to such woes. She also understood why her dad's mother got out of Texas as soon as she could every spring, claiming she was leaving before tornado season hit, and stayed in New Mexico until Texas began cooling down from the extraordinary summer heat, returning in the fall to Lubbock, where she lived with her youngest daughter and her family.

Dolly had three older siblings living at home until her oldest brother graduated from high school when she was almost three and a half. She remembered him being on an outing with them during which he pushed her older sister off a big log that served as a bridge over a creek. She was pretty sure that took place when they stayed at the rental cabin that summer in the Jemez Mountains. She was small enough that she wasn't allowed near the water by herself, and remembered watching the incident from a distance. She was quite an obedient child, probably because if she weren't, her parents used a thump on the head—her father's method, or a swat on the behind—her mother's method, to let her know what wasn't allowed. She hated both their methods, which could easily become actual spankings on the behind lasting a few moments, not just swats and thumps, depending on the seriousness of the infringement of the rules she was instructed to follow. Avoiding the physical enforcement of the household rules was first priority when it came to how she managed her life, beginning as soon as she understood these things. Walking and talking by eight months meant she understood them sooner rather than later.

All she knew was that she had a vivid memory of that stream and the big log that lay across it, and of watching from a distance as her sister was pushed off, then sat on it as she took off her shoes to pour water out of them after the incident, sobbing in anger at their brother, who was laughing at her and jeering from where he stood on the bank.

She knew from an early age her brother had a mean streak as she often saw him bully her sister, who was ten years older than Dolly, her brother fifteen years older. So much for a protective, loving older brother. Those two never got along. When she was older, her sister told her he teased her mercilessly from the time she was old enough to remember. She was dark complexioned, with dark hair and eyes as well, and he was blond, with pink and white skin and sky-blue eyes. She said he had her convinced the first few years of her life that their parents got her from Sandia Pueblo, which was a few miles up the dirt road from their rural home. Dolly had vivid memories of seeing the Pueblo Indians slowly going past her front yard in their horse-drawn wagons. So it would have been easy for their brother to convince her sister they might take her back to the Pueblo. She didn't completely get over that fear until she was in grade school, she had told Dolly, because she knew she didn't look like the rest of the family, so she believed him. Dolly was not a blonde like their brothers were, but her hair was a mixture of light to medium brown with hints of gold and red if she spent much time in the sun. Her skin was extremely fair, her eyes blue-green. When she was in her twenties, and not getting any sun on purpose, Estee Lauder didn't offer a makeup base as light as her skin. Their mother with her golden olive skin had black hair and the same blue-green eyes as Dolly, which actually were green, but looked blue with certain clothing colors. And although their dad had hazel eyes, he was as fair-skinned as Dolly except where sunlight tanned his skin. Her father didn't have any hair so they didn't know what color it had been. Their mother said it had been brown while it lasted, since it was quite gone soon after they married. She said he lost all his teeth and his hair by about age twenty-five, when he got his first full set of false teeth, a story Dolly always found strange, growing up with regular dental visits and having to brush her teeth twice a day from a young age. But all that was a long time ago. Both parents were gone, Dolly herself now a woman of a certain age, as the French would say. The Jemez Mountains remained basically unchanged since her toddler days. They were one of the few things in her life that never seemed to change, which made her love them all the more.

Jemez Springs had changed dramatically over the decades, as every small town does, but its mountain setting had not. Now, instead of a private, secret center for what her mother used to describe as "renegade priests," the retreat center, run by the Paracletes and open to the public, not just Catholics, was named after the priest who founded the original healing center way back in the middle of the twentieth century.

Father Gerald Fitzgerald was born in the late nineteenth century in Massachusetts, where he also was educated. Dolly wondered if he belonged to the family tree of President John Fitzgerald Kennedy, but her online searches had come up blank so far. Given the controversy around his healing center, and its resulting sexual scandals, the Kennedy family probably wouldn't want the familial connection made public if there were one. Ironic, Dolly thought, given how synchronicities ran rampant throughout her life, if they were related. One of the Kennedy family members, infamous for his sexual shenanigans, had been her next-door neighbor in Albuquerque one year in the 1990s while doing a medical residency. Sen. Ted Kennedy's black limo rested outside her home one afternoon in the Victorian historic district, the only one in Albuquerque, while the senator visited his nephew, but she didn't get the opportunity to catch a glimpse of him coming or going unfortunately, much less get to meet him. For all its faults, she felt the Kennedy family had been good for America. Most families have just as many faults, often probably more, but don't do nearly as much for others, nor for their nation.

She learned of the assassination of President Kennedy while on her way to fourth period choir in seventh grade at Taft Junior High School in Albuquerque's North Valley. It was one of the most memorable events of her entire life. Years later Don McClean sang about the day the music died in his huge hit, "American Pie," but for her the music didn't die, it just changed, but oh so dramatically, on that day, and she knew she never could go back to the way it was before, a fact confirmed when men kept getting killed—Martin Luther King, Bobby Kennedy, all those soldiers in that useless Viet Nam War, her school chums who died in tragic car wrecks, including a horrific train-car crash near her old elementary school, in which boys she had known since first grade were killed, when she was in ninth grade and they were high school sophomores. Her fifth grade teacher, who still taught at the school at the time, had to identify the bodies. He later told her it was one of the most difficult things he ever had done.

Death began filling her teenage years two months before she turned thirteen, on that day in fourth period choir as her choir teacher cried openly in front of the class, the first time she ever saw a man cry. He taught her that it was okay for a man to cry, just as it was okay to love your President enough to cry that hard. So yes, she loved the Kennedys, all of them, followed their trials and tribulations, thankful they bore the burden for the rest of us so publicly, showing us the way in so many respects, all the while trying to make it all better for the rest of us. She was raised as a Baptist by her family and church members in Albuquerque to make the world a better place, but ironically, it seemed the Catholic Kennedys were better Baptists in that regard than most Baptists she ever had known, with the exception of a special few, including some relatives.

She pondered all of this as she sat in the blissful forest setting, complete with the loud sounds of the running water before her. Despite being called a river, by the standards of most places in the world, it was barely a stream. But for this state, and these mountains, it was a large body of water coursing through that valley. If it was too wide, deep and fast to wade across easily, it was a big mountain stream. She learned all about the New Mexico categories of mountain streams in those early childhood days. She smiled as she remembered her various family members teaching her these details. And if one dared to wade in the bigger streams, it was always wise to wear an old pair of tennies in case fish hooks had been left in the water by the dozens of trout fishermen who traversed the Jemez waters during the warm months. Many people in New Mexico fished not only for pleasure but also for sustenance. A fishing license for dozens of fish each year was far less expensive than paying for dozens of meals from other sources.

Not natural sporting men, by nature nor heritage, the men in her family rarely caught many, no matter how hard they tried. She had uncles and cousins who seemed to know all the tricks, but not her immediate family. When they did catch something, her mother could turn the fish into a delicious fried fish meal in no time. Her cooking skills weren't lacking despite the fact her men lacked the ones for catching the fish in the first place. She cleaned the fish too, giving the men more time to fail at catching more.

Amazing how being in these mountains brought such a flood of memories from her early life. The air grew colder as the sun dropped lower on the high canyon horizon. It disappeared early in the day this time of year, the canyon was so deep. Dolly was glad she had brought a coat as well as worn layered sweaters. Once the sun began disappearing, the temperature dropped dramatically and would continue to drop throughout the night. But she had no desire to go inside, wanting to experience dusk by the river while listening to the mountain sounds, breathing the fragrant air of the ancient forest, letting old almost-forgotten memories surface.

Once the sun disappeared behind the canyon walls, she sat down on the ground, cross-legged and closed her eyes. She wanted to spend some time in meditation before it got any cooler, especially since no other guests nor staff members seemed to have any interest in enjoying the beautiful setting on this particular evening. She began the breathing routine she always used to begin her ritual.

A few minutes into her meditation, she heard the faint hooting of an owl.

She knew the great horned owls, often called hoot owls by locals, but known also among scientists and birdwatchers as tiger owls, due to their immense size, were in the Jemez. They lived off the small critters in the forest, and on cats if people let them wander outdoors. Something about the sound of the hooting always thrilled her. One rarely saw them, so she didn't bother to open her eyes, just integrated the soft sounds, which didn't seem that close, into her inner meditative zone. She knew some would say perhaps a guide from the bird kingdom was communicating with her, but she didn't interrupt her meditation to dwell on the possibility. She took her natural affinity with the world's animal kingdom for granted, they all were connected to each other if one just paid attention. Meditation to her meant keeping the mind clear, and she mentally recited her favorite mantra again to get herself back into that blissfully blank space. Her owl continued to hoot every now and then.

Suddenly, without warning, she felt a whoosh that was so close, it rippled her hair. As she opened her eyes to see a huge shadowy form flying away, she realized she was hearing another sound. Wailing? Wind howling?

There was no wind.

And the sound was becoming louder and louder, drawing nearer and nearer, not flying further from her, not at all. Owl or not, whatever was making that sound was coming closer.

Definitely wailing. A crying wail, not a howling wail.

Goose bumps erupted all over her as a chill ripped through her spinal cord, reverberating out through her extremities as dramatically and quickly as the creature had flown over her. But this was no bird. This was something otherworldly.

She knew its name. La Llorona. It came to her as though someone had dropped it in her brain while flying. Terrified, as the wailing, seemingly wind-driven, grew ever closer on the still night, she jumped up from her spot on the ground, grabbed her bag and fled up the hill to the center.

She ran into the lobby, grabbing the first person she saw, demanding to know where Father Marquez was. The startled woman, obviously a guest, looked at her in bewilderment, then said she had no idea. "Look in the dining room." Dolly did. He was nowhere to be seen. She asked one of the dining room employees, who told her he probably was in his room but didn't like to be disturbed. "This is an emergency," she cried. The woman gave her his room number, not wanting to argue with the urgency in Dolly's voice and demeanor.

Finding the room, Dolly pounded on his door, which opened quickly. He seemed shocked to see her, or shocked at how upset she obviously was. "What's wrong?"

"She's here, isn't she?" Dolly demanded.

"Who? What are you talking about?"

"La Llorona. You know she's here. She just flew over me. I heard her wailing out there."

A look of deep, tired resignation passed over the old priest's face. "So she came to you too, did she?"

"Yes. You see her don't you? How often? What does she do? Does she say anything or just keep up that awful wailing?" Dolly's words tumbled out over her pants and gasps.

"Here," he said, pointing to an easy chair in his sparse but comfortable apartment. "Sit down, catch your breath. Would you like something to drink? How about some Scotch."

"Yes, please, on the rocks with plain water please, no soda. Thanks."

Many psychic types over the years whom she knew or about whom she knew, justified their excessive eating and/or drinking habits by saying they were too sensitive and their excesses numbed them a bit, made them less sensitive. She never was sure if that were true or just an excuse, but right now a Scotch served by an old priest seemed to be a good combo. "Make that a double please, Father."

He set the crystal glass on the coaster already in place on the table in front of her chair, then sat down on the couch facing her, holding his own double in his hand. "I like the Irish whiskeys," he said, obviously feeling the need to explain should she notice it wasn't from Scotland.

"I'm Irish and Scottish, so my genes appreciate either," she said, smiling at him. "Thank you. Now tell me about her, please."

"I realize you aren't writing a story for the media, so I don't need to ask you to keep this off the record, but I do want to ask you to respect my privacy if you feel the need to share anything I tell you with others working on the boys' cases. If you give me your word about that, promising to ask me before you tell anyone else my secrets, I will be glad to have this discussion with you. I knew you were a sensitive the moment I met you. Second Sight, the Irish call it, don't they? Doesn't surprise me you are Irish then."

"A bit, but mostly a Northern European mongrel. You have a deal, Father. Yes, I see ghosts, have premonitions, feel the presence of spirits, you name it. Now tell me what you know. Please. Despite these abilities, I am not used to being frightened like that. Is she really the bearer of bad news the legends say she is? I'm convinced. If that is what she wanted, it worked."

The fragrant pinon wood crackled softly in the fireplace as the dusk turned into darkness outside the windows of the apartment. The two had more than one refill of Scotch as their evening together progressed. Eventually Father Marquez brought out snacks, to suffice for the dinner they were missing. Guacamole, blue corn chips, salsa, cheeses. "One of the staff members makes them for me, so the guacamole and salsa are homemade."

"La Llorona has followed me around all my life," he began. "To this day, I don't know why, only that when a death of a child is about to happen or has happened, and my life somehow is touched by the deaths, she makes her presence known to me. It doesn't matter where I am geographically, as you can see for yourself. That young victim was going to be an altar boy at my former church, where my sister still works. I am nowhere near there physically, yet La Llorona visits me here deep in the mountains, a couple of weeks before it happens. Why not my sister in Santa Fe, or one of the priests there?"

"How are you so sure she doesn't?"

"Because my sister thinks I am *lleno de tonterias, un poco*, touched in the head, and always have been, because of this La Llorona thing. I know the priests and staff in the parish. If someone had experiences with her, I would have heard about it. They all know about my lifetime haunting by her, as I have not tried to keep it a secret from the priests, nor certain staff members, which has left me open to gossip, I am quite aware. But my theory about these things is that transparency, within reason—it is the Catholic church after all—is better than secrets and lies and cover-ups. Even where ghosts are concerned."

"Sounds extremely progressive for a Catholic, Father." They both laughed.

"You are trying to help solve a murder, two now perhaps, from what you have told me. Now that we are being so frank with each other, I want to point out an observation that may be useful to the investigation."

"Please, of course."

"I assume you are familiar with the La Llorona legend, most native New Mexicans are?" She nodded in affirmation.

"Then let me remind you, she impulsively and with uncontrolled anger, killed her small children, only to regret it, which is why her soul is so tormented. But despite the scary ghost image that mothers and grandmothers have used to frighten their children through the centuries into staying close to home, especially at night, she actually only appears to people who have lost or are about to lose a child, as you know. I have studied everything I can on this subject for decades, and spoken to many who have experienced her. My parish in Santa Fe was filled with those folks, more than anyone realizes. What I know is that when the death of a child happens at the hands of a *woman* she appears. She is quite specific with her appearances."

Dolly stared at him a moment, then said, "The police, and I, are convinced the mothers did not commit murder."

"I don't disagree, the police are well trained in recognizing suspects close to the victim. And you know the cops personally, plus have your instincts. I don't doubt those conclusions. I simply am saying quit looking at the men and start looking for a woman."

"Does your sister know how you feel about this?"

"Yes and no. She hates to discuss my ghost experiences, so it is difficult for me to be frank with her when I have no proof of anything, which was the situation with that 1980s murder. I do know I suggested the female angle and she scoffed, which I expected, so I never brought it up again. Maybe if you speak with her, without bringing me nor our ghosts into the conversation, she will at least help you and the police find out what women are involved with the altar boys through the church activities, even if it only is carpooling."

"Does La Llorona appear to you often up here in the mountains?"

"No, in fact this has been the first time since I moved here, which is why I wasn't surprised when you called, as I knew about the little boy's death, first because of La Llorona, and then of course, the nightly news. I do watch it a bit," he smiled.

"But you were expecting me because of La Llorona?"

He smiled. "Basically, yes."

"I admit, I am amazed. One doesn't expect such frankness from a priest, even a retired one. Thank you, Father, for being so open. I think it will help the investigation tremendously. I am close to the primary detective on the case. We have worked together for years and even have discussed La Llorona. I would like your permission to share your information with her, but I see no reason why she nor I would have any need to share it with anyone else. Would that be okay?"

"I will defer to your judgment. I know several members of the Santa Fe police force have had experiences with La Llorona and know of others who have as well, so it may seem ironic, but I would trust my information with one of them more than just about anyone else. I just ask that you keep anything I have said away from the media. The Catholic church doesn't need this kind of press. And Jemez Springs doesn't either."

"Of course, Father, and thank you."

"How long are you going to be here?"

"I only had planned to stay the night. Why?"

"I would like to hear some more about your other-worldly experiences. La Llorona doesn't appear to just anyone. Would you care to share? I am free tomorrow. I would suggest we meet for breakfast or lunch, but given the subject, we probably should meet in here. After breakfast perhaps? I am an early riser, so anytime after eight would be fine with me."

"It is eight now. I had no idea it was so late, the time has flown. I am an early riser, I will be here at eight if you promise to have coffee ready."

"Done," he said as he rose to walk her to the door.

She arrived promptly the next morning with her little bottle of organic grassfed-sourced cream in hand. "I believe cream is good for us," she said as she walked into his apartment and the old priest's eyebrows shot up in askance as he stared at it. "If it is natural, the way God and cows make it, not meddled with by mankind. Good source of omega seven essential fatty acids too. Want some?"

"No, I think I will pass," he smiled. "No offense. I've spent most of my adult life avoiding pure cream, so at my age, why start now? Let me get your coffee. Sugar, sweetener?"

"No thanks, just a spoon please. Father, are you just going to quiz me this morning, or will you share some of your La Llorona experiences with me?"

"Certainly I will, this is a two-way street, I try to be a fair and equal priest." He smiled as he handed her the mug of coffee and the spoon. "Do you want to regale me with your stories first or listen first?"

"It doesn't matter to me. I do have questions for you."

"Then I would like to hear what you are willing to tell me, so that when I do share my secrets, I will have a better sense of who you are. I would be most comfortable with that. Would you?"

"Yes, that makes perfect sense. I am not a medium and I don't go around seeing ghosts all the time, so I really have little to share, to be honest with you. But I am not discounting the validity of my experiences when I say that. Sharing experiences of this sort always is difficult if we don't have a strong sense of the other person's experiential context. Believing in such things isn't the same as experiencing them."

"Couldn't have said it better. Can you begin with childhood?"

"No, not really. I know that most people who are sensitive, shall we call it, begin realizing it at a very young age. Even though many say they assume everyone is like they are, and only as they get a bit older do they realize they are different. But that wasn't my experience. I was raised Southern Baptist in the middle of the last century, and took my religious education very seriously from the beginning, starting around age three when I graduated from Sunday morning nursery to an actual Sunday School class taught by my aunt, a highly educated woman for her generation, with a master's degree in music. And she was the preacher's wife. She taught music, but also enjoyed teaching us little children about Jesus every Sunday morning, about how He loved us and so we should love Him back. I did.

And I loved the stories about miracles and angels, and the songs we sang about Jesus loving the little children and the animals, like the pictures showed. And I believed every word of it.

"But other-worldly experiences? No, not a one. I did have a healing that resulted from praying to Jesus in early grade school, but I call that my miracle, not an other-worldly event. No ghosts, just a simple healing, the kind Jesus did all the time, according to the Bible. And although I don't mind sharing the details, it doesn't fit with what we are trying to discuss now, so I would rather skip that story if that's okay."

He nodded, and took another sip of coffee.

"I began having premonitions of the future when I was in fifth grade that did come true, but again, I don't think those relate to what we are discussing here. I have had them ever since in various forms. But they have nothing to do with ghosts in my opinion."

He nodded and sipped, in full priest-as-listener mode.

"Basically, I have had three profound experiences with ghostly beings, in my opinion. Other experiences were less well defined, I would say un-provable, but to some they all are. To me the others were, compared to the three I want to tell you about, which I would swear on my life happened, while with the others I probably would forego the swearing part," she laughed.

"The first two happened when I was in my twenties, working for newspapers. And before I began a formal meditation practice, at age twenty-eight, which definitely enhanced my so-called psychic abilities, but didn't add to my ghost sighting record in any noticeable way.

"My first newspaper job after college was that of an arts writer and editor, in an area of Central Texas that actually had a thriving arts community, believe it or not. A local housewife who had won a poetry contest called me one day to see if I would do a story about her, since she had won a poetry award. I went to her house for the interview, and long story short, over time we became friends. She won some more awards, was published. She actually was a songwriter and guitar player and thus performer as well, more than a poet, so several opportunities arose to make announcements about her in the paper, run photos and so forth, and to visit with her through our work.

"The first time I interviewed her in her home, her husband at work, her kids in school, I was aware of an Indian standing behind her when she sang for me and played the guitar.

"Now let me define that the way a clinical psychologist explained definitions to me a few years later, one who had clinical experience in the parapsychology department at Duke University determining if a person was psychic or crazy. I learned from her that an hallucination is when something you think you see is as real as everything else in the room, such as the furniture. Since I never have done hallucinogenic drugs like so many of my peers have, this was helpful for my frame of reference. A psychic sighting, known by the Irish as Second Sight, is something that you can see but you know it isn't real in the way everything else in the room is, such as the furniture. You know you can touch the furniture. And you know you can't touch what you see with Second Sight. This Indian was the latter—he wasn't like the furniture. On a different plane of reality is the best way to explain it.

"But he was such a cliche, with the long black hair. And he was huge. She felt a strong connection to Native Americans, and her songs reflected it. Some could have been written by one of them in the long ago instead of by a white Central Texas housewife in the mid-seventies. The follow-up stories and announcements I did on her didn't really merit a visit but we both liked the excuses to get together during the day.

"I kept seeing the Indian when I was in her presence, especially when she performed for me in her living room, singing and playing her guitar. Finally I had seen him enough and felt comfortable enough with her that I was ready to say something, figuring if I was seeing him that much, so was she.

"She was shocked when I told her—but not dismayed—that was clear to me immediately. Almost in tears, overwhelmed by what I revealed, she said he was her guide and helped her write all her songs. She was amazed I could see him too, the only person who ever had to her knowledge. She was a very private person, with few friends, and none with whom she could discuss things of this nature, plus a husband with whom she didn't confide such things. He managed a local business, a nice guy, ordinary Bell County white guy, but not someone who would want to know his wife had Indian spirit guides who helped her write her songs, and could be seen by others.

"By telling her that I saw him too, in detail—she wanted to know when I first saw him, the whole story of my experience up to then, was so grateful I told her—that we immediately became fast friends and stayed so for more than a decade after that, despite enormous changes in both of our lives that caused each of us to move to different cities, even states. She divorced and remarried and created a new life, but never did much with her music and poetry after that period where she won those local and regional awards and did a bit of local performing.

"My second experience was only two or three years later. I had relatives in San Antonio, and lived with them a few months the first year I lived there after landing a job in the magazine and arts department at a major daily newspaper in the days when the town had two. About five years earlier, my relatives had lost a teenage daughter in a traffic accident in that city. I come from a gigantic family and haven't even met all my first cousins to this day, so it wasn't unusual that I didn't know this family until I moved to San Antonio. Thus I never knew the girl who had died.

"I stayed in what had been her room. She showed up more than once, the same Second Sight experience with which I had seen the Indian, and seemed to just be looking at me, no messages. The Indian didn't talk to me either, was always standing behind my friend. This girl never got close to me, always was across the room. After two or three visits, I asked my cousin what her daughter had looked like, she showed me photos, as well as gave me verbal descriptions, she already had told me in great detail the circumstances around her death.

"It was her I was seeing. I felt comfortable telling my cousin of my experience, assuming if I was seeing her, that my cousin or other family members may also have had similar experiences. Mystical experiences ran in that family, my mother's, I knew because of things my mother's oldest sister had told my mother and me, and one of their brothers had told us as well on one of his annual visits to our home, when I was a teen.

"But my cousin and her family had not seen the girl. My cousin was open to the information, even seemed grateful for it. I got the idea it comforted her. The irony to us was that after I told her, the appearances stopped. We concluded the girl was curious about who was staying in her room and once she knew her family was okay with it, she was too.

"That story has an addendum. Several years later, five maybe—can't remember for sure, I only lived with them a few months, so this was long after I had moved out—my cousin made the decision to move to Dallas. She had quit her job and was free to move there, where her husband, a Baptist minister, former Navy chaplain and high school counselor, had been working and living during the week for years, only coming home on weekends. That same red-haired daughter appeared to her and told her not to go. My cousin heeded the advice and never made the move. A few years later her husband retired and moved back home to live full-time. That was the only time the girl, who was her youngest daughter, ever had appeared to her, or given her a message, but it was a profound one for my cousin, because she went back and forth for years trying to decide whether to move or not. Once she decided to make the move, her daughter felt so strongly about the decision, she intervened, discouraging her. My cousin actually seemed relieved, was my take on it when she told me the story. Given a lot of circumstances in the various family members' lives at the time and later, I feel it was the best decision and am glad her daughter helped her make it.

"The other situation is more complicated. So much so, I am not sure I want to share it with you yet. It takes a lot out of me to talk about these things. Is that normal? They are energy drainers."

"Yes, that is normal," he said. "Partly because no matter whom you tell, there always is a trust factor at first. You don't know me, nor I you, and our culture teaches us that anyone who has experiences of this sort is crazy. Mentally ill or delusional or both. Or on drugs. Intellectually you may trust me, but emotionally you can't because you don't know me well enough to have that kind of bond, so it drains you to tell me these things because you are creating your own emotional protection as you go. Let's take a break, why don't we. More coffee?"

7

"WOULD YOU BE UP FOR A WALK, OR IS IT TOO COLD FOR YOU," she asked him. "I am about coffee'd out."

"So am I. A walk is a great idea. I take several walks most days, but find very few are willing to accompany me. Good thing I don't mind the solitary life," he said with a smile.

"Show me one of your favorites then, if you would, and tell me about your La Llorona."

They put on their coats, hats and gloves and headed out the door. It was a beautiful fall day in the Jemez, a bright sun shining over the canyon walls. He led them down the stairs, out the door of the retreat center and across the grounds to what she realized was a relatively hidden path not easily seen by the public unless one knew it was there. No breezes. With little traffic on the highway, the silence of the beautiful day made it easy to chat as they walked, single file, along the path, which ran near the river, but not next to it.

"La Llorona has been my lifelong companion," he began. "I almost didn't go into the priesthood because of her. That in itself is a long story, and like some of yours, not for our discussion today. Another time, though, and I will be glad to share it with you. Suffice it to say it took me years to accept that she was real, and that she wasn't going to leave me alone.

"Rather than share specific stories today, for I have many and it could take hours, or more, I want to tell you my conclusions, my theories, give you my overview of her, at least in relation to how she has acted in my life, for there are many tales of her behavior worldwide as you know, and they often seem to contradict each other. Some legends, and people's actual experiences with her, indicate she is a demon, dressed in black, who portends only evil. Others say just the opposite— that she only wears white, is like an angel who protects children, and tries to warn of evil in hopes of preventing it. I think she does all of it."

"Really?"

"Yes, I do. That shocks you doesn't it?"

"Yes."

"Because it doesn't seem logical? Is too inconsistent?"

"For starters, yes."

"Have you studied any of the similar legends and actual experiences of people through the ages in relation to demons, angels, saints, even ghosts?"

"Well, some, but probably not like you have, I am gathering from your question."

"You are correct. I did a masters and a doctorate in such things, with a focus on the legends within the Church. I didn't include contemporary experiences of people who are living, or lived in the last century or so, but I did study as many as I could find while doing my research for my degrees.

"I thought I had researched you quite well, but I had no idea you had so much formal education in these subjects.

"Most people don't. I was pushing the envelope to get approval for them, as you can imagine, and the agreement was that we would label the degrees and my thesis and dissertation in such a way that no one would realize what they were about unless I told them or they actually read them. The dissertation never was published, on purpose, for that reason. It was as though my degrees were secret ones. I had friends in high places or they never would have happened. Even during the Vatican II culture, my work was just too controversial. The Church wants no association whatsoever with La Llorona, despite the fact all the legends of her specifically come out of the Catholic population. Other cultures, such as Japan, have similar stories but the names and details are different. La Llorona, white dress or black, demon or angel, is pure Catholic in origin and perpetuation. But the Church sees her as only a demon, never an angel, and thus she doesn't exist except in the mind of deluded souls who believe in Santa Claus, the Easter Bunny and witches at Halloween in black hats with pointed tops.

"Because she is so forbidden by the Church, a strong thriving subculture has built up around her in every Catholic culture, large and small, for centuries, driven by the power of institutional suppression. Yet even the Church won't go so far as to come out and formally say she is of the Devil—and it does believe in a Devil, that is doctrine."

"You really have taken an intellectual approach haven't you?" she teased.

"You could call it that, I guess. Some of my colleagues just call it bat-shit crazy."

She laughed. "Father, your vernacular doth amaze."

"Seriously, though, what are your conclusions, since you obviously have come to them from both the intellectual and experiential?"

"Let's sit down here on these rocks in the sun and catch our breath while I tell you. We will be ready for brunch when we return. Will you join me?"

"Certainly. I am your faithful companion as long as you want to talk, Father."

"As I told you earlier, she only has appeared to me when a child has died and a woman has been involved, responsible actually, either from neglect or through overt action. It took me a long time to realize that, but when I did, it was so obvious I couldn't understand why I hadn't noticed the pattern sooner. But not having many, often any, humans with whom to toss ideas about this back and forth, I was slow to wend my way through her mysterious ways. And I don't know if that is true with everyone who experiences her, or just me. So far, when I have heard stories I could research on my own, I found that deaths appearing to be caused by men on the surface could be traced back to a woman, but often law enforcement and medical teams didn't even realize that. I had an advantage as a priest because of the confessional. Women are much more consistent about going to confession than men, which probably doesn't surprise you. And they tend to confess all, unlike the men, who will pick and choose what they confess, generally speaking. I often was able to fill in what turned out to be blanks in the men's confessions by what the women confessed. As a result, I learned things through the confessional that no law enforcement nor medical person ever could have known, nor would know, given my vow of secrecy. That vow of the confessional has been God's greatest gift to me."

"So tell me why La Llorona has hung around you, surely you have an answer, at least a theory," she said with humor in her voice.

"Oh, I do," he said with an apt smile. "I do. Shall we start back now? How about lunch? I promise I will talk the whole time."

"Deal."

They got up and began the trek back through the forest on the beautiful late autumn day in the Jemez. They walked silently for a while, single file. As they neared the retreat center, he asked if she wanted to eat there or go to one of the restaurants. "My treat," he said.

"I didn't make a reservation for a meal at the center. In fact I think I am supposed to be checking out by now, aren't I? Was it eleven or one? I didn't expect to stay this long so didn't pay close attention."

"Don't worry about it. I'll check at the desk to make sure no one needs the room today. I need to go to my room and get my wallet."

"I'm going to run to my room, too," she said, "and check my phone. I actually didn't bring it with me, you witnessed a miracle today Father, and didn't even realize it." They both laughed.

They met a few minutes later in the lobby. "Shall we walk or drive?" he asked.

"I'll walk if you will," she said.

"Let's do it. Which restaurant, Mexican food or the hamburger joint?"

"Which will give us more privacy, do you think? The Mexican restaurant, because of its size?

"Yes, it will. Let's go there. I always enjoy their food. I might even have a beer. I took care of things for you at the desk. You can stay another night if you want, as my guest, which means you don't have to pay."

"Oh, thank you Father, that is very kind of you. I need to check some things at home, I have a pet sitter, but I will do that after lunch. I am happy, and able, to pay for my room again. I will let you treat me to lunch though, if you let me buy your beer."

He laughed heartily.

"I am of German and Spanish descent," he said, serious again. "My mother was German, her parents were German immigrants to New Mexico. My Spanish lineage goes back several centuries in this state, as does the La Llorona legend here. Some say it began in South or Central America, or Mexico, or Spain. No one really knows. But there seems to be agreement on the fact it has been around since the Spaniards came to the New World, which was more than 500 years ago. No indication of her existence can be found before that in Spain, so no one knows whether the legend began in Spain or in the New World. My hunch is that it began in the New World, simply because of the timing of the earliest stories that we have on record, then made its way back to Spain early on, along with many other New World exports: corn, beans, potatoes, tomatoes, chile peppers, tobacco, vanilla, pumpkins, avocados, several kinds of nuts including peanuts and cashews, squash. Oh yes, and chocolate."

"Is that all?" Dolly asked, dryly.

"No, actually the list is longer," he laughed. "but, you get my point. Many things the world takes for granted weren't known, much less available, before the Spanish discovered their New Kingdom. La Llorona seems to appear almost exclusively to people of Spanish descent, whether they are aware of their genetics or not, although here in New Mexico I have known of some exceptions, especially among Anglos born here. You said you felt her but you admit you didn't see her. "

"Okay, you caught me," she said, grinning slyly. "I was a Spaniard in a past life, several actually, which I recall, a woman each time. So would that count? Or are you a Catholic who does not accept the reincarnation theory? And furthermore, can a ghost tale be so gene-specific? I have to admit Father, that sounds ridiculous even to me, and I'm about as open a person to these things as you are going to find."

"I realize that," he said, "and I realize my theory sounds crazy. And yes, I am open to the idea of reincarnation, but like the famous Protestant writer and psychiatrist, Dr. Scott Peck, I don't want to believe it, prefer the one-lifetime-is-enough theory. As for ghost theories, my lifetime of research, and documenting all the anecdotal information I could find, has led me to this conclusion about La Llorona and the Spaniards. Now, thanks to your contribution just now, I will create a new file about past life identities. I consider my research scientific at this point, and am daring the Good Lord to prove me wrong with an exception to the theory. So far, He's kept his distance on the subject," he laughed.

"The ghostly world has patterns if you study it, I have learned," he said. "Most often, the legends and experiences people have with one ghost specifically have to do with place, and given that most of us believe ghosts are spirits of the dead who have not been able to move on to the next world, there is a sort of logic to them being place-bound creatures.

"But La Llorona is different. I don't consider her in the category of Mother Mary, for obvious reasons, but like Mary, she can be seen and has been seen just about anywhere, geography doesn't seem to matter. What does matter is whether people believe in Mary or La Llorona, and thus the experiences of them tend to reside in Catholic culture, although Mary doesn't limit her appearances to the Hispanic world, as you probably know."

She nodded.

"La Llorona does. I don't consider her a saint nor a holy being, while Mary is. But I don't consider La Llorona a ghost either, stuck in purgatory, nor an angel visiting from heaven.

"The chile rellenos please," Dolly said as she handed the waitress the menu. "Make that Christmas, and iced tea."

"And I'll have the special, red and green, just like hers," Father Marquez said, also handing the waitress his menu. "With a Dos Equis."

"So Father, please continue. But first I would like to ask, have you ever had any personal experiences with Mary? So many people have, it seems, throughout the world."

"No, I am not one of them unfortunately," he said, "but I have known several who have, and others who know people who did as well. Word travels fast when someone has an experience with her, and we priests usually are included in the gossip loop. That is one of the things I loved about my years as a parish priest, the confessions and the counseling. Kept me close to the people and their lives. Have you known anyone?"

"No, I have not, but I did have a next door neighbor in San Antonio who went to Medjugorje and her ordinary rosary beads turned to gold. She said that wasn't unusual at all. She showed them to me on her return. She was an Anglo who had graduate degrees in religious studies, theology, subjects of that nature, from famous colleges back East, I vaguely recall. She was in Texas because her husband was one of those second or third generation independently wealthy Texans who could live anywhere and chooses to stay there. I think she told me she converted to Catholicism, wasn't born into it. So she probably liked San Antonio given its strong Catholic influence, similar to the one here in New Mexico."

"Mary is not the same as a saint to Catholics, you realize?"

"Yes, Father, I do."

"And the saints themselves are in a category all their own. I have a theory that what we call ghosts or spirits also have a category all their own. Not all of them of course. But some. I believe in a hierarchy of spirits as much as I believe that saints really do help us and that we can and should pray to them, converse with them, honor them. Just as we do Jesus our Lord, God the Father, the Holy Mother and the Holy Spirit."

"So where does La Llorona fit into all this? She isn't a saint, she isn't part of the Holy Trinity, nor in the same realm as Mother Mary. Is she evil or good or both? Neutral perhaps, depending on the heart of the person experiencing her?"

Their food arrived just then, looking and smelling delicious. "So what is it? Your theory?" Dolly was beginning to feel he was putting her off by wandering into related subjects now for the last hour or more, so she dug into her food and put him on the spot. Time for him to explain.

This time he did. She ate, he talked, continuing to sip his beer, taking a bite of food only now and then. "I think there are many La Lloronas," he began.

She could see he wasn't joking. "I'm all ears."

"A contemporary cable TV series has run in recent years that included a plotline one season about a worldwide coven of witches, continuing from ancient times to the present. I believe that idea isn't so far-fetched, for I began suspecting the same of the La Llorona legend long before some Hollywood writer came up with the TV idea.

"I can understand Mary and various saints appearing to people throughout the world, as so many have claimed throughout the centuries. Some even claim to have seen Jesus, stories abound. Apparently his appearance before Saul on the road to Damascus was only the first among hundreds since, maybe thousands. I don't know how many the Vatican has documented, and it makes sense many more have gone undocumented. I accept that some people are delusional who claim to have these experiences, some even seriously mentally ill, hallucinating. But when hundreds, even thousands, of such appearances are documented, I agree with the Vatican, we must take them seriously, both historically and in the present, until or unless we can prove them not to be true. And rarely is anyone able to disprove the claims. If anything, others often are present at the appearances who corroborate the experience, not discount it.

"I think La Llorona is not in this category. When people throughout the Catholic world, especially the Catholic Hispanic world, have their experiences of her, see her, I don't think they are all seeing the same spirit. There are many La Lloronas. We know so little about the spirit world, good or bad. I don't think it is outside the realm of possibility that spirits can and do work as groups, even as hierarchies, just as we humans do on earth, and as we are taught the angels always have.

He took a few bites of food, and motioned to the waitress to bring him another beer. Dolly still was working on her dish of chile rellenos, refried beans and Spanish rice. She finished her iced tea, which she drank year-round at local restaurants, just as the waitress came over with his beer and the pitcher of tea for her refill.

"Are you with me so far?" he queried.

She nodded.

"I do feel the La Llorona coven, which is how I describe it to myself, is mixed. It has good and bad, and some who are both, maybe they all are. Ghosts and spirits are more similar to humans in their tendency to have both good and bad traits, probably because supposedly they are humans without bodies who haven't been able to move on to more advanced levels of existence after death. I don't believe the Lloronas are trapped the way we see most ghosts as being, but I don't consider them highly advanced or what we might call enlightened beings. Yet I am convinced they are helpful to humans more often than not. "

"You should eat, Father. Your food is getting cold. I find everything you just said absolutely fascinating. I am stunned, actually. I now have much to ponder. I hope you will allow me to visit you again in the near future, and discuss all this further. Plus, you still haven't shared your personal experiences with La Llorona, or with one of them I should say, or some of them. Only your theory, which leaves me much to ponder before we meet again. But given the profundity of what you just shared, even without checking on everything at home, I need to drive back now and consider all this, and not stay another night, if you don't mind, before we meet again. But I am going to hold you to your promise to tell me more."

He smiled and sipped.

Father Marquez picked up the phone, knowing from the caller ID that it was Rosalie. He knew what she wanted to discuss.

"Not over the phone," was his greeting.

"Then will you come here? You know I don't like to do highway driving," she said. "And we must talk. You know that."

"Yes," he sighed with resignation. "I will drive to you. Tomorrow. I'll be there in time for lunch."

"Connie, we need to talk. Do you have time now? I'm driving home from Jemez Springs."

"Yes, let me get to a more private location, I'll go outdoors. It's nice out today here in Santa Fe. You just now leaving Jemez?"

"Yes. Connie, what actual connection do we have so far between the murders and La Llorona? Any, or are they just talk and innuendo on the part of the mothers and some of the cops, including our retired guy in Mora?"

"Let me think a minute. When you say connection, what are you trying to find? You know everything I know so far, I think. Oh, there is something you probably don't know, since I just learned it late yesterday. Let me fill you in and see if it helps.

"Apparently one of the altar boys got sick and went to the hospital with food poisoning about the time little Anthony disappeared. And there is a La Llorona connection with this kid. Now that I think about it, I would say it is the most direct connection we have so far. A neighbor of the sick boy, an Anglo woman who lives across the street, a widow, swears she saw a Zorro character skulking in the bushes around the house while the family was away with the boy in the hospital. That is how she described it—like Zorro. Tall, with a black cape, long black hair. She wasn't sure about the Zorro mask—it was more the height and the billowing skirt of the cape that caught her attention, she told the cops."

"So help me get from Zorro to La Llorona."

"I don't. The cops did. Apparently some of the film locations have had reports of a Zorro-like creature hovering around at strange times, in strange places, always when children are involved in the films. One little boy disappeared for a few hours about the time one sighting happened, which is how the stories started, I was told. No formal reports were filed, the boy wasn't missing long enough, but the cops talked to a lot of people and learned all this. The thing is, the Hispanics were saying it was La Llorona. The Anglos, especially the ones from California, were saying it was Zorro, but the Hispanics told the cops they had it all wrong, it was definitely *not* Zorro, not accurate at all. It had to be La Llorona. There always was the sound of the wind with wailing around the time of the sightings. Zorro wouldn't bring sounds of wind, nor does he wail. Plus he's a fictional character, La Llorona is not, despite what skeptics say.

"So now the guys are saying the description the Anglo woman gave of her neighbor's visitor fits that given by the movie folks, so everyone is saying La Llorona is involved."

"What about the little boy in the hospital? How is he? What did he eat?"

"He's home now, but they still are doing tests, you know how slow the labs are. I will keep you posted as we learn more. But does what I just told you qualify as a legitimate La Llorona connection in this case? Is that what you meant?"

"Yes, given the boy with the food poisoning was an altar boy with the one who was murdered, I would say it counts. Wouldn't you?"

"Of course, but I don't know why you asked me. What did you learn?"

"I learned something from the old priest, at least I got pointed in a direction. He says look for a woman murderer. If La Llorona is being connected to the case, we need to be looking for a woman, not a man, no matter how obvious a man may seem as a suspect. The key is the La Llorona connection, do you see? It can't be rumors or legends, like the boys' mothers have brought to our attention. It has to be an actual sighting or an auditory experience at least."

"Yes, I get it. You are saying Father Sanchez isn't our man after all. But a woman. I'm going to have to ponder that, for we had not even considered looking at any women. There aren't any, but maybe that is because we have been so sure it was a man. Are you going to be home today pretty much, or do you have to travel again?"

"I have to get home to my pets, my sitter is expecting me, so I can't drive up to Santa Fe. Frankly, my time with Father Marquez was so intense, I need some time to chill. And to think about women. I guess we both will be thinking about women, a lot. Just text me if you want to talk and I'll do the same. I don't even know any women connected to this case except that nun, the sister of Father Marquez. And you know how that interview went. It didn't. But you have talked to the mothers and probably will think of others through your cop connections, so keep me posted. The more facts I have, the better my intuition will work for us. I have some things to tell you about my time with the old priest, but it can wait until we get together next."

"I have an appointment tomorrow with the mother of the boy who got the food poisoning," Connie said. "Want to join me? I haven't talked to her yet, as it was under my radar until yesterday, when the street cops shared what they learned. Her son is back in school, so I'm to meet with her about eleven."

"I'll be there. Can you meet me for breakfast or coffee first, so I can fill you in on my Jemez experience?"

"You saying it *was* an 'experience'?"

"One could call it that," Dolly laughed. "See you about nine? I'll pick you up at the station."

Rosalie said grace, and the old brother and sister silently began eating the meal Rosalie had prepared. Chicken soup and tortillas. Wine. Their somber mood permeated the small kitchen where they sat, well protected from alert ears.

"I don't know if I can protect him this time," she said. "We live in different times and people ask more questions, won't take what we say at face value just because it is us. No one trusts us anymore, not even us nuns when it comes to something like this."

"What did you witness?" he asked in a barely audible voice. He did not want to be having this conversation, aware that his sister, on the contrary, seemed almost to be excited by it.

"He was helping the boy dress in little girls' clothes. I saw them through my peephole. The boy seemed reluctant at first but never upset. The sessions went on for weeks. He would stay after the other boys had left, and they would put the clothes on the child together. Who knows where he got them or how. I didn't know he even had them again. The boy obviously enjoyed it more and more, so Father Sanchez certainly chose him well, recognized him as one of his own kind.

"But they only dressed the boy in the clothes? Was there any touching, fondling, love talk, lechery?"

"No," she said tersely, obviously hating discussion of the graphic details. "He could have been caring for an infant, it all seemed so innocent."

"Then why are you so sure he did it? We have to be sure before we accuse or hide him. We never knew for sure he did it last time, you of all people know that. You can't accuse someone of murder who helps little boys dress up as girls and teaches them to enjoy it. Perverted of course, but a crime? A sin? Lawyers would have a field day with a case like this if the truth ever got out. Further damage to the Church's worldwide reputation, to ours as Catholics here in New Mexico, to Father Sanchez. The child would be hurt the least—unless of course he was a murder victim as a direct result of the sessions.

"You are sure Father Sanchez never has done this with another boy in all this time until now? Why this one do you think?"

"He's a lot like the other one, physically. Same coloring, similar body type, angelic personalities, unlike some of the boys. Who knows what drives Father Sanchez? One would think wearing the robes of the priesthood would satisfy his strange desires to act like a female. Why does he need to teach little boys to act like him? If he showed them how to wear priest's robes, as though preparing them for the priesthood, no one would even think twice. But no, he keeps girls' clothes and uses them, including underwear and shoes and socks. And he wears his own robes the whole time, no disrobing, no adult women's clothes. It's as though he were dressing his daughter, except it's a little boy."

"Does he linger or seem to lust when the boy is changing into the girls underwear?"

"No. He shows him what he needs to put on—the panties and the slip and the socks, the pre-teen bra, the dress, the shoes, then leaves the room long enough to give the boy time to change. Just like last time. Nothing has changed. It is so harmless in a sense, if both boys hadn't turned up murdered, I'd never speak of it, not even to you, nor in the confessional, since I have nothing to confess. But now I feel I must tell you this, even if I have no sin for the confessional. I fear the wrath of the authorities coming down on all of us."

"Rosalie, do you feel in your heart that he is the one who kills them? I need to know."

She didn't answer him for a long time, slowly sipping her soup.

"I just don't know. It is as though God ignores me when I ask for His guidance in this matter, as though He has abandoned me the way Christ felt He abandoned Him on the cross. It has become my cross to bear. Last time was enough for one life, but now this? It seems too much to bear. I am eighty now. Too old. Why me, why now?"

They sat in silence until the light outside told them the noon hour was long gone, the sun beginning its afternoon journey in preparation for its usual dramatic

Santa Fe sunset. Finally Father Marquez stood up, gathering his coat and gloves for the drive home. "I need to meditate and pray on this, Rosalie.

"La Llorona has been visiting me again. I know you don't believe it is her, but an evil spirit. I am not saying what I see isn't evil, but you know I think it is the Llorona. She—it—has told me so many times. At least I know she isn't the Madonna. If only I had visions of Her, messages from Her, how much easier my life would have been."

Rosalie was clearing the table. She refused to look at him. She hated hearing about his visions of the legendary Spanish spirit. It terrified her. But he kept talking.

"I thought I was finished with her, just like you never expected Father Sanchez to start his activities again, or another boy to be murdered. I don't know what God is trying to tell us, but we must try to find out before we do anything. Keep an eye on Father Sanchez as best you can, but otherwise go about your daily activities as though nothing has happened. You are right, authorities will be scrutinizing all of you in ways you couldn't imagine the last time this happened. You can't give them any reason to notice anything out of the ordinary. My visit today can be explained away by the fact we are brother and sister, and everyone here is upset about the death of another altar boy. It wouldn't be considered unusual for me to come here to give my condolences.

"Remember, Rosalie, no priest ever has murdered a child in the world, that we know of. Even the most aberrant pedophiles in the priesthood don't seem to be killers as well, not like the secular pedophiles so often are, who kidnap and kill and give the media such immense fodder. I just don't think Father Sanchez has it in him. There is a mystery here, and I don't think the solution is going to be found with him, although if the authorities ever learn of his perversions, he could very well be accused even if he is innocent. With this second murder, the possibility of a demented serial killer looms large, someone outside the Church. I fear it is going to be a difficult process to find the truth, and I fear it may take us into great darkness, but we must solve the case this time. We must."

Father Marquez was lost deep in thought about his meeting with his sister. She troubled him. She always had. And with all of his training, innate intelligence, and spiritual and psychic gifts, he never had been able to understand her completely.

Oh, on the surface, one could say there was nothing to understand, nothing especially deep anyway. And he would have to agree, for whenever he tried to figure her out, he found nothing. He had been trying since he was a small boy. She was his older sister by three years. From his earliest memories, he knew he felt something off about her, and for 70 years, that feeling remained.

La Llorona herself held less mystery for him than his sister did, a fact he himself found extraordinarily strange. He had come to accept it over the years, hoping any mystique his sister might have would turn out to be benign at worst, non-existent at best. He could live with his own paranoia about her more easily than he could live with the discovery of truths about her that might cause him disappointment.

He knew she considered him abnormal, and that too, he accepted, for he knew why and the reason was because of something in her that most would consider normal. He had experienced the presence of La Llorona since he was a boy, and he started telling his sister about his experiences when they were both quite young, still in elementary school. She was the one who helped him recognize the wailing woman whom he heard, always with wind heard but not felt, and whom he occasionally even saw.

He always had found it ironic that even though she recognized La Llorona from descriptions of his experiences, and thus taught him about the fabled ghost woman, she didn't believe him. He tried for years to convince her his experiences were real, that he wasn't making them up, but she refused to believe him. She always insisted he learned about the witchy woman from his playmates at school, and then he played dumb on the subject just to see how she would react when he told her about his fantasies. She was certain he was playing games with her, trying to scare her, trying to get her to admit she believed in ghosts and witches.

It always had struck him as so strange that Rosalie claimed to feel the call of God to become a nun, but beyond that, seemed to harbor absolutely no mystical awareness whatsoever. He went into the priesthood because of his continuous awareness of other realms. He considered himself a mystic first, a priest second, well aware that not all priests, many actually, were not the least bit mystical.

Mother Teresa admitted she had felt the Lord's call to do His work, but for most of the rest of her life she never felt that deep mystical connection again. She was to be commended for having the courage to admit that publicly, how her Lord disappeared on her for half a century. Yet she had been named a saint.

He knew many men went into the priesthood for reasons having little to do with their inner spiritual life, but he always had the impression most nuns did have a deep inner spiritual life and thus chose their path accordingly. His sister was a minority in that respect.

He had no statistics of course. There were no studies on such things, and he wasn't sure most would be able to answer the questions honestly if there were studies. His life-long observations led him to conclude many priests and nuns were profoundly self-deluded. It would be impossible for them to give factual answers in a study that raised questions requiring accurate self-knowledge.

Sister Rosalie entered her private greenhouse, reveling in its warm moisture, as always. Her morning routine never varied. Awaken at three, say a few prayers while still in the warmth of her bed before arising. After minimal toiletries, while the morning remained dark and silent, she went to her special place in the cathedral where she loved to pray and meditate in its vast and sacred quiet, the lights, if any, only those from the few candles still glowing from yesterday. Some mornings many still glowed, others nary a one. But even on those days she didn't need a light to know where to go to commune with her Lord.

After an hour, precisely, she rose from her knees and went to her favorite place on earth after the cathedral, her tropical greenhouse. She grew plants in its moist warm climate year-round that normally could never be grown in this dry, high altitude climate. She loved Santa Fe and never wanted to leave it, felt blessed by the Lord Himself that she was able to live out her life and serve Him in His blessed cathedral. But she loved tropical plants, especially flowering plants and herbs. When she was a girl, she was torn between becoming some kind of agronomist and a nun. Eventually the call of the Lord won out.

Once she learned that she wouldn't be denied expression of her love of plants as a nun, she was eager to go into the convent, eager to grow and learn about plants as she grew in her bliss as a Bride of Christ. She chose as her favorite flower, in honor of Him, the ancient Palma Christi, or Palm of Christ, which now grew in her greenhouse in forms from many countries, filling her life with its varied and brilliant beauty year-round.

She wandered down the aisles, fondling her beloved plants, which she had collected from many countries, grouping them by families according to their names and height: the Gibsonii, with its red-tinged leaves and veins and pinkish-green seed pods, its sister, the Carmencita Pink with its pinkish-red stems and the other sister, Carmencita Bright Red with her red stems, dark purplish leaves and red seed pods. Some of these were almost five feet tall now.

A smaller family included the Impala, with reddish foliage and stems, and Red Spire with its red stems and bronze foliage.

The tallest had no family, but stood alone, like Christ Himself: Zanzibarensis, with large, mid-green leaves that could grow as long as twenty inches, with white midribs.

She thought of the beans from the plants as gems of Christ. They made beautiful beads for jewelry, and she gave hers to a local bead shop run by a devout Catholic woman, and some to individual jewelry makers, also devout Catholics in the parish. In return, since her vows as a nun prohibited her from running a business for profit, they gave her generous cash donations in birthday cards, Christmas cards, Easter cards, Advent cards, thank you notes. The correspondence from them was generous as were their donations, which she used to fund her little greenhouse offerings to the Lord, for she saw it as an altar to the Lord God and His Beloved Son.

Wandering the aisles, tearing off dead leaves, straightening new growth, checking for moistness in the soil, seeing to the daily tasks of nurturing her beloved plants, she pondered the problems her priests were facing as a result of the little boy's murder. What was the Lord going to do for them, how was He going to protect them from erroneous and misdirected accusations? Her heart was heavy as the thoughts weighed on her soul that morning. The visit from her brother had brought her no peace. Quite the contrary, it had only brought her a state of anxiety, one she could not quell, no matter how much she prayed and wandered among her flowering plants. Thank goodness the Archbishop was keeping his distance from all this. No meddling was needed here now, she muttered to herself, thanking her Lord Jesus.

Thoughts of her brother swarmed in her brain, despite her efforts to make them dissolve. She knew he truly believed that the fabled La Llorona existed. And she knew he really believed the witch had something to do with both boys' deaths. Crazy. It was so hard to admit to herself he was off in the head, lleno de tonterias, poco loco. He'd been like this since childhood.

He had been a good priest before he retired, being loco hadn't hurt him professionally. She doubted anyone realized it but her—she certainly hoped so. Priests were so isolated from close relationships, from any kind of intimacy, emotional as well as physical, they were protected from certain realities of life, or if necessary, from their own base nature.

Becoming a priest had been a good choice for her brother for that reason. The priesthood protected him from himself. He could keep his nuttiness a secret, his entire life, from the people in his life. Everyone that is except her.

8

MRS. CERVANTES WAS OBVIOUSLY SHOCKED TO HEAR ABOUT the possible connection between her son and the boy who had been murdered.

Dolly was surprised, but at the same time, she realized that a devout Catholic like Mrs. Cervantes wasn't in the habit of connecting the dots between a child's illness and a murder, even if the two boys were in the same group of altar boys. It wasn't in her frame of reference, Dolly was thinking to herself as Mrs. Cervantes obviously was trying to keep her composure while absorbing the shocking news.

"What did your son eat before he became ill?" Connie asked. "I realize the doctors have been over this with you already, but I need to ask you to go over it again. I am sorry to have to trouble you this way. I know it is hard."

"The hospital people said they checked with Johnny's school and learned that no one else had gotten sick, and since Johnny and the rest of my family had eaten the same food, and he was the only one who got sick, they didn't think our food could have been the problem. They never mentioned anything about the altar boys, although I told them refreshments always are served and that is where he was after school that day. I assume they checked, though." Her brow furrowed as she remembered the chain of events from those frightening days when her son was so sick.

"Is your son especially close to anyone in the group of altar boys?" Connie asked. "Someone who might have been paying close attention to what he did that evening—what he ate or drank, any unusual behavior? Sometimes boys know things about each other, and don't remember it is important unless or until someone asks them. Is there a friend of his we could ask, or even a member of the church staff who is especially close to him?"

Mrs. Cervantes' brow furrowed even deeper as she was lost in thought for a few moments before answering, her careful, conscientious manner amazingly intact even when she was under great stress as she obviously was now.

"Actually he was closest to the boy who died," she said. Dolly had to work hard to keep her face from showing her shock. Connie didn't blink. "And Father Sanchez. Both boys were his favorites, Johnny always told us. He was proud of that. But none of the boys like Sister Rosalie," she said with a wry smile. "I don't know any young boy who ever liked nuns, even when I was growing up. I guess some things don't change."

"Did Johnny know his friend had gone missing before he got sick, Mrs. Cervantes?" Dolly asked.

"Oh no, of course not. We were all at the hospital with Johnny, so my family probably was the last to know Anthony had gone missing. No one called to tell me because they knew we had enough to deal with already, and we weren't paying any attention to the news. The hospital staff also was quite protective. If our neighbor hadn't reported that Zorro character in our yard, we wouldn't have been talking to the police about any of this. That is how you found out about Johnny, isn't it?" she asked, looking from one woman to the other.

"Yes, it is," Connie said. "The guys who talked to you and your husband realized how important it might be that your son was also an altar boy, which is why I called you. It just doesn't seem like it could be a coincidence that your son almost died and another boy, his best friend, did. We are wondering if someone also tried to kill your son. We are waiting to get test results back from the lab to see if the boys may have eaten the same thing, although given the circumstances we don't know how much information they will be able to give us."

Mrs. Cervantes nodded in agreement with Connie. "I feel so sad for Anthony's mother, knowing we almost lost our Johnny too."

"Have you heard if any of the other boys showed any signs of illness that day? Even the slightest? Have any of the mothers called you with that kind of information?" Dolly asked.

"No, most of the altar boys' mothers have called me, since Johnny got home, yes, but none have mentioned their sons being ill. We all are in shock at Johnny having to be hospitalized, and then Anthony's murder. It is almost too much for any of us. The mothers were as protective of my family as the hospital staff was, so we didn't know about Anthony until we brought Johnny home. Then everyone started calling and dropping by. We all are just so shocked."

"Do any of you mothers help with the refreshments for the altar boys?" Dolly asked.

"Oh no, all they expect us to do is get the boys there, and pick them up, on time, and we coordinate with each other as best we can. We live all over town, so carpooling can be a challenge. The church staff understands the scheduling and transportation challenges, so they don't make any other demands on us. They are grateful we support our children in being servers. Like the priesthood, it isn't as popular to be one as it was when I was growing up. Girls usually aren't interested much now either. It was such an honor for the boys when I was young," she said with a look of regret in her eyes as she remembered the old days. "Now it seems we are always having to reassure everyone it is safe for our children to serve that way, that not every priest hurts boys. After Anthony's death, I confess I am not so sure now."

"Are you considering pulling Johnny from the group?" Connie asked.

"I would let that be his decision, but if he is frightened, I wouldn't force him to continue. He hasn't said anything yet. We made it clear he had to get well first. And the parish is providing free counseling for all the boys with professionals to help them deal with Anthony's death. I want him to participate in that, but I won't force him. He's been so sick, we haven't really talked about any of this yet. He still is weak. Today is his first day back at school."

"So who provides the refreshments for the boys, Mrs. Cervantes?" Dolly asked.

"Oh, Sister Rosalie, of course," she responded immediately, obviously without even having to think about it. "She always handles the food for the boys. I think she does it all herself too, without help. But like I told you already, the boys tolerate her. I wouldn't say they dislike her as much as they don't like her, does that make sense? They so love Father Sanchez, the contrast is easy to see. Some of us mothers have talked about it." She laughed.

"I'm sorry, I shouldn't laugh about the boys not liking a nun, especially an elderly one like Sister Rosalie, but right now, I am surprised anything can make me laugh, so I should thank God for her if she can cause me to laugh."

"We understand," Connie said, "no apologies necessary. We have met her and can see how little boys might not warm up to her. Has she always been the one who provided the refreshments?"

"As far as I know, at least since Johnny has been an altar boy, but he is only into his second year. I had heard mothers mention her in that regard though, for years, now that I think about it. Mainly because the boys don't think her food choices are so cool," she laughed again. "You know how little boys can be about food. Even altar boys at church, especially today when they are so used to all the unhealthy treats available everywhere. I remember hearing about how she tried to give them milk to drink instead of sodas, a few years back. You'd think she had tried to get them to eat liver. Amazing how strong a protest a group of little altar boys can create, but they did. The milk idea died quickly."

All three women laughed.

"What do you think makes Father Sanchez so special to the boys?" Dolly asked, fearing she might be treading dangerous waters with the question. "Do they actually tell you mothers why they love him so much, or is it just something you know instinctively?"

"Both," Mrs. Cervantes answered immediately, again without having to ponder the question. "He's just a wonderful man, a wonderful priest. So loving and sincere, yet so reverent, so humble. He seems to make the boys want to be good, want to love God, want to make Jesus and their parents happy. A lot of religious leaders and teachers and parents can't do that, you know. So when someone comes along like Father Sanchez, it is special. He is a special man."

"So it would never enter your mind that he might have hurt one of the boys, even murdered one?" Dolly asked.

A horrified look came across her face. "Oh no. Of course not. I already talked to the other cops about this. Father Sanchez is the last person who would hurt one of the boys. He is a protector, he would defend them to his death if need be, I have no doubt. I know the other mothers feel the same way. We all adore him as much as our boys do."

Connie was careful with her next question, not wanting to break the rapport they had with Mrs. Cervantes. "Are there any other women involved with the church or the altar boys, besides the old nun and you mothers? Anyone who helps out? We have reason to believe a woman might have been involved in little Anthony's murder, and possibly with your son's food poisoning."

"Ay dios," Mrs. Cervantes exclaimed. "What a horrible thought. Let me think for a minute," and she went silent, gently rubbing the rosary beads she had been holding in her hand the entire time.

"No, there just aren't women involved with the basilica the way the nuns were when I was young. So much has changed in the Church with how things are done now.

"Do you all think a staff member would be capable of poisoning your son, or do you feel that was just an accident, some bad food he ate, and no one's fault?"

"I did think it was just an accident. We know when we send our children out into the world, we can't control everything they eat, whether or not they wash their hands, or whether others do, you know how it is. But when Anthony disappeared at the same time my boy got so sick, it seemed to me to be much more than a coincidence, especially since they are such close friends. They usually hang out together when they have those refreshments, so it would be easy for them to have eaten almost identical things. My son almost dies and the other one shows up dead. Do you all know yet exactly how he died? No one could drown in that river. That's a joke."

"No, he didn't drown," Connie said. "We can tell you that, but not anything more, really. Tests are being done, and we are looking for poisons, just like we are with your son. More extensive tests than the ones done initially."

"This is all so hard on everyone. At least I have my son. I feel so so bad for Anthony's mother, poor thing." Tears began gently falling down her cheeks.

"We need to be going, Mrs. Cervantes," Connie said quietly, almost whispering the words, as she put her hand on the grieving woman's arm. "Thank you so much for helping us today. If you think of anything please call me immediately, no matter what time it is, day or night. You have my cell number."

The women were silent as they left the house, climbed into Dolly's vehicle and belted up. Dolly had shared some of her conversations with Father Marquez.

"I just don't see how it could be a woman." Connie broke the silence first as Dolly pulled out of the driveway.

"I can't say I disagree with you, not after that conversation."

"We talked to all the mothers and the altar boys, and all the brothers associated with the cathedral in any way, as well as the priests. We took DNA samples from everyone too, did I tell you that yet? We've been so busy with basic police work, I forget what I have told you and what I haven't."

"No you didn't tell me about all the DNA testing, but I'm glad to hear it was requested. Frankly I am surprised the department would spring for such extensive testing."

"It probably wouldn't have if it weren't for that old case thirty years ago," Connie said. "Getting DNA from drowned bodies, even if they weren't killed by drowning, is challenging as you can imagine. But they are trying. And now with the food poisoning angle appearing to be connected, the more DNA collected, the more suspects can be eliminated. We started out with so many, it could have taken years to eliminate most of them the old fashioned way. That is why the old case went cold. We just can't let that happen this time."

"So were the priests and the old nun tested too?"

"Of course, they were first. But we made it clear to them it was elimination testing, knowing that if they were innocent, they would welcome it, and if guilty, they might slip up enough that the rest of the testing wouldn't be necessary. Unfortunately they haven't acted the least bit guilty, so we've had to order tests on everyone. We won't get them back for a while, that is the downside."

"The thing is, I don't need to tell you, all the boys would tend to have DNA from the priests and the nun, because of their association with the altar boys every week, including the food they eat. So finding DNA matches to the murdered boys wouldn't tell us much, would it? It would be DNA from one of the brothers perhaps, or one of the mothers, or even one or more of the other boys that might be more helpful. Am I right?"

"Yes, you are. But until we get results back, it doesn't do us much good to second guess the process. It's frustrating, all the work and all the waiting."

"But," Connie continued, "back to the old nun. Doesn't it also seem totally unlikely she would be involved since she is the sister of Father Marquez? If he thinks a woman is the likely murderer, and from what you say he does, enough to point us in that direction anyway, surely he meant everyone and anyone except his own sister?"

"One would assume that," Dolly said, "but with him, I don't assume anything. The more he shared with me, and I with him, the more I realized how complex a man he is, and how brilliant. I'm not saying he would protect his sister if he thought she were the murderer, don't get me wrong. I don't mean that at all.

"I'm just saying that I think we can't assume anything about what he means, and must take what he says at face value. Often the most brilliant people are able to communicate complex ideas in the simplest manner. That is a reflection of their brilliance, that ability to create simplicity where others leave only confusion. If he said to look for a woman and not focus as much on finding a man, I think we should.

"Our problem is that the main woman we would immediately look at happens to be his sister. I don't think she is the woman he meant. I didn't get the idea he had any specific woman in mind. He was using his knowledge and experience to point us in the direction of a woman, because he felt that would make our search more efficient. But I didn't get the slightest hint that he had a specific woman in mind. That is our job—to find one."

"Yet, from what you say, the irony of his sister's position in all this surely hasn't been lost on him," Connie said as Dolly nodded in total agreement.

"I noticed you didn't bring up the La Llorona angle with Mrs. Cervantes," Dolly said.

"No and I am glad you followed my lead on that. I felt we needed to dig for facts today, and that sighting by her neighbor can't be considered pure fact, you know that. She may have seen someone lurking around the house, that is fact, but her description of him as Zorro or a tall woman in black wasn't where I wanted to take that conversation just now. Plus, we have our reputations to protect," Connie said as they laughed in unison. "The street cops take La Llorona sightings in stride, but we homicide detectives have to be careful to stay on the side of science and legal facts. A case like this makes us walk a tightrope, especially when you're brought into the mix," she said, laughing again.

Dolly smiled. "Here we are, unless you want a coffee to continue this conversation, girlfriend."

"Yes, I would. I want to ask you about something, but waited until we finished all our business today on purpose, you'll see why. Let's just go down the street to our usual place."

Coffee ordered, Dolly said, "Okay, what's going on?"

Connie laughed. "Well, it's not so much that anything is going on...have you heard the news about Baylor and gays?"

Dolly just stared at her for a few seconds, trying to see if she was serious or joking. "What *are* you talking about?"

"Good, you haven't heard then."

"Heard what and why is it good?"

Laughing again, Connie said, "It was important you be sitting down. And good that I get to be the first to tell you. Baylor has gotten rid of its ban on homosexuals. You know my partner and I follow Baylor's girls basketball team closely, and so we pay attention to news stories about Baylor too. The fact you went there also makes me pay attention, I admit."

"We know you two follow Baylor sports way better than I do," Dolly laughed.

Their coffees were ready. Connie got them and sat back down."I want to know what a ban on homosexuals meant and what it means to lift it."

Dolly finally spoke, deadpan face. "They wouldn't let anyone dance on campus from 1845 until 2001, and yet they're letting the gays come out so soon?

"I didn't know they had a ban on gays. How do you ban gays? Take a survey to see who says they are gay and then tell them they can't be there?"

Connie laughed louder than ever. Others looked at the women.

"I just thought you would want to know," Connie said, still giggling, but quietly so people would quit staring at them. "It's all over the internet apparently. You've been out of touch lately, chasing ghosts and priests."

"A little bit," Dolly smirked. "My head is spinning. I'm going to read all about the details when I get home and then we'll talk. Did they talk about gay marriage or gay sex or what? What isn't banned now? That's what confuses me. What specifically about being gay was banned that isn't now?"

"You got me," Connie said. "That's what Anna and I were asking each other. We thought you would have all the answers."

"Not this time. All I know is anecdotal, but from good sources, shall we say. Baylor was the main college in Texas at least—not sure if the reputation extended beyond there or not—where gay guys knew they could go and be comfortable when I was there. One dormitory in particular had rumors circulating that it was the gay dorm. I learned all this years later, but it made sense to me. I realized I had heard things when I was there about that dorm, but at the time hadn't really understood what was being said. Now I do.

"And, one of the primary drama professors was known to make passes at pretty male students, I know because one of those pretty boys told me that is why he left the department after his first semester at Baylor. Technically it wouldn't have been pedophilia given the age of the students, with occasional exceptions of course, such as those who began Baylor after their junior year in high school. The friend who told me about his experience was destined for fame regardless, and found it as a writer instead of an actor. Someone else in a major men's club there told his mother, who then told me, that it was filled with gays, that is where he learned to have gay sex and get in touch with his bisexuality. He later died of AIDS, one of the early waves of deaths beginning to sweep the nation by the mid-eighties. It was sad.

"I could go on and on, but my point is that no one talked about a ban on gays. No one talked about gays. We didn't use that word then. Homosexuality and homosexuals were terms out of science books, or psychology books, not terms used in everyday conversation. I guess we called gays fags in those days, but there was so little talk about any aspect of the subject while I was there, I honestly don't know what people said, now that I think about it. My friend never called his prof a homo, just said he put his hand on his leg with a certain smile, causing said friend to decide right then and there he didn't want to be a drama major. And yes, I do know Johnny Mathis is gay, but that isn't why I said that. No one knew he was when his "Certain Smile" hit came out. He remains one of my all-time favorite singers. He can cook too. I even got to interview him once, it was heavenly."

Connie managed to roll her eyes at the pun on the famous album, but still was giggling between sips of coffee as Dolly drug up the memories.

"So is Baylor coming out?"

"What do you mean?" Dolly asked, looking puzzled.

"Well you said it was known as a school for gay guys all those decades ago, had an established reputation among gay teenage boys was what you insinuated, so I am just wondering if a school like that has been in the closet since who knows when? Maybe it decided it was time to come out of that closet, since the Supreme Court gave its blessing to gay marriage last month. That must be what precipitated Baylor to do this, don't you think?"

"Well I doubt Baylor approves of gay marriage. Did the news articles say that?"

"No," Connie was giggling again. "But you know what happens when we gays come out of our closets. We want to get married in front of God and Country and Kids and everyone."

"Okay, time for me to go home and talk to friends and read up. Sounds like the news cycle is a good day or two ahead of me. Have to catch up. You want a ride back to work?"

"No, I'm good," Connie smiled as they left the coffee shop. " Talk to you soon. Go see Father Marquez again. You must get some La Llorona stories out of him this time. I wonder if he is gay. You should ask him. A famous priest and author wrote twenty or thirty years ago that more than ninety percent of Catholic priests in America were gay. Now we know too many of those men also were pedophiles, but maybe the Church has purged most of them by now. One would hope. You should ask Father Marquez about those stats. He probably knew that author, he's dead now."

"When the time is right," Dolly replied as they parted ways. "When the time is right."

9

DOLLY COULDN'T WAIT TO TAKE HER FURRY SWEETHEARTS out that evening in the autumnal dusk, a favorite time of year for her walks in the Rio Grande area. Actually every season gave itself a reason to be her favorite, and she thus played fair as each one's turn came around year after year. Oh, how she loved her New Mexico and the many gifts it had bestowed throughout her life.

Some years the golden and beige leaves left the big cottonwoods early, some years they stayed late. She loved the years they stayed late, which usually meant they had turned from green to the golden spectrum late as well—a warm autumn. But it could just as easily mean the fall was so dry, no leaves had been removed by falling rain, much less snow, but instead, allowed to ripen for months, not weeks, to full winter dormancy before floating to the ground.

After their walk, everyone got fed and she went to her meditation area, knowing they all would join her, one by one, once they filled their tummies. They loved to lounge around her while she meditated, and she loved their ethereal presence, for all seemed to know instinctively it was time to enter another zone.

On this night, the meditation went long. She had been doing it so many years, the meditations led her, not the other way around. When it was time to end, she was brought out of her reverie automatically, but rarely at exactly the same time. Sometimes the meditations lasted a long time, more than an hour, other times only 20 minutes. She learned long ago to let them be, and not force the timing, at least not in the evenings. Morning meditations sometimes had to be cut short by a timer, which is why she relished her evenings when no timers were needed, no phones had to be attended, no noisy traffic could be heard.

After almost two hours, it ended. Rising slowly, she whispered to her babies so as not to startle them, and moving slowly, they all went back outdoors, back to the ditch bank, where the gently flowing water in the old Clear Ditch made a gentle rippling sound, barely audible.

After deep and lengthy meditation, she often found clarity and solutions.

This night was no exception. As they wandered slowly next to the almost-silent water, taking in the sweet, fresh, earthy aromas of the night that only can be found in high desert climates near flowing water, she realized she needed to wander through the cathedral grounds in Santa Fe. She sensed a beckoning, but knew that her imagination easily could be adding drama to her meditation suggestions, for it often did. Her lifelong dilemma always had been separating out her imagination from her psychic ability. She tried to stay receptive and open-minded by allowing them to work together, hoping for better results. Often she was rewarded, sometimes she was not. Until facts could be found in any given situation, she never knew which result she would get.

Decades ago, her poet friend with the ghostly Indian guide had been beckoned intuitively. To Marfa. After Dolly met her, she had joined a yoga class, and in a few months, transformed her once flabby, overweight housewife body into a svelte, tall woman who looked much like the seventeen-year-old version of herself. Her marriage was lifeless, so when she felt an intuitive beckoning from Marfa, she went. There she met the man who became her second husband. An artist, her new husband led them on a nomadic life as his work became more and more famous throughout the Western world. What if her friend had refused to answer the beckoning call when it came?

As it had turned out, the artist and husband-to-be had known he was going to meet his soul mate and was waiting for her to arrive in Marfa. He too understood these things, but he also knew when he needed to stay put and not move, to be still and wait. He had waited for years, biding his time, he had told her. Once they found each other, they never lived in Marfa. It had been a place for him to learn patience and hone his talent, not a place for them to carve a life together.

Dolly knew being still and waiting were not for her path this time. She was the beckoned, not the one doing the beckoning. But who or what was calling her?

She must, absolutely must, tour the basilica grounds, and on her own, no guided tours, preferably at night, although pulling that off might be a monumental task, she realized. If only she were Catholic, she could come up with some sincere spiritual reason to want to be there after dark. Connie was, albeit a bit lapsed. Had she been ex-communicated for being gay? Was that something Connie was supposed to confess? Dolly couldn't remember what her status was these days, nor the latest edict that had come down from the pope on the subject, if any. All her adult life it seemed Catholics were in disagreement with each other about all sorts of things, some on board with whatever pope had the title, and many often not, especially here in America. But apparently everyone took the popes in stride, just like Americans took their presidents in stride, once they got elected, regardless of whether your choice was the selection or not.

But she had answered her own question. Connie had to go with her. Two women without status as Catholics was better than one in this situation, no question about that. At least Connie would know enough about Catholic rituals and needs and acceptable behavior to help them wander the grounds and as many building interiors as possible after dark, while raising a minimal amount of suspicion. Connie would know what to tell whom too, with no eyebrows raised. Dolly knew if she approached the staff, more than eyebrows would be raised. She couldn't even make an accomplished sign of the cross. Baptists taught her to be into the Risen Saviour, not the crucifixion. They found all the focus on the dying and dead Jesus on the cross quite morbid.

Dolly found herself smiling. One never would find a Penitente among evangelicals. But then for a century or more, Catholics hadn't wanted to claim association with Penitentes, the secret Catholic brotherhood found in New Mexico and Colorado.

When they returned home after a long walk on the dark and cloudy night, she texted Connie.

As Dolly drove to Santa Fe the next day, she went over everything she knew about the case in her mind. Connie and she had worked together enough now that they didn't waste each other's time going over every detail of the case at it was learned. Connie brought things to her attention when she felt the need, and Dolly asked questions in the same vein—when there was a need. But she was stymied now, and she felt Connie was too. She knew all the usual interviews had been done—the staff, the parents, the children, as well as the routine searches for possible forensic evidence at the cathedral and in little Anthony's home. She knew not to pressure Connie about the results of interviews, or the scheduling of them, but her patience was running thin on this. Why had no one seen Anthony leave that day? It was as though he had vanished into thin air. Who or what was the elephant in the living room they were missing? She hated to turn to pure psychic ability and technique to break cases. The validity of science and good fact-gathering always should be the foundation for any case. Intuition and so-called psychic ability should only be add-ons to basic police work. She felt strongly about that, and knew that was why she was hired and why people with whom she worked respected her, and her work. But this case was coming up so cold, not counting the actual cold one from all those years ago, she was beginning to wonder if she needed to be going to psychics for help.

When she left the Bell County newspaper and took a job at the Hearst daily in San Antonio during the final era when evening newspapers still existed, Dolly soon stumbled across people who were professional psychics. Until then, she never had known one in her life. The closest she had come to a psychic was by reading in the Sunday magazine in the Albuquerque morning paper about Jean Dixon, the famed Washington, DC, psychic the press loved to both adore and disdain when Dolly was a girl, especially after President Kennedy was shot. Years later, the Wall Street Journal wrote an in-depth front page investigative piece about Dixon, portraying her as a complete and utter fraud.

Eventually she formed a theory that if you are going to go to a psychic, you must never go to just one. Make appointments with three within about the same 30-day or so period, or don't go to any of them. She had learned the hard way how easy it was to give up all your power to one, to get too hooked into what one told you, in ways that weren't healthy, supportive or frankly, character building. Letting someone else direct your life could only end in disaster, no matter how accurate the psychic might be.

No psychic ever is one hundred percent accurate, for it is as much art as science. Just finding three psychics you could trust was a challenge. She never had found even one in New Mexico in all these years whom she found worth their salt, much less her money. But San Antonio was blessed with some really good ones, and thus over time, she developed her Theory of Threes. Two psychics might tell you the exact same thing, or give you totally unrelated, even opposing information. So two weren't enough for an accurate psychic photo of yourself at any given point in time. A third was essential.

By the time you heard what that last one had to say, you most likely would have heard at least one thing, if not a few things, that were the same. But you also would have heard a lot of differing information among the three as well. Over time you learned which ones were the most accurate, but that could take years.

She had had psychics tell her things that happened exactly as they said they would, but years later. Most psychics will tell you that their timing usually is bad, for usually it is. It helps if they are honest enough to tell you that. She was told her husband was going to buy her a car in February, which she assumed, when said like that, meant the next February, a few months away. But no, it was several years later, the details of how it all came to be exactly as the woman had predicted. By then it was a wonder Dolly even remembered her prediction, but it was so exact in terms of how she had described the situation, she certainly did remember.

The best way to use psychics was to find their Themes for You, and by going to three in the same general time frame, you got an expanded view of their Themes for You as well as their accuracy abilities. The one who might tell you things quite different than the other two also might be the one who turned out to be the most accurate. After spending years figuring all this out with her footwork among the psychics, as she liked to think of it, detective work, reporter work, whatever, she concluded it was easier, cheaper and generally more reliable, to learn to meditate, do it regularly and thus develop your own intuition.

Some of those San Antonio psychics had become good friends of hers as well, or were her friends before they became psychics. Some still were. One even worked with the royal family of England when Princess Di was killed in that horrid crash that had so much mystery surrounding it. If she ever felt the need for a cadre of psychics, she had them, some well into their ninth decade by now, but still practicing their trade, one with a clientele that read like a Who's Who of the Powerful, Famous, Rich in Texas. One had died, sadly, another in her seventies had been doing serious body building for about two decades now. Amazing women all. Dolly had gone to men psychics now and then, but never found them as helpful.

If Connie and she didn't get a break in this case soon, she was going to have to tap into her personal San Antonio Psychic Line, as she often labeled it.

The women met for lunch at Tomasita's, for two reasons. It was Dolly's favorite restaurant in the world and had been for more than two decades, and it was so wonderfully noisy in general, but with an ample amount of nice big private booths, they could converse about sensitive matters without fear of being overheard nor of attracting much if any attention. Just two more Santa Fe women at lunch, no big deal.

Connie heard Dolly out on her reasons for wanting to explore the grounds, reminding her that their little tour was going to arouse a lot of animosity, "I'm just saying."

"Exactly why I want you with me," Dolly replied. "But I need to get some things clear in my mind about where we are in the case before we go over there. It has such huge gaps, more like a cosmic black hole actually.

"For starters of course, when was Anthony discovered missing? How was he supposed to get home? Haven't you all traced his presence from where the altar boys were that afternoon to when he disappeared? Or did he just evaporate into thin air? I haven't bugged you about these questions because I know you well enough to know you will tell me when you have adequate information, but usually it comes long before this point in our investigation. What's going on? This is me bugging you."

"Well, as usual, your timing is perfect. You can bug. We still don't have all those answers, but what little we do know wasn't learned until yesterday. That was why I suggested lunch today before we go over there so I could tell you. I agree, this has been the big gap in our investigation, and it's because Johnny and his mother are part of it. "They are?" Dolly was astounded. "But we just talked to her yesterday. You didn't say anything that would have made me think that."

"Exactly. I wanted you to meet with her minus any preconceived notions I might provide you. After you and I left, one of our officers who knows the family well, including Johnny, met with Johnny by himself, in their home. His mother was there of course, but she left them alone in the room to talk. She wasn't approached about it until you and I left. We didn't expect it to happen so soon, but she was quite willing to help us, and so was Johnny. She told him it was his choice, which we encouraged her to do, knowing we would get better information from him if he didn't feel pressured nor coerced. Everyone felt it was important Johnny be as comfortable as possible with the person doing that interview. You can see why now that you know the two boys were so close.

"Dolly, your text last night didn't surprise me at all. In fact, if I hadn't heard from you, something, anything, I would have been surprised. I know how you work by now, your process. I was going to call you today and tell you about the interview. Your text last night made me decide to just wait and tell you before we went over to the cathedral. I must say I am surprised that you want a tour of the cathedral buildings and grounds, that wasn't quite what I was expecting. I am not sure what I was expecting, though, I confess. You never fail to surprise me," she laughed.

"So here is what we know now. Johnny's and Anthony's family members usually take turns taking the boys to and from their meetings. Apparently the two mothers coordinate everyone, since several extended family members are involved, depending on work and school schedules.

"The day of the disappearance, Anthony was supposed to ride home with Johnny. The boys' mothers told them who would pick them up from school and drop them off, and who would pick them up at the cathedral. The boys themselves, being so young, didn't pay much attention, for they knew where the cars were supposed to be each time. They looked for the cars, not the drivers or the boys going with them. Sometimes other boys rode with them, always arranged by the mothers."

"Sounds like a perfect set-up for someone to go missing without anyone figuring it out quickly."

"You got it. That day, when Johnny's cousin, the designated driver du jour, picked him up, he already was feeling so sick, neither the cousin nor Johnny paid attention to the fact that no other boys were riding with them that day. The boys always ran out to the waiting cars as a group and got into the one for them. No one expected a boy to get in the wrong car, or worse, not run out to the cars at all."

"In other words, you are telling me the boys were expected to know who was driving them, but the drivers didn't necessarily know which boys they were driving?"

"That's correct. Turns out it wasn't just Johnny's and Anthony's families who operated in this manner, other families did too. It takes a village and all that, you know."

"Well, this village isn't doing a very good job. I trust the parents will be changing their system?"

"One would hope. The lack of consistency in the transportation arrangement enabled our murderer, it is becoming increasingly clear."

"So let me get this straight. You really are saying Anthony disappeared from a group of altar boys at one of the only basilicas in the American Southwest, and no one, and I mean no one, seems to know what happened? And it wasn't until late yesterday that you became absolutely certain of this, after the interview with little Johnny?"

"That's correct," Connie said, regret wreathing her words. "No one."

"Why didn't you learn any of this from Anthony's mother herself? Something strikes me as deeply amiss that apparently you didn't."

"True, and I haven't brought it up because I had nothing to say, but kept hoping I would. I still do, have hope that is. For right now, we don't have squat from her. She is out of her mind with grief, and basically isn't rational, to put it bluntly. They've got her on so many drugs, she barely knows who she is when she is awake. Most of the time she sleeps, I am told. More than one of us have tried to interview her, but we can't get into the basic details of how that day evolved. Her whole *modus operandi* now is *not* to think about how that day changed her life forever, destroyed it forever as far as she is concerned. We assume one day we will be able to speak with her calmly about details such as who was supposed to ride with whom and so forth, but not now. It could be days, weeks, even months. Maybe never. We just don't know. And the father doesn't know anything, for she handled all those transportation and communication details. Also, the husband is extraordinarily protective of her right now, as to be expected, but he also isn't real pro-cop, we realized almost immediately, so he isn't supportive of us trying to find out what she knows. We would like to think he would call us when she is up to talking with us, but we aren't expecting any miracles. So we walk a fine line between contacting them regularly to see if she can talk, and harassment, at least in his eyes. It's a delicate situation, to say the least."

Dolly motioned for the waiter as she asked Connie, "Want something else?"

"No, I'm good." Connie smiled at the waitress. "Too bad we have to go back to work. I would love to have one of your famous margaritas, best ones in New Mexico."

"Then come back when you finish work," the waiter smiled back.

"We may need to," Dolly and Connie chimed together, giving each other a knowing look.

"Before we head over there, let's review what we know from my perspective, okay?" Dolly asked her.

"Of course," Connie said. Police Perspective vs. Psychic Perspective. Their Principle P's. Merging the two was how they solved their cases.

"Okay, for starters," Dolly began, "we have several La Llorona connections to this case in terms of timing. One, Father Marquez experiences her for the first time in years, after thinking he was free of her, she had been gone so long from his life. Two, the neighbor sees someone or something that could be a description of La Llorona, at the home of the best friend of the murdered boy. That report is less substantial than Father Marquez' in my mind, because the Anglo neighbor thought she was seeing Zorro. The only reason I give it credence is because of the reports of a similar character on the movie sets, confirmed by the Hispanics present to be a La Llorona character, not Zorro. So whether someone is dressing up to be one or the other, or is the witch herself, I buy the Llorona description, not Zorro, my childhood TV hero.

"Three, I have an experience when visiting Father Marquez that I explain as La Llorona, but have absolutely no way to prove that except that I felt it was her. Again, about as solid as the Zorro-Llorona descriptions, as in melted ice, and thus useless as facts but useful in terms of signs and symbols, synchronicities, all that New Ag-ey stuff."

"Well, it also is science, you know, " Connie said, "Have you hung out with the astrophysicists and think tank folks around here lately? It isn't just New Agers who think patterns should be taken seriously. It's about thinking outside the box. That is why we have you."

"Okay, thanks for the vote of confidence, for right now, I'm stalled and it is driving me nuts. Moving on here. Fourth. The priest who immediately was the prime suspect and certainly the most obvious candidate, to the superficial observer of the situation, anyway, has a strange and one-of-a-kind history of dressing up regularly as La Llorona when young. He goes so far as to admit his fascination with her as a child on the record, but attributes it to a phase he went through, nothing more.

"And now the clincher to all this: Father Marquez says when a situation has a La Llorona connection, we have to look for the woman behind it, not a man. I have thought about what he said a lot, and how he said it, since I was with him as you know when he told me that. I plan to query him some more on this, but for now, let me say I choose to interpret what he said to mean a woman could be the reason or cause of a crime, but not necessarily the perpetrator of it. Or, she could be both."

"Aha," Connie leaned forward, obviously excited. "But in this case, we don't even *have* women, unless you count an ancient nun and the mothers of the altar boys, all of whom have alibis that have cleared them. Finding the woman behind the man or the woman without the man isn't going to be easy. What a Chinese puzzle."

"What do we know about the nun? Have you all researched her carefully?"

"Yes, we have and she is a strange one, but then what nun isn't when you start putting their life under a microscope. People think priests are strange. Nuns escape most of the scrutiny, certainly the public eye, in a way priests do not. My conclusion is that the nuns are the weirdest ones of all, for that very reason. They can lead such secretive lives, away from prying people of any kind, from both the public and within the Church, in a way a priest never could.

"As for Sister Rosalie? For starters, she maintains an amazing greenhouse where she grows flowering plants and medicinal herbs. She even has an extensive collection of Palma Christi plants from around the world."

"Those being?"

"I wondered if I would stump you with that label," Connie laughed. "Those are the plants that produce castor beans, and thus are the source of castor oil, as well as beautiful beads. And the poison, ricin.

"Ricin? Are you kidding me? Why hadn't you told me this before?"

"Again, I didn't have complete information. The hospital was told to test for it in the food poisoning case, but it was too late by the time we found out about her little hobby. They did tell us little Johnny's symptoms were consistent with that, if a bean or part of one had been put in his food. He didn't die so it wouldn't have been more than that. Three can kill an adult. But frankly, his symptoms could have been from bad seafood, which he ate the day before, or many, many other things. Seafood is the source of something like one in four food poisoning cases in this country. And food poisoning is so hard to pin down, especially if it is only one case like that was."

"Okay, so she's weird, has a green thumb and loves beautiful plants. I suppose the Palma Christi name has a special meaning for her?"

"Of course, the Palm of Christ, because, according to the old Romans, who gave it the Palma Christi name, the leaves supposedly look like the bleeding palms of Jesus on the cross. Some say it also has that name because the plant's healing qualities remind us of how Christ could heal people, supposedly with his hands. Although you and I know he didn't always use his hands in the Biblical miracle stories.

"I buy the old Roman reason for the name myself. Edgar Cayce, the famous healer and clairvoyant as you know, recommended castor oil packs for all kinds of maladies, and I suspect the healing hands of Christ theory came about during his era, but that is only my simple opinion. You can find all kinds of info online if you want to know more.

"The plant grows naturally in warm climates, and can be a potted plant, a bush or shrub, or even a small tree, depending on many factors. Our nun has them in pots and some are definitely growing into small tree size. It grows everywhere in the Mediterranean countries where Catholicism got its start. It seems obvious to me why a nun with a green thumb and access to a greenhouse would grow it, simply because of the Jesus connection, but she probably understands its medicinal uses even though I truly doubt she processes those beans into castor oil.

"I think the poison bean aspect is just that, an aspect, and a minor one. How many people avoid growing oleanders because they are so poisonous? Not many, yet they are everywhere in warm climates, we all love those gorgeous flowers."

"That's true, I've certainly had them in my yards, even with all my pets. They are all over the place in the South, and in Arizona. I had them around me for years in San Antonio before I even learned they were poisonous."

"But, one thing we learned about the old nun does concern me," Connie continued. "I hadn't told you yet because I wanted to discuss it in person, and it's not like we have had tons of time. Plus I only learned this the other day. She is a type one diabetic and has been all her life. She injects insulin daily. My hunch is that she has taken such an interest in medicinal herbs and plants because her health always has been so fragile."

"Insulin." Dolly felt a zing of energy go through her entire body. "*Insulin*," she repeated.

"Yes, insulin," Connie said, "and yes, I know what you are thinking. But come on, a nun? And how, when and where would she do it? Where would she put him if she did? I knew this would set you off in a direction, and I've already been obsessing about it ever since I learned of it. But I just can't get anywhere. It just doesn't seem possible. How could she throw him into the river? She's a nun for God's sake, Jesus Christ's too, and an old one at that."

Dolly pulled a folded piece of paper out of her tote. "I wrote up a list for you, in case the office staff or Father Sanchez stonewalls you. Actually typed it on a PC and printed it out." She laughed.

"So I see," Connie said. "You couldn't have just texted or emailed it?"

"Sometimes there is nothing like old-fashioned hard copy," Dolly deadpanned. "It's bullet point, you can scan it later, and show it to them if you need, or have it for reference so you don't forget something."

"Does this really need to be so complicated?

"Yes," Dolly replied, handing it to her.

"They have a security detail. The Vatican has its Swiss guards, does our basilica have Sikh guards? Since it is to Santa Fe what the Vatican is to Rome?"

"Well, I hadn't thought about it that way, but now that you point it out..." Connie muttered, looking at the list. "I should know who does their security, but now that you bring it up, I realize I don't. I know the guards were interviewed. They saw nothing unusual. I don't remember anyone saying they were Sikhs.

"Since our home-grown Espanola Sikhs became world-renowned as a result of nine-one-one, it would be fitting for them to be the guards here. But the basilica doesn't have quite the funding the Vatican does. Local retired Catholic cops would be my guess for here," she laughed.

"If we could text a security guard as we leave each area, that would help them keep track of us as well as get each area locked again as soon as we leave. It really is important we don't have people actually accompanying us on this nocturnal escapade, you understand that, right?"

Connie nodded.

"Or they may want us to text them to unlock each area as we are ready to enter, which would be okay too, as long as they don't want to come along with us, I emphasize again."

"I get it," Connie said, a bit impatiently. "You can't feel the vibes with a leering guard in your presence.

"Who said he would leer?"

"They all do when you show up."

Dolly laughed. "Every year that fact fades a bit, you realize. Being in one's sixties, no matter how well preserved, probably is my final decade for gathering leers, except from really, really old men.

"Anyway, once you get permission for our little tour, I trust you can work out these logistics. And Connie, try to get us access to everything, including the bell towers, basements, the green house—especially that green house.

"I understand the apartments being off limits, but nothing else should be. And don't let them stonewall you. The throne of the third archbishop here, Placid Louis Chapelle, that rests in the cathedral, was stored for decades in some basement on the grounds, I've read. And that crucifixion scene above the confessionals?"

Dolly looked hard into Connie's eyes, toying with her Catholic guilt. "You know which one, right?"

Connie nodded, not quite meeting her gaze, too many years since she had been in a confessional, including that one, which all good Catholics who grew up in Santa Fe went to at one time or another because it *was* the basilica confessional, and thus, according to some, Dolly had been told, an especially sacred experience compared to confession at the other Catholic churches in the area.

"Well, that crucifixion scene was stored forever in one of the bell towers. My point being, we should be able to access the bell towers, the basements, tunnels if any exist, old cellars, every nook and cranny."

Continuing to stare at the list while Dolly talked, Connie nodded, "I get it."

"You have the right to get a warrant for all of this, not that I need to remind you. I'm actually trying to shore up your strength here, because I have no idea what kind of reaction our request will get, and you don't either. Just remember, religious privacy does not supercede the law when a child disappears in plain sight from the basilica grounds as little Anthony did."

Connie was strangely silent. Dolly knew all this was hard on her. Dolly never had seen anyone raised as a devout Catholic, no matter how lapsed they might have become later, who was able to shake off all of that early training, just as she herself knew the same was true for so many raised among seriously loyal Baptists as she had been. When the world weighed heavily, those early teachings provided the foundation for whatever belief system one used in the present, consciously or unconsciously. All her life she had observed so-called non-believers do and say things when under stress that indicated they actually held the same fear of Jehovah, of Yahweh, as they were taught to have at age five. It was those Jewish underpinnings of Christianity that held people in their thrall. Jesus didn't scare folks, but Yahweh did, all that flailing and anger and smiting for which he was world-renowned. Still could keep people in line.

"What a case. We are stumped, that is true. It isn't our first time and it won't be our last," Dolly said, picking up the check as they stood up. "Lunch is on me, I am the one with the expense account. Let's go explore the American Southwest's equivalent of the Vatican. See you this evening. You'll convince them to let us in then, I have no doubt."

10

THE TWO SLEUTHS HAD DECIDED TO MEET AT THE STATUE OF the first Indian Catholic saint. Not a New Mexico Indian, Kateri Tekakwitha was from a complex East Coast lineage and heritage, an orphan raised by Jesuits. The statuesque sculpture of her that graced the front of the cathedral so proudly was done by a Jemez Pueblo woman. The stories of St. Kateri were the kind that gave Dolly confidence in her own ethereal experiences. As she grew beyond her Baptist upbringing, Dolly studied experiences of many of the Catholic saints, and Hindu saints as well, which helped her understand some of her own, not that she was anywhere near the status of a saint. But they helped her understanding and acceptance of herself, and of others whom she knew personally with similar experiences to her own.

Many Bible stories did the same thing. In fact when she was young, those were all she had, but she soon realized her fellow Southern Baptists weren't big on psychic experiences. Members of her family were, some of those also devout Baptists, since most of her family was Baptist, except for the uncle who turned Mormon when he was almost sixty. He had some astounding psychic experiences, through dreams, as did his daughter. They had shared them on a visit when Dolly was a teen.

Before college, Dolly believed all those miracles in the Bible stories, but she didn't find a lot of support in her Baptist-dominated environment, at home nor at church, for believing such things could happen in the present day. Which made her wonder, what was the point? Why learn these things only to find they are out of date?

Her religion classes at Baylor, taught mostly by highly educated Baptist ministers, advanced her religious education tremendously because they provided science, history and archeology to show how so many of the Bible stories probably were true and not myths nor fairy tales. The Old Testament prof, a former pastor of Waco's largest Baptist church, who smoked cigarettes throughout class, provided facts and figures that strengthened her spiritual understanding in leaps and bounds, not because they had anything to do with God per se but because they indicated miracles are as much a matter of perception and knowledge as of religious faith. They didn't discount perceptions of God and man's story of Him, as much as they made Him and His potential more real, less a fairy tale for children to outgrow.

Dolly found herself recalling some of her early childhood frustrations with her religious education while walking the short distance from her room at the La Fonda to meet Connie. She was grateful to Baylor for the kind of religion teachers it provided her, before it, and so many Baptist seminaries, began purging that sort of fact-based thinking, along with intellectual perspectives on the meaning of sin and redemption, about the time she graduated, as the ultra-conservative, anti-intellectual element of Southern Baptists took over throughout the nation, a coup that had lasted most of her adult life.

"So are we on?" Dolly asked as she walked up the stairs from the street to where Connie sat on one of the benches near the dramatic statue.

"You are," Connie smiled mysteriously.

"I am? Okay, what's happened?"

"We have permission. But Father Sanchez wants to meet with me privately right now. I am to join you later. I have *no* idea what he wants."

"Ah, interesting. And what about the list?"

"I was told we have full access to the cathedral, but not the living quarters of the nun, nor of Father Sanchez, both of whom live in apartments on the grounds. Other priests and staff, some monks too, live across the river. They gave me a map employees use, which has more details than the ones for the tourists."

"What about security staff?"

"Well our famous Espanola-based Sikhs, whose clients include Homeland Security, you know, are a bit out of the price range of the Catholic church these days. All those lawsuits, you know," Connie deadpanned, referring to all the pedophile priest settlements worldwide in recent decades.

"Two retired cops, one from California and one from Arizona, which is why I didn't know about them, and don't know them, are it. Seven days a week. Only at night when everything is closed. Joe is on duty tonight, he knows every nook and cranny, I was assured, and can open anything for us, for you. I'm texting you his number right now. He knows not to hover, but to be vigilant. He *was* a cop, after all, and we are doing police work. He won't come around until you text him to let you into something, since I trust you are going to wander around outside a bit first?"

Dolly nodded.

"So I guess you are good to go. I can only imagine what Father Sanchez wants. Sounds like a police matter, since he wants it to be only me. Maybe he's going to confess."

"Stranger things have happened. I don't want to keep my phone on the whole time because I don't want anything to interfere with my experiences, assuming I have even one, much less several," Dolly laughed. "So feel free to leave me voice mails or texts and I will check them as I move around, since I obviously will have to turn on my phone to communicate with our guard. As for finding me, I would suggest you text him, not me, when and if you are ready to join me. I may reach a point where I need to be completely alone and if that happens, I will let him know to tell you that, okay? Actually this sounds like a good system we have, for I knew I probably would need to do some of my work alone tonight, but at the same time, needed you involved. I may feel the need to spend the entire night here, I just don't know. Depends on what I stumble across. I am so excited about that map. It will be a huge help. And I brought a flashlight."

"The office staff asked me how long we would be," Connie said. "I told them I had no idea, and they didn't seem surprised, fortunately. Oh, and they don't have security cameras. I thought I remembered our officers being surprised about that when Anthony disappeared. But I asked, just in case they decided to install them since then. I guess filming people in church and on the grounds just goes too far, even today, at least here it does. I was glad to learn they didn't."

"Being in a house of worship with cameras watching me is creepy, I agree," Dolly said. "Frankly, Connie, I don't mind doing all of it by myself, I think you realize that. If Father Sanchez should confess, you would have to take him down and book him, wouldn't you?"

"Yes, that is true, but do you really think he did it, and that he would? I don't. But," she laughed, "I know you just needed my credentials to get in here."

They laughed together, releasing nervous tension, both realizing the importance of the coming hours, as they stood up and went their separate ways,

Dolly to the park next to the cathedral now that it was dark, and Connie back to the office building just south of the cathedral, which also housed the rectory.

Dolly had been feeling the inner *pull* to this place for a while, but now that she had answered it, her psychic radio seemed to have gone dead. Or was overwhelmed. She wasn't sure which. As the evening hours wore on, and the town quieted, she knew some of the vibes left throughout the day by tourists and parishioners would recede, but that wasn't the problem.

Although a cemetery wasn't on the grounds of the old cathedral, unlike so many others throughout the world, plenty of famous and many not-so-famous dead guys were buried in crypts beneath the floors of the cathedral, most on its north side. The cathedral and other buildings were filled with statues and other forms of art depicting famous saints, even some famous sinners, as well as Jesus and Mary, of course. All of these collected vibes, whether ghosts and spirits or simply the energy of the devoted who focused their sorrows, grief and prayers onto specific ones. This place probably could use a major ghost-busting, spirit-cleansing team, she thought to herself. Centuries of psychic residue covered every inch of this place. No wonder she couldn't feel anything, for she actually felt all of it, far too much to sort. Like being rolled up in a psychic rug. How was she going to *feel* anything? This place was filled with too much psychic debris. Yet the irony was that she wouldn't dare want the place cleansed first, because that could erase all clues she was seeking.

The cathedral grounds had a violent and erratic history, adding to the complex energies of the location. She wandered around the park on the north side of the cathedral, mulling over the location's history, priming her mood, trying to be an open channel for whatever might drift her way. The night air was crisp, not too cold, no breeze, the sky clear, star-filled.

The Spanish apparently were living in the Santa Fe area by 1607, the year Jamestown was founded by the British in Virginia. It wasn't until 1620 the British refugees who later became known in history books as the Pilgrims associated with the First Thanksgiving arrived in Plymouth, Massachusetts. Those British Puritans, extremist Protestant evangelicals, came from the Netherlands, where they had been living among the Dutch for many years to avoid persecution in their homeland because they refused to adhere to the teachings of the Protestant Church of England.

Santa Fe was given its present name and declared the capital of New Spain in 1610. But the official Spanish Catholic presence existed in New Mexico long before that. The Spaniards began conquering the New World, with great passion for money, especially gold, and for dominance, with the arrival of Christopher Columbus in 1492. It went without saying that beating the competition was a primary goal, since other things, better things unknown yet, might be found. Out of such hopes came the stories of the Seven Cities of Gold in what became the New Mexico area, and those fables, as they turned out to be, drove massive exploration and settlement efforts in the area. The trips were long and arduous. Only the strongest survived.

Dolly continued her slow meandering through the park on the north side of the cathedral as she remembered her early American history, this cathedral such an essential part of it, even though most American history books excluded it.

About thirty miles north of Santa Fe, where the Rio Grande and Chama River meet, Juan de Onate brought more than five hundred men, women and children, and about four thousand animals from Spain to colonize the area. About a hundred of the men were soldiers. With the group were about a dozen Franciscan priests and friars. There the first parish church in the American Southwest was dedicated to St. John the Baptist, and the first mass was celebrated on the feast day of the Nativity of the Virgin Mary, in September 1598.

Given the Baptist influence that eventually overtook New Mexico in large waves, beginning in the nineteenth century, when the state was almost exclusively Catholic, and strong even today, Dolly always had considered that first John the Baptist dedication as a perfect forecast of the future of the area, where Baptists and Catholics so often lived side by side, sometimes in harmony, sometimes not, both dominant forces in the state's culture and politics.

The tiny colony soon became embroiled in disputes. Seeking peace, Pedro de Peralta, the Spanish governor appointed to replace Onate, gave Santa Fe its present name and moved the little colony there, officially establishing it as the capital of what now encompasses the American Southwest. He built a church on the grounds where she now strolled. It was the first capital established by Europeans in what eventually became the United States.

Dolly had loved the several old Spanish missions when she lived in San Antonio, but hadn't realized when living in that lovely Texas city that New Mexico's missions pre-dated those in Texas by 120 years, and in California, by 170 years.

Now that the Catholics had their first pope named after St. Francis, Dolly thought some recognition should be given New Mexico because it was declared the New Kingdom of St. Francis by Fray Marcos de Niza, a Franciscan missionary who also was an explorer for Spain. But he didn't make that declaration and plant his cross in Santa Fe in the 1600s as might be assumed. It was done in 1539 at Zuni Pueblo

The Spanish had trouble with the Indians from the start, according to them. She smiled wryly to herself. She would say the Indians had trouble with the Spaniards, remembering some of the stories, horror stories of cruelty all too often.

By 1680, they had had enough of the Spaniards and mounted the Pueblo Revolt, one of the most famous events in New Mexico history. It sent the Spaniards who lived through it back to Mexico, for a while. The Santa Fe church was destroyed in that revolt.

This piece of land in the heart of Santa Fe today had seen an inordinate amount of violence, for priests were a primary target of the revolt. The Pueblo Indians wanted their land and their religion back, their culture re-established without Spanish soldiers and friars forcing them to change it, making them slaves and worse. These cathedral grounds probably experienced a great deal of passionate violence as a result of that anger almost 350 years ago.

The Spanish returned by 1693, and eventually, built another church on the site, the first to be named for Santa Fe's patron saint. Work on the present cathedral was begun in 1869 when French-born Jean Baptiste Lamy became the first archbishop assigned to the area. Rather than tear down the one built in the early 1700s, he had his massive new structure built around and over the old one, planning to remove the old when the new was finished.

Some aspects of Lamy's construction project weren't completed until the twentieth century, although most of it was done in the first twenty years. Most considered the cathedral a finished building by the late 1980s, although a few things had been added since then, decorative, not structural.

She continued to meander, and recall what she remembered, which was quite a bit, in part because she had a brother-in-law whose grandfather was brought to New Mexico from France by Lamy among the specialists he brought in groups to the project. That grandfather was a master bricklayer. As life and fate would have it, one of her oldest sister's and that brother-in-law's three children had married a Northern New Mexico hippie rancher a decade or so after his father had been the contractor who built the old PERA building, as famous for its La Llorona and other ghost sightings as for its official function. The niece was almost Dolly's age, the marriage a long and apparently successful one, producing a couple of kids who turned out well by any standards—New Mexican, Anglo, French, Baptist, Catholic, educated or bricklayer. These were the stories that made New Mexico so special with its diversity of peoples and cultures.

But problems, politics and sheer fate, or God's will, caused countless problems with the initial construction efforts of Lamy's architects and craftsmen, creating a series of stop-and-go efforts. Some of the problems probably were enhanced, if not caused, by the fact that Lamy was French, not Spanish, and he brought architects and builders from France, who were expected to supervise and train local Spaniards and Indians, few if any of whom would have been fluent in French. By then New Mexico Spanish was not quite the same as the Spanish spoken in Europe, even if those Frenchmen did know Spanish. Lamy didn't live to see the project for which he became most famous finished, but he did get to live long enough to see it used as a house of worship.

As Dolly walked and mulled, and let herself feel the energies surrounding her, from the street, the cathedral, Santa Fe in general, her history lessons and her memories, she felt no energy whatsoever around the interior of the huge structure. Her *pull* wasn't coming from it, she realized, as she found her way back to the front of the cathedral, since locked gates and fences prevented her from walking continuously around the entire cathedral.

Even though not a Catholic, she knew that in the fall of 2005, when this, the Cathedral of St. Francis of Assisi was named the Cathedral Basilica of St. Francis of Assisi, by Pope Benedict XVI, it was a big deal. Already the mother church for the Archdiocese of Santa Fe, it now was the only basilica in New Mexico, and one of few in the entire American Southwest.

What was pulling her here? Two boys had been murdered here, three decades apart, she suspected. If she was right, were their ghosts here? Or would spirits of great saints, even some of those old priests and archbishops buried down in the basement, rise to the occasion and help her tonight? Help her solve this crime? And what about La Llorona?

Yes, she thought to herself, what about La Llorona? She never had heard of any sightings of her in relation to the cathedral. Yet she had her probably-elegant Spanish handprints all over these crimes, if one knew how to follow the clues with Second Sight, as she and Father Marquez and so many others understood. Including some cops.

She decided to visit the only part of the old church built in the 1700s that still existed, the small chapel dedicated to Our Lady La Conquistadora. A statue of the Virgin Mary resided there, the oldest representation of Mary in the United States, having been brought about 1626 by a friar in a wagon train, supposedly from Spain, But she had read that tree rings found in the wooden statue indicated it was made sometime during the 1400s or 1500s, or just before it was brought to Santa Fe. Historians claim no one ever seemed to know who made it, nor even where it was made. It was a mystery. Almost two feet tall, the wooden statue was taken to El Paso when the Spanish fled during the Pueblo Revolt, in which about two dozen priests were killed.

The seeds of Protestant extremism were planted in New England, at Plymouth, at the same time the brand of extremist Catholicism that was perpetrating the Inquisition upon Europe was being seeded in what became the American Southwest. Many settlers in the Southwest, especially the Sephardic Jews who settled in the New Mexico and Colorado area, were fleeing the Inquisition, but secretly, pretending to be Catholic converts publicly. Many of the old Spanish colonial names are of Jewish origin, and the present-day bearers of those surnames can be found everywhere in New Mexico, and southern Colorado.

Like the entire church built on the grounds when the Spanish returned after the Pueblo Revolt, the little chapel was made of adobe, unlike the present cathedral with its Romanesque architecture and materials. If anyone could help with La Llorona mysteries, Mother Mary could, Dolly thought to herself. Even though not a Catholic, Dolly always had loved Mary as she learned of her in her Baptist upbringing, sad that the Baptists didn't give her more importance than they did. Growing up around all those Catholics made it easy to know they gave Mary far more respect, and she liked that. In New Mexico, Christmas especially was a time when Mary was honored with special holiday lighting on manmade grottos in people's yards and on church grounds. So beautiful. After all, she *was* the mother of Jesus. God must have thought she was really, really special to choose her for that role. So she should be glorified. Dolly thought the Catholics got that right, and Christmas was a wonderful time to honor her, on the day of her son's birth. That made sense to her then and now. But Baptists only glorified Jesus year-round—and some preachers, she noticed through the years. Never women. Not that Catholics had a history of treating women great either. Monotheistic religions in general needed a lot of growth and development when it came to having respect for women. Some were further along than others, but at least the changes in attitudes were happening, in some places, slowly, others more quickly.

She texted Joe. He arrived so quickly to open the doors for her, she knew he had been aware of where she was all along. But he seemed to be nice enough, easy going, not a threatening goon or anything, she thought to herself.

She entered the little chapel, lit by some low lights and a few candles still burning, and sat down on one of the benches. How nice to have the place all to herself at this hour. She immediately went into a deep meditation. When she came out of it, she learned an hour had passed, as she texted Joe to let her out, for he had locked the doors behind her at her request. If murderers lived on the grounds, or worked there, she didn't want any of them disturbing her during her own holy moments.

Unlike the thousands of people, Catholic and non-Catholic alike, who claimed to have had personal experiences with the Madonna, she had not. Tonight, she felt a deep, deep peace after her meditation, the kind one feels after a long, deep, sleep. But she had more clarity than ever that she was not going to find the clues she sought in this holy sanctuary.

As she was rising to leave, a glint of light from La Conquistadora's eyes caught her gaze and she found herself staring straight into the eyes of the statue. And they were staring straight back at her. Was she imagining the little Madonna's eyes were holding her own in its gaze? Then she heard Joe opening the door and the electric moment was gone, the glint left the ancient Madonna's eyes and they returned to their usual wooden gaze into space, not at her.

In a heavenly state of shock as Joe let her out, she did remember to ask him if any cellars, new or old, existed beneath the little chapel, or any other parts of the basilica. "Not the basements, and crypt areas, but actual cellars, like for wine or food, or even a bomb shelter, since this place was pretty much at the heart of the Cold War, given its proximity to Los Alamos."

He laughed. "No, at least none that they've told me about, except the one beneath the green house, and it's just an ordinary cellar, for canned goods I've been told, and things like apples, potatoes. The old nun takes care of that green house, so I guess she is the only person who uses that cellar. I can show you where its door is. They wanted me aware, since it would be a good hiding place for a fugitive if one ever should try to hide around here."

Chills were creeping up and down Dolly's spine as he spoke, not quite the same experience as having a Madonna stare her down, but electrifying in their own way.

This was what she was seeking. She could feel it. The Madonna had given her a signal that she was on the right path now. Had it really been Mary, or some other spirit, or force, working through the statue? Or her imagination, fueled by the circumstances?

"Is the greenhouse close to Sister Rosalie's apartment? Does she have a private entrance from it to the greenhouse?"

"Honestly, I don't know. I've never seen the interior of the apartments. They have shown me the tiny walled enclosure at the back of them, again, so I would know the layout in case we had to chase down a fugitive on the run. The entrance to the greenhouse that I can access is outside that wall around their yard. If you are ready to go over there now, I'll show you."

"I am."

As they walked to the greenhouse, which had been built on the edge of the huge parking lot southeast of the cathedral grounds, Dolly asked him again how Sister Rosalie accessed her greenhouse.

"I don't really know. I only work from dusk to dawn, and so I never see her. I understand she rises before dawn for prayers in the cathedral, but she manages to come and go without me seeing her. She has her own keys of course. I spend most of my time keeping an eye on the outer perimeter of the grounds, especially in the back, where the hotel is. That is where we feel I need to keep a look out for wandering tourists, to help them if they get lost if nothing else. And I've had to help a few," he laughed.

"I can imagine," she said, laughing with him. "It's so easy to know who the tourists are, they all seem to look lost most of the time, so I can see how they could really get lost around here at night. And they always look so out of place, no matter what part of town they are trying to traverse. Santa Fe residents just don't look like the Americans who visit it, that's for sure. And of course, all the international tourists just add to the eclectic mix.

As they approached the greenhouse, after he had opened the gate in the fence to the parking lot for them, she asked, "Doesn't Sister Rosalie have her own entrance from the rectory area, or does she have to come out here too?"

"Oh no, I doubt she ever comes out here. There is an entrance from the rectory, a gate in the wall. But like I said, I don't know if she has one also directly from her apartment. That greenhouse was built outside the old wall because the grounds had no space for it, I've been told. So they just took away enough space from the parking lot to build it, including digging that cellar, and then building enough of a wall around it to connect to the old wall, which already had a gate that could be used to access the little yard the greenhouse was given. It's a nice set-up. Apparently when the nun's brother was a priest here, they were able to get that done for her, to get it funded. Amazing when you think about it, I doubt that would happen today."

"You mean Father Marquez?"

"Yes, that must be his name, since I know her last name is Marquez. I've never met him. They hired me after he retired and left Santa Fe.

"Anyway, the rest of us have to enter the little yard to the greenhouse through this gate out here in the parking lot. But no one does except delivery people and occasionally a security guard like me. That is why they give us keys, in case we think someone jumped over the wall. They worry about vandals smashing the windows and damaging the plants, since anyone can see it is a greenhouse, the walls aren't tall enough to hide it, obviously."

"And do you know where the cellar door is?"

"Yes, I do. We keep it locked too, and I do have a key for it. Are you sure you want to go down there? Even I think it's spooky, I must admit. I had to go down there after the little boy disappeared."

"Did anything seem unusual?"

"No, not at all, but then I'd only been down there a couple of times in the past, it's not like I hang out there," he laughed. "It's filled with canned goods, she apparently does a lot of canning. And she has a lot of books there."

"Books?"

"Yeah, I didn't try to really look at any, they are all on shelves, but I did notice some of the titles seemed to be about plants, trees, herbs, gardening, things like that. She keeps it nice and tidy. It even has a nice smell, like she burns incense down there. It has plumbing—a big sink and a counter and cabinets. But no bathroom. It's just one big room. The lighting is good. It is her little domain. The staff tell me she is a fabulous cook, still does some cooking for them, although now that she is so old, some volunteers help with that."

"Interesting," Dolly said. "She sounds like a lucky nun."

He laughed. "I guess so."

He opened the gate and they walked into the tiny yard area, which was not lit, she noticed, but she could see what looked like grow lights inside the greenhouse itself as he unlocked its door. "Let me show you where the cellar door is."

Dolly was amazed at the little universe she had entered. The place was magical. And no one knew about it. It could be an important tourist attraction, it was so beautiful, even seen from the outside, if the space had lent itself to viewing. It didn't. Not even parishioners got to enjoy its benefits. She found it almost puzzling that Sister Rosalie worked so hard on this, for obviously she did, and kept it all to herself. Actually Dolly found it beyond puzzling. It was downright strange, too weird. Something wasn't right.

She thanked Joe for his help as he left her, promising to check on her if she hadn't texted him in two hours. She explained she might spend some time meditating and praying, it was so nice in there. He seemed to understand, taking her at her word, since he obviously had no idea why she was here. He just knew she was someone from the AG's office who worked with the cops, that the other cop was talking to Father Sanchez, and that they had permission to see the grounds. She asked him to tell Connie not to disturb her until she texted him, a request she could tell didn't make sense to him, but he didn't question her, thankfully. She asked him to lock the greenhouse door after him, she didn't want Sister Rosalie walking in on her unannounced, assuming if the old nun had to unlock the door, Dolly would hear her entering.

As he left, she realized Connie should be finished with Father Sanchez by now. She checked her phone just to be sure she hadn't missed anything, although she knew she hadn't. What was taking Connie so long? Just as well, though, because what she needed now was total solitude in this place. She turned her phone off and began meandering up and down the rows of plants, many with which she was not familiar. The beauty of the plants, some with flowers, was stunning.

The door to the cellar, which was in the floor, was the way Joe had left it—open. The gaping hole seemed to glare at her. She did not like the vibe coming out of that cellar. What a contrast to the joy and beauty the greenhouse seemed to emit above the ground.

Completing her little tour, noticing what she assumed to be the many varieties of Palma Christi plants, which truly were worthy of being named after Jesus Christ, in her opinion, she found the light switches and turned off all the lights, including the one that controlled the grow lights. Using her flashlight, she found her way back to the hole in the ground that was beckoning her, against her will, she realized. She wasn't eager to enter, but knew she must. Some light was coming up the stairs, so she knew the cellar was lit, but she kept her flashlight on anyway. She didn't want to be surprised by any New Mexico bugs, although more than likely the place was sprayed regularly. Unless the nun went natural and used things like lady bugs, but right now proper ecology wasn't a high priority for Dolly. She just wanted to see if creepy crawly things were part of her environment at the moment.

This place itself, even if bug-free, was totally creeping her out, she thought to herself, as she slowly, carefully descended the steps. It wasn't the physical place. These were not even difficult stairs, probably built to enable the old nun to utilize them well into old age, which she was doing. The entire place was incredibly well built, it seemed. A lot of planning had gone into the building, and now the maintenance, of this place. It surprised her that a nun would be given so much latitude outside of a convent situation. Father Marquez must have made a huge difference in how her life as a nun played out. Few nuns would be allowed to live the life she had for decades here at St. Francis.

The greenhouse had a pleasant, soothing energy and wonderful smells. The cellar didn't seem to have either. She hadn't seen any evidence of marijuana plants in the greenhouse, but had expected to find at least one or two down here, since medicinal pot was legalized in New Mexico in the 1970s, the first state to do so, but the law had not been implemented until the 21st century. So far she didn't smell any. Many older people found pot to be a better malady for their various health problems than pharmaceutical drugs, and without the side effects of the latter.

The closer Dolly got to the cellar floor, one stair at a time, slowly, reluctantly, telling herself she was looking for bugs but knowing she was just dawdling out of dread, the creepier the place got. She never had enjoyed smoking pot, unlike so many folks she had known since her college days at Baylor. But right now, a joint might be just the thing, she smiled wryly. She thought of her sessions with Father Marquez and his single malt scotch selections. She wished he were with her now.

The cellar was deep below the greenhouse, and had the look and feel of a bomb shelter, regardless of what the guard had said. No dirt floor nor walls here, as she stepped into the room, which had a really high ceiling, surprisingly. No wonder there had been so many stairs, but the railing was solid, making it easy to ascend or descend. The walls were completely covered on all sides from floor to ceiling with shelves and cabinets, and the sink area Joe had mentioned.

There must have been hundreds of books. And hundreds of jars of God knew what. Various herb-like greens and some small branches were lying in bunches on one of the counters beside the big, actually, Dolly realized, huge, sink. Looking more closely at some of the jars, she realized not everything in them was canned food. All kinds of strange and interesting things seemed to be in the jars, along with what appeared to be ordinary fruits, pickles, vegetables. But no pot.

Scanning book titles with her flashlight, for she still hadn't turned on all the lights in the cellar, she realized a massive library about plants throughout the world was on those shelves. The expected gardening books were there, of course, but along with them were what appeared to be books from medieval times, modern copies, about healing plants and potions, even some books that she recognized as falling in the category of witchcraft, some Wicca-related publications, but not all. As for white or black magic, who knew, Dolly thought to herself, not wanting to touch any of them.

In front of one wall of shelves was a big comfortable easy chair with a reading lamp. How convenient, Dolly muttered to herself. What better place to get away from it all, given what *it all* included upstairs on the basilica grounds in the heart of Santa Fe. A reclusive personality wouldn't be comfortable surrounded day and night by hundreds of tourists, parishioners and coworkers. Going underground was a solution that made sense.

Finding the light switch, Dolly flipped it and found herself bathed in light so bright it hurt her eyes. Did the nun have bad eyesight? Few normal sets of eyes could stand so much light for long. Maybe that was why several lamps graced the room, all well-positioned for whatever tasks might take place in it, from working with plants by the sink, and on the big table in the center of the room, to being able to see titles on all the shelves.

Flipping the switch, Dolly slowly walked around the room, switching every lamp on and off, checking for she wasn't sure what. Differently-colored light bulbs? Various wattages? She continued to flip on and off switches, but found nothing unusual. All shed extra light to specific areas in the room, nothing strange about them at all.

Realizing her growing frustration, Dolly decided to keep every light off, including the one by the stairs that lit them, and her flashlight. Why was she here? A child could have been hidden in here, but she knew from what Joe said the cops had been all over it and so that meant no evidence was found to indicate anyone but the nun and the security guards ever came in here. And even if the nun was their woman, how would she get a kid down here, kill him, get him into a car and dump him in the river at night? It just didn't make any sense. Nothing made any sense. She had felt such a *pull* to this place and now that she was here, nothing. Nothing. Except an ancient Madonna statue catching her eye, *maybe*. She wasn't sure even about that, given the low lighting in the chapel.

So there she stood, in the center of a room below ground in the heart of old Santa Fe, on grounds where dozens had died violently through the centuries, whether by acts of war or in building accidents, and dozens more were buried in the crypts. No wonder she was creeped out. Wasn't she too old to be scared like a kid in a cemetery at Halloween? Yes. She smiled at herself. Humor wasn't going to take away this creepiness.

Switching on her flashlight, she turned to the chair and sat down in it, switching the flashlight off again. The silence was almost boisterous it was so huge. She leaned back and shut her eyes, keeping the flashlight in the chair with her, just in case. Again she smiled. Mainly just in case a bug crawled across her. At least the place seemed spotlessly clean.

The St. Francis Basilica hadn't escaped the gay pedophile scandal that had roared through the Catholic church internationally like a raging, out-of-control grass fire in the last 30 years or so. Many would say it turned the Church into a train wreck, never to recover. Affairs with women, under-age or not, also got caught up in the outing of bad priests.

Pope Francis became the head of a Church so badly wounded, it seemed no saint, including St. Francis, could help the situation. Pope Francis seemed to be bringing some hope back, but many thought it too little too late. Only time would tell.

Sadly, New Mexico had been badly scarred by the untreatable pedophile priests, perhaps beginning earlier than just about anywhere in the nation, in large part because priests had been released from the Jemez Springs treatment center and assigned to small parishes throughout the state in towns and villages, unheard of and unknown by, most Americans in the latter half of the 20th century. But Albuquerque, Gallup and other cities in the state had not escaped the plague either.

Immunity didn't seem to exist in this state from the time it began releasing the patients, due to the location of the national treatment center in the heart of the state. For many years it was the only one in the nation until one opened in Wisconsin. New Mexico parishes bore the brunt of the releases, especially in the years before more treatment centers, and thus geographical locations more convenient for release from those centers, became available. When the press began learning the truth about the Jemez Springs center, in the early 1990s, it wasn't long after when it was shut down.

Dolly remembered when, as a child and teen, her family would drive through Jemez Springs regularly during summer months, and more often than not, see priests in their robes strolling along the highway, standing around town, being quite visible. Her mother always said the Catholics sent their "renegade priests" there, including the ones who became addicted to alcohol because of all that wine they had to drink during mass. Tee-totaling Baptists like her parents found that practice abhorrent, and blamed the Catholic church for subjecting its priests to a temptation that set some up for addiction. Her mother had alcoholic brothers and thus understood all too well how many factors, including genetics, could cause some people to have weakness where alcohol was concerned if they risked taking "that first drink." Dolly heard various versions of this litany just about every summer as far back as she could remember, her parents using it to instill in her and her siblings a terrific fear of alcohol. None of them had a clue the priests were there for far more than just alcoholism and mental illness, the latter being an assumption on the part of her parents. They felt the lifestyle of priests would drive any normal man mad. Baptist preachers in general had a reputation for being oversexed. It was accepted as part of the personality type needed to be a good preacher and pastor of one's flock, so the idea of asking your pastor to be celibate was downright crazy in their eyes. The Catholic church was the reason those priests needed that retreat, not the priests themselves, Dolly was taught. Thus she learned to pity them.

As she continued to relax, or try to relax, in the big, comfy easy chair, her eyes still shut, resting her head against the back, she again found herself thinking about how unusual the crime of murder was within the Church. And here, there had been two, and children at that. Why here? The parish had cleaned up its pedophile scandal only to be saddled with murdered children, over 30 years time. Horrifying, and more so because the first one never was solved. And if Connie and she didn't have a break soon, she feared the second might not be either.

Despite the creep factor, this cellar felt like a reflection of the cathedral's 'good history,' not the violent, murderous one she knew continued on the grounds above her through several centuries. Maybe it was just an illusion because it was so spotlessly clean.

The question remained. Were those boys killed on the grounds and taken from here to the river? Was Johnny poisoned here, or by a meal elsewhere the family mentioned as a possibility?

Sitting there in the dark, dark silence, she felt the burden of the unanswered questions overwhelming her, drowning her almost.

Her eyes flew open and she sat up so fast, the chair creaked.

She had been so deep in her reverie, it was like being in a dream, and she had felt like she was drowning, for a split second.

Olympic medals were won and lost by hundredths of a second, proof that important experiences really did happen in the blink of an eye, the proverbial split second.

The boys hadn't drowned, the coroners proved that. But they had been placed in water because someone wanted everyone to think they had. She was in the right place, this had been another sign, but *she* wasn't going to drown here. The sensations of drowning were not meant for her literally.

If she were a Catholic, which saint would help her if she asked? Maybe the magnificent Indian whose statue graced the front of the cathedral grounds. She was named a saint for many, many reasons. Several claimed to have had visitations from her after she died, and ever since her death, people claimed to have miraculous healings after praying for her help. This church, this parish, this town, so many families, needed a healing. Barely able to pronounce her name properly, if at all, Dolly simply said, "help us." A saint would know when she was needed, Dolly trusted. Names were only the symbols, it was Dolly's plea to her that counted.

Also, if La Llorona were involved in any way, she trusted the earthly spirit of the Indian saint could handle her.

Dolly leaned back into the chair. Closed her eyes again.

Now what?

The darkness. The silence. She thought of the famous horror story writer, a thought she did not want to be having right now. He made a story about a woman stuck in a car with a mad dog outside one of the scariest literary events of her life. What would he do if this were one of his stories, instead of her life?

Why am I thinking about a man whose entire career has been the portrayal of evil in all its forms, she wondered. I'm trying to tune into a female Indian saint, not a man who has spent decades writing about the dark forces.

So what was she waiting for? She had no idea. Or too many.

She could make a list. Maybe that would help her focus. She began counting on her fingers, realizing she had to do it by category, she didn't have enough fingers for individuals.

An Indian woman saint, a Spanish ghost-witch, an old nun (she did have keys, after all, so she could show up at any time), Mother Mary, any number of ghosts of dead Indians, padres and friars spanning five centuries, the ghosts of either of the two murdered boys, then there is always St. Francis, and of course Jesus Christ himself, although she had no illusions about her status among the famed deceased, so she had no expectation of them coming around, but she put them on her list, just in case, given her location in the world right now, with the ancient towering cathedral only yards away, and their recorded abilities to appear through solid walls.

This is nuts, she said out loud to herself. The sound of her voice almost scared her, in its contrast to the silence to which she had quickly become accustomed. She remained in the chair, standing up so she could sit back down cross-legged, beginning a mantra for clearing the mind she learned decades ago from Paramahansa Yogananda's meditation teachings. Oh, yes, he needed to be on her list too, for he *had* shown up in her presence several times. Even another person had seen him once when that happened, in one of her Elisabeth Kubler-Ross classes. It took that acquaintance a couple of years to get up the courage to tell her he had seen Yogananda standing by her that day when they were discussing him in class. She had felt him that day, standing behind her chair, although at other times, she had seen him with Second Sight. Having someone else confirm her experience had been a wonderful assurance that she wasn't crazy when these things happened, as others had often tried to tell her when she dared to share her experiences.

Where oh where was a good ghost when you needed him, or her? The Sanskrit mantra quickly carried her away from such thoughts.

11

WHEN DOLLY CAME OUT OF WHAT HAD BECOME A DEEP meditation, she had lost all track of time, but did not want to turn her phone on and break the ambience of silence and darkness. As she sat there, getting back in touch with the reality of her situation, she knew without a doubt she had to explore the books, that her clues lay with them. This could take days, not hours, much less minutes, she thought to herself.

Shutting her eyes, and calming her mind yet again with her mantra, she visualized the shelves as she searched for the energy spot she was seeking, for she knew now there was one. She soon found it, but continued to inwardly scan every single shelf in the room, and the cabinets and counters, even the floor, the table, before she stopped. She didn't want to miss anything, now that she seemed to be in some kind of psychic research process. Eyes still shut, she smiled at her own dry humor. It would have been easier if a ghost had just shown up and told her something, but she wasn't complaining, just observing. Being grateful for everything was probably as useful an attitude with ghosts as it was with life in general.

She continued her reverie a few minutes after she finished the mental scan, then she did some deep breathing, which was recommended before beginning the mantra but she actually had forgotten given her strange circumstances.

She opened her eyes. Total, total darkness. Blackness actually. And the silence. She could hear herself breathe, probably could hear herself blink if she tried. Slowly, she uncrossed her legs—ever so grateful that she could sit that way for long periods of time—and stood up. Just as when she entered the cellar, she felt nothing. The room had no vibe, which she found strange, given how much time Sister Rosalie obviously spent in here. Did she cleanse it regularly with some potion? How did she keep it vibe-less? Or were her personal energies so bizarre, she left none behind when she exited?

Dolly knew she would be pondering these questions for the rest of her life most likely. But now, she needed to get to work. She found her flashlight. And her phone. For a moment, she considered checking it, but decided against it. One word or two in a text could shatter all her progress so far, she didn't want to risk that. She would rather live with the regret of delaying an important message than the regret of possible lost opportunity in this strange cellar.

She turned on the super-bright overhead light, shocking the blackness away, the contrast shocking her too for a moment as her eyes adjusted. Once they did, she went immediately to the shelf section where she had found the energy in her scan and began browsing titles. The shelves on that wall were floor to ceiling, unlike some of the others in the room, and her area was filled with what appeared to be reprints of historical texts dating back to ancient Greece and Egypt. She pulled some out to find some even were written in Greek and Latin, with no accompanying English translation.

So the old sister is quite the scholar, she thought to herself. No surprise there, given how brilliant her brother was. Rosalie probably didn't get the education he had, but given this vast library, she had been a masterful self-educator.

As she bent down to pull out a huge Egyptian tome to see what it's language was, she thought she saw something on the wall behind where the book had been. Dolly was tall, so she got down on her knees to get a better look, shining her flashlight into the space. What was that, cracks in the wall? No, it was a perfect square. Those weren't cracks. But what? She had read enough books, watched enough movies, since childhood, to know about bookcases that open doors to secret rooms and tunnels. But she didn't dare get her hopes up, how often did one come across those in real life? Usually, never.

She pushed. Nothing. She felt all around the square. Nothing.

Getting up, knees protesting, she went to the sink area to see if she could find a knife. She did, in a drawer, several. She took one, and was down on her unhappy knees again in a jiffy. She poked the knife through the crack on the right, nothing. She tried the other three sides. When she did the bottom, she heard a strange noise, so she slid the knife back and forth within that crack.

The square *opened*.

She was staring at some kind of knob, like somebody's bad idea of an artsy door knob. She turned it, for the box-like space was large enough she could get her hand around the knob.

Jumping to her feet in terror as a creaking sound broke the immense silence, she found herself looking inside a room as the shelf next to the one with the knob box slowly moved to reveal it.

Stunned, she stepped into it, but barely, fearing the door would shut behind her.

The room contained a large sofa on one wall and a cot on the other. She thought she saw human forms in both. Small, children? Sleeping under their covers? Or dead and covered up? Chills raced throughout her entire body as she tried to keep her senses about her.

More afraid than ever of getting locked in the secret room, she stepped back into the main room and used the huge Egyptian tome, which she had put on the floor, as a doorstop. At least now she wouldn't lock herself in, but that didn't mean someone or some thing might not. No wonder she had thought of that horror writer tonight and his imaginary forces of evil. Only hers were *real*.

Stepping back inside the inner room, she saw the couch and the bed were empty, the covers smooth, as though no one had slept nor lain in either.

Now she was not liking the fact she had come alone, this was too scary. Should she go find Joe or Connie?

Calm down, she told herself. Think.

She didn't have to think long to realize the two boys who were killed had lain here, some 30 years apart. They showed themselves to her. *They* were the ones who showed up to help her tonight, the boys themselves. Her tears began flowing, tears of gratitude to the children for believing in her, tears of sadness and compassion for what they had to experience. Tears of joy mingled with tears of grief and sorrow.

This had to have been the work of Sister Rosalie. Was she a serial killer? Had she killed more?

Why?

Exploring the room quickly, she was careful not to touch anything since a forensics team would be arriving soon. She saw a door, but did not touch it. Where did it lead? Was there a tunnel to Sister Rosalie's apartment? Or a tunnel to somewhere else?

A nightstand stood between the couch and the cot, with three drawers and a lamp on top. What was in those drawers? She didn't want to disturb any evidence. Why didn't I think to bring gloves, she chastised herself. Connie would have had some if she were here.

Thinking of Connie, she realized it was time to get her, to get help, to get everyone involved. If the nun didn't commit the crime, they soon would know who did, she was certain.

Leaving the room as she had found it, she moved her doorstop, and turned the knob so the shelf creaked itself back into place. She left the lights in the main room the way she had found them, in case someone entered it who might try to destroy evidence if they knew she had been there. Making sure she had her flashlight, she texted Joe to come get her, and headed up the stairs. Connie had texted her, she noticed, but she didn't read it. She had to get out of this place now.

Setting the lights back to the way they had been in the greenhouse, she told Joe to treat the entire area as a crime scene as he let her out and took care of the locks. He didn't ask her any questions, just gave her a knowing look. "I will contact everyone, you just keep a look-out for anything out of the ordinary over here, and try to keep an eye on Sister Rosalie if you find her out and about anywhere on the grounds or in the buildings. *Don't tell her anything. She's the suspect.* I'm going to walk back to my room at the La Fonda now while I contact the proper authorities. I don't want to be seen by anyone who lives here, if they haven't seen me already."

"Got it," he replied.

She walked through the parking lot to the street, stopping only after she was almost in front of a La Fonda entrance. Eleven o'clock, the street was empty. Turning to face the majestic cathedral at the end of the street, she finally read Connie's text, which was sent two hours ago.

"Where are you? SOS!"

Dolly had lost all track of time while in the cellar. She and Connie had met on the grounds just before six. How did so much time pass? Yet given the nature of her experiences tonight, this wasn't unusual, she knew that. Still, it never failed to surprise her when hours could pass in what seemed like minutes.

Connie had texted her again, an hour ago, with all caps. "CALL ME!"

She did.

"He said the nun did it!" Connie gasped into the phone.

"I know."

"You do? Did you talk to him too?"

"No, I found her hiding place for the boys."

"You did?" Connie's voice was shrill.

"We've got to get a forensic team over there tonight, before the nun does anything. She may realize we are on to her and try to destroy evidence. She has a cellar beneath the greenhouse. Joe's keeping an eye on it for us, but I need to meet you there to show you how to access the secret room in the cellar. He doesn't know about it."

"Father Sanchez told me he is quite sure she did it, but he doesn't know how. Do you?"

"Not exactly, that is why we have to get that forensic team there ASAP. Where are you?

"I'm in the lobby of the La Fonda, waiting for you."

"I'm right outside on the street."

Dolly's phone went dead, the call lost. A moment later, she saw Connie walking out onto the sidewalk, talking on her phone.

"Yes," she was saying, "I will tell you everything, but we've got to get control of this before she ruins the evidence, or worse, flees. Oh my God, what if she commits suicide? I gotta go."

As the two women entered the parking lot area, two police cars were pulling in too, from different entrances. Relieved they didn't use their sirens, Connie asked the guys, who included Rodriguez and Johnson, to be as quiet as possible, and to alert any others who were on the way to cut the sirens, and to work with stealth. She asked them to secure the greenhouse, and to continue to keep an eye on the rectory as well, but without disturbing anyone inside of it. Silence was important.

Joe unlocked the doors for the women. Dolly left the greenhouse lights as they were. The forensics team would be taking charge soon, and she had seen everything she needed to see. She took Connie down the stairs, and into the secret room. Connie had pulled out gloves for both of them as they entered the greenhouse.

"What's in the drawers?"

"I don't know. I didn't have gloves with me."

Connie was opening them as Dolly spoke. Both women gasped when they saw all three were filled with diabetic medicines, including syringes and liquid insulin.

"I am going to assume she used insulin until someone proves me wrong," Connie said.

Dolly just nodded. She had determined hours ago that ricin had not been used, although what herbal poisons were to be found in all those jars in the other room? The challenge with all of them, including the castor beans, was preparation and effective delivery into the body.

"Okay, let me get forensics in here. I told them to park a block away so as not to arouse suspicion while you showed this to me. And I've got two guys waiting to go with me to make the arrest. I've alerted Father Sanchez that we are going to do it tonight. When I left him, I thought we could wait until morning, but obviously now we would be foolish to wait."

Dolly nodded and said, "May I go then? You have lots to do before there will be any time for the catching-up stories."

"Of course. Text me in the morning when you wake up, get plenty of sleep, and I'll meet with you when I can. I doubt I will get much sleep tonight, as we are going to try to get a confession immediately. Good work, Dolly."

Dolly needed to unwind with indulgences. She hoped it wasn't too late for room service as she walked back to the hotel, still feeling like she was in an altered reality. She so missed her pets right now. When she got back, the restaurant was closed, as she knew it would be. The bar was not, but that was the last place she wanted to be tonight. Taking the stairs to her room, she found the room service menu, dialing the extension as she scanned it.

Two silver margaritas and one chile rellenos plate later, she no longer felt like she was in a trance, but normal wouldn't be an accurate description either, with her thoughts still focused on the evening's events. What had Father Sanchez shared with Connie? And what caused him to rat out the old nun? He wouldn't break the confessional pact, she was certain of that. But if he knew something outside the confessional, he was morally obligated to share it with the police, she also knew that. But how many priests would have, she wondered? A newfound respect for the man whose integrity she—and a whole lot of others—had questioned from the start had been formed tonight.

She turned off the lights and crawled under the covers, putting in her earplugs and turning off both phones. The Do Not Disturb sign already was on the door.

The next day came too early, even though Dolly slept until 8:30. No texts, no phone calls. She was in the dining room by nine, drinking coffee with cream, no sweetener, no food either, texting Connie to let her know she was ready for the day, Connie texting back, "you aren't going to believe what's happening." They arranged to meet for brunch in an hour, in the dining room, where they could find a table with some privacy, not always easy in downtown Santa Fe's cadre of restaurants.

Dolly returned to her room to pack, assuming she wouldn't be staying another night. And to put some finishing touches on her makeup that she had skipped in order to get her coffee, not in the mood to use room service for it.

By 10:30 she was downstairs again, this time with a perfect table for them on the sidelines of the huge dining room, her bag already in her car in the parking garage. She knew Connie indulged what she considered to be Dolly's bourgeois La Fonda tastes. Native Santa Fe folks rarely went there, preferring the dozens of hole-in-the-wall cafes and non-tourist attraction restaurants. But the tourists always flocked to them anyway, making all of them crowded and noisy. Old people with style could be found dining at the La Fonda, some regularly. They'd been doing that all her life, and now she was one of them—old that is, the style part a matter of opinion.

Connie rushed in, looking stylish herself. "Are you dressed for this restaurant, or for your office?" Dolly kidded her.

"Both," she laughed. "I don't have a lot of time. Let's order and then you just sit while I talk." They did, huevos rancheros—Christmas, Dolly requesting four eggs instead of the usual two with the refried beans, and then she obeyed Connie, quietly sipping an iced tea with lemon and stevia while they waited for their food.

"Sister Rosalie didn't resist arrest last night, although I don't think she was expecting us, nor had any idea Father Sanchez had talked to me, yet she remained calm and stone-faced until she learned of your discovery. Then she registered shock and dismay. We didn't tell her about that until we got her in the interrogation room. She never asked for an attorney. Once she learned we knew of the cellar, she asked everyone to leave the room except me. Then she told me she wanted to confess, but not to us, only to Father Sanchez. I said this wasn't a Catholic confessional and the kind of protection she would have with that was outside our legal parameters, so no, she could not. Then she explained that she didn't want him to exercise the confidentiality rules of the confessional, she just wanted him to hear her story. She said he could record every word, but she didn't want anyone else in the room.

"I asked her if she intended to kill him too? I was dead serious, and she knew it.

"'No,' she said, 'I need to say some things to him, and I just want him to hear the whole story first. It'll be easier for me that way, probably for everyone else too.'

"'You realize we will have follow-up questions, don't you?' She said she did, but she was adamant he was the only one who would get her complete version initially, so I said okay. They are meeting now. We kept her in the interrogation room all night, bringing in a cot for her to sleep if she wanted. No way would we put her in holding with all the malcriados."

"So what did Father Sanchez tell you last night?"

"That he knew she killed Anthony. He said he suspected all these years that she killed Danny too, but he hadn't been here that long and didn't know her well then, didn't have a grasp of the situation enough to suspect her for sure at the time, much less tell anyone of his suspicions. He admitted they were fleeting then anyway, for he tried not to think about them. Easier to do in those days, frankly. He felt as long as he was innocent, and he was, he had no business focusing on who might be the killer. Obviously his sense of morality has strengthened since then. He said this time, he had no doubt it was her, almost from the very beginning. And he knew, also without a doubt, that he had to report her. He was just waiting for the right time."

"Right time." Dolly almost snorted her tea.

"Yes, I know, it sounds weak, doesn't it? Given how long it has been already. I guess he was waiting to see how much we would figure out on our own. Who knows? I haven't asked him that yet, and he hasn't said. But I will. You know me.

"When we sat down together last night, he simply said he knew who did it, and he wanted to tell me in my official role as a homicide detective, so if I needed to record him or take notes, it was okay with him. I did both."

"Does he know why she committed the murders? Does he think there are any more?"

"More?" Connie looked puzzled. "You think there might be more?"

"Well, we have to consider all possibilities."

"No, he didn't mention more. What he did say was that she murdered boys to whom he was closer than any of the others the entire time he has been here, so he knows it has something to do with him, but he has no idea what, or so he says. He still claims he is not a pedophile. He said the only thing he has been able to conclude as a possible reason is that she has some kind of strange attachment to him, due to their living and working arrangement, and his friendship with the two boys was threatening to her. She feared they were taking him from her. He said he realized that sounded sick, given she is a nun and older than he is, bigger than he is too, physically. Not exactly a couple in which one would expect to find possessive tendencies on the part of either.

"He tactfully inferred he thinks she is quite deranged, and her life as a nun has kept her from spending it as a mental patient. I reiterate, very tactful."

"Wow, I wonder if Father Marquez has any idea about any of this. Do you think he does, and that is why he told me to look at women, making me think it was because of La Llorona? I will have to talk to him when all this is settled. I actually feel sorry for him, his own sister, a murderer. A two-time murderer, of children no less. He will be so thankful he is retired and safely squared away in the Jemez as this news breaks. Can you imagine if he still were here, and working as a priest?"

"I asked her if her brother knew about this, or helped her. She was adamant he does not and did not. I felt she was being sincere, she seemed terrified and saddened both, knowing the truth no longer could be kept from him. I almost felt sorry for her at that point. Almost, but not actually. Thinking about what she did makes me find her utterly repulsive. I may be a Catholic, but compassion isn't in the cards for me in this situation. I do have compassion for the brother, and Father Sanchez, but not her. No way."

"Can he legally take her confession?"

"She agreed to let us record it, both video and audio, and to sign a statement with her written confession if we let her meet with him, as long as we didn't watch them through a hidden window. I told her we couldn't do that, a law enforcement officer had to be in the room or watching and listening from next door. She didn't like the restriction, but she didn't resist us. She knows it's over. She's in our system now, not the Church's. She hasn't even asked for a lawyer, but Father Sanchez said he is getting one for her. I asked him if he would wait until after her confession and he agreed to the request. I was afraid he wouldn't. A lawyer would refuse to let her say a word.

"Of course, we told Father Sanchez where the button was he could push if she tries anything. She is a lot bigger than he is, and we know she is strong, and a murderer, not exactly a trustworthy nun. I sure wouldn't take her word for anything.

"I've got to get back. We don't want to put this off, in case she changes her mind. She wanted to do the confession only in Spanish, but I told her we couldn't allow that. We're waiting for Father Sanchez to arrive so we can get started. The women ate their food quickly, in silence, then left together.

Father Sanchez and Sister Rosalie sat facing each other across a table in the drab, barren interrogation room. Dolly and Connie could see the faces and body language of the priest and the nun from where they sat watching on the other side of the one-way window.

So this was to be the conclusion to the nightmare in which she felt she had found herself, found all of them, for too many weeks, Dolly asked herself. Oh, those grieving mothers. And poor Father Marquez. His own sister.

Sister Rosalie began. "Thank you for seeing me, Father. I don't expect you to absolve me, that isn't why I asked for you to hear my confession. I wanted to explain to you why I did what I did."

Father Sanchez remained silent. She continued.

"Yes, I did kill both boys, Danny all those decades ago, and now Anthony. I did it to save them from you, Father." He remained silent, but now seemed to be willing himself to be stone-faced, devoid of all emotion.

"You see, I knew what you did with them when you were alone with them." She was watching him closely for reaction, but he gave her none. "I had a peephole where I could see you in the room where you took them and gave them girls' clothing to wear, how you helped them with it. I know you didn't do anything physical with them, but I feared you eventually would. I decided I had to kill them

176

to save you from yourself, Father. You are a good man, a good priest, which is why I took it upon myself to help you, and to save the boys from you as well. I am sure they are resting in heaven now where they belong, far from the tragedies of humankind on earth."

"How did you kill them?" At last he spoke.

"You know I practice martial arts, have since I was young, to help keep my diabetes under control. I got each boy to come to the cellar with me to help me carry things out, and once they were inside, I used a rear chokehold that when done properly, makes the child instantly unconscious. The boys never knew what happened, they didn't suffer, felt no pain. I made certain of that.

"The cellar has an invisible door, accessed through the book shelves, which opens into a secret room. An old tunnel ran from my apartment in the rectory to where we had the greenhouse built. The entrances had been closed years ago, but the builders discovered it when working on the greenhouse and studying the documents for the entire grounds archived by all the earlier builders over the centuries.

The tunnel went from the rectory to an old cellar, which is how I got the idea of having one under the greenhouse. We just made the original dirt enclosure far bigger and safer, of course. The builders suspected the tunnel and cellar may have been built originally in case of more attacks by Indians, for it appeared to be quite ancient, built long before the present rectory was built. For years I expected someone to come forward asking about the original, someone whose family member or friend had told them, or who had family records with information about it. Most of the men who worked on the building crews through the centuries either lived here when hired, or remained here after being brought from elsewhere. I expected someone to have passed a story or two down the generations about the tunnel. But no one ever did.

I had the greenhouse builders open up both entrances, and swore them to secrecy all those decades ago, getting them to sign confidentiality agreements that I never let near a lawyer, wrote them myself. Letting a lawyer get involved would be the best way to prevent secrecy, she snorted. No one else ever knew it existed, assuming those builders kept their promise to me.

"I have a little cot in the secret room, where I carefully laid each boy before giving him an insulin injection where no medical examiner would be able to find evidence of it after the body was found in water. Enough insulin to take him to heaven, Father, but never to be discovered during an autopsy.

"And my complete confession to you must include the fact that if I felt I were strong enough to have done the same to you, I would have, when I saw your activities with Danny way back then. But I knew I physically couldn't manage it, even then, when I was so much younger and stronger than I am now. I barely managed it this time, wasn't sure if I was going be able to finish placing the body in the river, but the Lord gave me the strength.

Father Sanchez grew paler as she spoke.

"The Lord Jesus Himself inspired me to use my beloved Palma Christi plant to help me with Johnny, knowing I might not be strong enough to finish my plan, that I might have to change it at the last minute if my body wasn't able to lift Anthony the same way I had Danny, sacrificing them to the Lord, saving their little souls. I chopped up a castor bean, the smallest one I ever had found over the years, and put it in little Johnny's cupcake, knowing he would get sick but not die, and knowing he was Anthony's best friend and that they often shared a ride to and from the altar boy meetings. I knew it was important that everyone be distracted by his sickness, in case my weakness caused me to take care of Anthony more slowly than I had Danny back in the day. God rest their little souls."

She crossed herself. Father Sanchez got up and left the room, quickly, not waiting to learn if she was finished. He looked like he was going to be sick.

Sister Rosalie stared straight ahead, as though he never had been in the room.

"Are you going to arrest him?" Dolly asked, breaking their stunned silence.

"No, we gave him immunity. That is what took so long the other night. I had to contact Pacheco and get that agreement worked out right then. He was at some fundraiser with his wife, took a while to get him on the phone. A dancing DA. Did you know he goes dancing all the time?

"Anyway, Father Sanchez will be retiring and leaving the state. He wants to work with an organization for people who are doing gender transitions, but doesn't have to stay in New Mexico to do that, not these days. He didn't have to offer her up, we realized that, so we decided to honor his requests. But it looked like even he was shocked at her motive. He didn't see that coming, you could tell by the look on his face as he left the room. Nor did I.

"He's her victim too, regardless of what his motives were with those boys. We will find out, trust me, immunity or no. The DA will be the one to decide if he wasn't forthcoming enough with us to complete the deal we made with him. The motive she gave for her actions focuses the spotlight on his behavior to an extent we hadn't expected."

"What I want to know is how did he manage to spend time with the boys without anyone else knowing? How did he get them home after those sessions? Drive them himself? He must have, but that information never came out in our interviews with the parents. We weren't looking for it though, and Anthony's mother hasn't really let us talk with her at length. She is the one who would know the answer."

"This isn't over. The DA is going to be livid when he hears what happened today. Not sure he'll be dancing with joy this week."

EPILOGUE

SITTING COMFORTABLY IN HIS COZY APARTMENT ON A COLD spring day in Jemez Springs, Father Marquez and Dolly sipped Scotch and nibbled on blue corn chips and salsa made in New Mexico. It had been six months since they learned the truth about the two murders.

"How is she doing then?" Dolly asked him, broaching the sensitive subject of his sister. They had not seen each other since the previous fall, but had kept in touch a bit by phone.

"As well as can be expected. Better, probably."

"Does she consider herself a recipient of God's grace—or unlucky?"

Father Marquez laughed, dryly. "Good question. A bit of both, I would say. We talk on the phone once a week. She knows what she did was wrong in terms of the Church and the law, but she really doesn't think she did anything wrong in the eyes of God. Of course, that is exactly why she is where she is now and not in a prison here. As you know, she was diagnosed as not insane enough to send to the state hospital for life, but not sane enough to send to an ordinary state prison for life."

"I have heard that you pulled some strings for that federal country club location where she's serving her life sentence."

"Yes, I did, and I don't regret it nor feel I did anything wrong, in the eyes of anyone, God or man, or woman for that matter. Taking away the freedom and independence she had in Santa Fe is torture enough for her. She suffers."

"If I may be so bold," Dolly began, but he stopped her before she continued.

"You may. Ask me anything. That is why you are here, I realize," he smiled kindly at her.

"Well, in part, yes, but I did want to see you and see how *you* are doing. You too were a victim in this situation, in some sense of that word. Those two were your immediate family, you lived in the same place, for so many decades. This must be extraordinarily difficult for you."

"Difficult, yes. Extraordinarily? No, I wouldn't say so. I always knew something wasn't right with my sister, but never could quite figure out what. I just knew she had a screw loose, to use an old saying. I knew she was better off as a nun than in secular society because of that loose screw.

"Frankly, it was Father Sanchez that shocked me the most. He too suffers terribly, I know, for I speak with him regularly too, although not as often as with my sister. He feels he caused her to commit those crimes and no amount of confession, nor discussion, nor counseling, is going to change his mind about that, it seems. You know he wanted to help those boys deal with their gender identity issues, for he recognized them, having experienced them himself at such a young age."

"I know he never meant them harm, but you know that many say he should have used common sense at the very least in trying to help them. I don't mean to sound insensitive, nor judgmental, Father, but his approach to helping them was what some might call sleazy, even if he had no sexual agenda with the boys. Are you saying he was only naive?"

"I guess I am, knowing even as we both use that word, it doesn't work in today's world as an excuse. But I know his background, our background as priests in our respective generations, and yes, I stick with that word, naive. But it never would hold up in court if any of this had gone that route. Fortunately for all, it did not."

"So you think it was best for the boys' families that it didn't as well?"

"Oh yes, don't you? Think what having all the details drug out in a highly publicized trial for months, even years, would do to those families, to that parish, to Santa Fe, to the state, even to the country. And to the Church, I must add. I am not saying this to protect it, but to prevent further pain for all. Can you understand that?"

"Yes, Father, I can. You come from a place of compassion. I wouldn't have expected anything less, frankly. If all priests were like you, we wouldn't be here, having this conversation.

"What I started to ask you earlier had to do with Father Sanchez. Did you have any idea he had gender identity issues? Do you think he came to that awareness late in life as the culture's awareness changed?"

"First, no, I did not. But the very nature of the priesthood makes those things easy to hide, for obvious reasons. We wear skirts. If a man wants to wear women's underpinnings, no one would be the wiser as long as he does his own laundry," he laughed.

"As for his own awareness, he hasn't said a lot to me about it, but I gather it was something that developed slowly over his life. The confessional gave him extraordinary insights, as it turns out. Even people with gender identity sometimes want to be devout Catholics, and ask for their priest's help. He began having deep self-understanding as a result of some who sought him out for support and compassion in his role as their priest. He is well-suited for the work he is doing now, far, far away. For him, the punishment in the situation is that he cannot spend the rest of his life in his beloved New Mexico. Otherwise I gather he is quite content, aside from feeling like it is his fault those boys died. That is his cross to bear and it will never leave him. God may forgive him, may not even blame him, but he won't forgive himself and does blame himself and only himself. He puts no blame on Sister Rosalie. He knew she was a bit off too, he told me, and he thinks he caused her to go off the deep end. He refuses to blame her."

"Father, I didn't know the Handmaids of the Precious Blood had left Jemez Springs before all this happened. I knew Father Fitzgerald started the order in 1947 when he opened the treatment center here, so he had nuns here whose sole purpose was to pray for the priests, but I thought they were long gone. Did Sister Rosalie know any of them?"

"Not well. But they knew of her and she knew of them, of course. I got to know the ones still here before they moved to Tennessee as well as any priest could get to know them. They were more than willing to be Sister Rosalie's contact with the outside world there in Tennessee. The fact their new location is so near a federal prison that was an appropriate kind for her had to be Divine Providence. Their understanding of her background, their shared lives in New Mexico, their understanding of the complex problems that can lie beneath the surface of the Church and the people within it, they are a perfect match. With no immediate family near her, they are and will be her family, with compassion and understanding. They also keep in touch with me, which I appreciate, giving me regular updates.

"They have made it very clear to me they too see Divine Providence in all this, because in addition to being Sister Rosalie's family contacts there, they get to talk with me regularly, for sometimes two or three of them will put me on speaker phone, and they insist I give them all the local news, gossip too, nice gossip anyway." He laughed. "And they get me to send them New Mexico foods too, which I am happy to do of course."

"So it sounds to me like they really miss living here?"

"Oh yes, they spent years debating whether to leave or not. The reasons kept adding up—the nudist colony moved in here, the Buddhist ashram has been here for years of course, as you know, a bed and breakfast opened near their convent that marketed itself to the New Age crowd, professional psychics have been moving in here for years now too, making this quite the mecca for such things. The hippies that started coming in the 1960s never really went away, they are just older and a lot shaggier now, and sometimes deranged, but from senility, unlike the old days when they would seem deranged from hallucinogenic drugs.

"But the final sign, if you want to call it that—they do—that caused them to make up their minds was when a bullet shattered a window of the room where they were doing evening prayers."

"Oh my goodness. And with all you priests long gone, for whom were they praying anyway? That is why I thought they left years ago, when the last of the priests did."

"With the internet now, anyone can and does ask for their prayers, and gives them donations. They work for the entire world now. Times have changed. And they pray for anyone who asks, not just priests. Life seems to be going smoothly for them in Tennessee too. It is such a conservative part of the country, unlike this little village, which contains a fairly full spectrum of humankind in this small canyon."

"Well, Father, may I treat you to dinner tonight?"

"I thought you would never ask."

Glossary

TRADITIONAL NEW MEXICO SPANISH DIALECT IS BASED ON SPANISH, Arabic and Latin brought from Spain and Mexico, and on Native American Indian languages in the Americas. It evolved among New Mexico families, of which many members never have left the state since arriving in one century or another after 1500 A.D. Recent immigrants from South of the Border have added to the mixture of Spanish dialects now heard spoken in the state, but those influences are not reflected in this glossary.

Conversational Words and Phrases

abuelita literal: little grandmother; vernacular: term of endearment used affectionately to mean (*my*) *dear grandmother.*

adobe: Spanish word for *al tub*, an Arabic word meaning *the bricks*; the Spanish introduced the Indians to the Moorish technique of mixing straw into clay, then putting the mud into wooden frames and sun-drying them, improving on the masonry already in use by the Indians.

ándale literal: get going; used locally, it means *awesome* or *right on.*

Ay Dios! literal: Oh God!

bueno literal: good; often pronounced *way-no* by both New Mexico Hispanics and Anglos, the word is used frequently to punctuate any phrase or expression, especially near the ending of conversations.

casita literal: little house; vernacular: refers to a cottage usually attached to a larger house and used primarily for short-term and long-term guests; Anglos have given the term a more expanded definition today that includes any small house for any use, especially for sale. Realtors have made the term well-known.

claro literal: clear, distinct; used to indicate that you have understood what has been said, or to clarify that a previous statement made by you or another is truthful and correct.

el cura literal: one who cures, and an example of the variety of Spanish words ending in *a* that are masculine in gender; vernacular: priests--the term *padre* never is used by New Mexico Hispanics to describe a priest.

el niño literal: the young boy.

en ninguna manera literal: in no way.

es muy simpático: a meaningful literal translation is irrelevant; the phrase is used to mean someone who is more than nice, someone with whom one feels an empathetic connection.

ese literal: that; this term only is applied to someone to whom you are speaking, the insinuation being similar to English vernacular, such as *hey, you there*, and is used to casually demean the person to whom it is directed.

estos literal: these.

estos pendejos curas vernacular: these *asshole* priests, or something similarly demeaning, such as the use of the f-word in English.

gracias literal: thank you.

hace 30 años literal: it's been thirty years.

hola literal: hello.

ijo literal: shortened form of *ijolá*, which means *wow*, and frequently used in the 20th century by New Mexic o Hispanics, but rarely in the current century.

lleno de tonterías, un poco literal: a bit full of stupidities.

mala leche literal: bad milk; vernacular: an extremely derogatory expression used to describe any nefarious person—supposedly someone who is bad because they received bad milk from their mother.

malcriados literal: badly raised ones; vernacular: refers to those whose behavior reflects lack of, or bad, parental upbringing, especially maternal.

me entiendes? literal: do you understand me?

mesa literal: tableland; vernacular: also used in modern times by Anglos to describe vast expanses of undeveloped, dry, high desert areas, such as Albuquerque's east and west mesas before real estate development covered them after WWII; the undeveloped portions still described as mesas, especially the west mesa.

mi esposa literal: my wife.

pendejos literal: pubic hairs; vernacular: extremely derogatory description of a person, male or female.

pero literal: but; vernacular: often used as a rhetorical filler, similar to how the phrase, *you know*, is used in English.

pinche literal: petty; vernacular: used to mean pathetic, and as a put-down to anyone or anything.

pobrito literal: poor little boy as in a pathetic and sad situation, not necessarily economically poor.

poco loco literal: a little crazy.

sabes literal: you know; vernacular: often used as a rhetorical filler, similar to how the phrase, *you know*, is used in English.

sí literal: yes.

tenía sólo eight years: phrase mingling New Mexico Spanish and English, meaning he was only eight years old.

People, Saints, Ghosts

Anaya: Spanish surname originally found almost exclusively in New Mexico.

Anglo or anglo literal: used as an adjective or proper noun, a person of English descent; vernacular: originated in New Mexico and now used nationwide, it originally referred to about 2,500 American soldiers led into Santa Fe by Brigadier-General Stephen Watts Kearney in 1846 during the Mexican-American War; since Spanish people are Caucasian, Anglo does not mean Caucasian, but its use in New Mexico tends to include anyone of European descent who is not also Spanish, Indian or Black.

Armijo: Spanish surname originally found almost exclusively in New Mexico.

Hernández: a few centuries ago, the Spanish language in Spain underwent a major sound change, when certain F sounds were replaced with a silent H; the name *Fernández* was one such casualty; many refused to make the change and kept the old spelling, resulting in two spellings of the original family name.

La Conquistadora literal: the conquering virgin—an interpretation found in Mexico and New Mexico for the role of Mary, mother of Jesus, as a conquering Christian warrior, a perspective not shared by the majority of Catholics worldwide, and apparently abhorred by the Indians of Mexico and New Mexico.

La Llorona literal: weeping woman; central character in a legend known to Hispanics worldwide, but no one seems to know where it originated; apparently it was unknown in

Spain before the Spaniards came to the Americas, so the assumption has been it originated in the New World; New Mexicans like to think it originated in their region when it was part of Spain, and they certainly have kept the legend alive—one would be hard-pressed to find a New Mexico Hispanic who does not know who she is, and it is safe to say most New Mexico Anglos know about her as well if they were raised in the state.

Rodríguez literal: sons of Roderick, the Visigoth king who ruled Spain after the Roman era; surname often found in New Mexico.

Rufina: common given name for Hispanic women in New Mexico, especially before WWII.

Sánchez: Spanish surname of Sephardic (Iberian Jew) origin; in recent decades much information has become available revealing many New Mexico Hispanics to be of Sephardic descent.

Tafoya: Spanish surname of Basque origin found almost exclusively in New Mexico until recent generations.

Secundino: common given name for Hispanic men in New Mexico, especially before WWII.

Zorro literal: fox; the name of a popular Southern California Robin Hood-like character who apparently became legendary during the Spanish Colonial period in that area, but historians have failed to confirm whether he actually existed; Hollywood made him famous with movies and a TV series in the twentieth century.

Places

Alameda or alameda literal: a grove of cottonwood trees; common name for streets and old communities in New Mexico.

Albuquerque: originally Alburquerque and now the largest city in the state, it was named for Francisco de la Cueva, tenth Duke of Alburquerque, when it was founded in 1706 by Francisco Cuervo y Valdés; the Spanish name has origins in two languages: *abu al-qurq* means father of the cork oak in Arabic, and *albus quercus* means white oak in Latin.

Barrio or barrio literal: neighborhood; vernacular used frequently to describe neighborhoods founded by and/or predominantly populated by Hispanics.

Belén literal: Bethlehem; a town south of Albuquerque founded by Spaniards.

Bosque literal: forest; vernacular: in New Mexico, *the Bosque* or *El Bosque* refers specifically to the immense cottonwood tree forest lining many portions of the banks of the Rio Grande as it flows through New Mexico from Colorado to Mexico.

Córdova: New Mexico's own version of the original Spanish name *Córdoba*, it is the name of a town in northern New Mexico and a road in Santa Fe as well as a commonly found surname in the state.

Corona literal: crown; an old tiny Spanish village and the closest community to the location of the famed Roswell UFO incident—debris from the apparent space ship was found on a ranch near Corona.

El Paso literal: the pass, as in passage through a difficult terrain; during the era of Spanish and Mexican rule, the city of El Paso, Tex., was an important stop along the *Camino Real* (Royal Highway) from Mexico City to Santa Fe.

El Rito literal: the stream; name of a town in Northern New Mexico.

Española literal: Spanish; town north of Santa Fe settled soon after the Spanish arrived in New Mexico.

Estancia literal: landed estate; vernaculur: describes large agricultural properties and usually translated as *ranch*.

Jémez: the name the early Spaniards gave both the northern New Mexico mountain range in which the atomic bomb later was created, and the Walatowa Indian tribe, many of whom still live at its pueblo, known as Jemez Pueblo.

La Fonda literal: the inn; famous hotel still in existence at the geographical end of the Old Santa Fe Trail, which began in Independence, Missouri, and terminated at the Santa Fe Plaza.

La Villa Real de la Santa Fe de San Francisco de Asís literal: The Royal Municipality of the Holy Faith of St. Francis of Assisi—a *villa real* was land allowed by Spain to be the personal property of the King of Spain; today everyone just calls the now-famous town *Santa Fe.*

Las Cruces literal: the crosses; town in southern New Mexico.

Las Vegas literal: the meadows; town in northern New Mexico.

Las Tusas literal: prairie dogs; tiny village near Sapelló named by the Spanish for the abundance of those particular rodents in the area.

Mora literal: choke cherry; northern New Mexico town founded by Spaniards and named for the abundant choke cherry bushes they found in the Mora Valley.

Plaza or plaza literal: town square; vernacular: descriptive term, and/or the proper name of an important area in a town.

Pueblo or pueblo literal: community; the name and description the early Spaniards gave the Indian tribes and villages that practiced *kiva* culture—societies based around circular underground clan lodges, often made of stonework.

Río Grande literal: big river; in Mexico, it is called *Río Bravo*, meaning wild or spirited river.

Rio Rancho literal: *ranch river*, but grammatically incorrect, as though the people who chose this for the name of the New Mexico town were not fluent nor literate in Spanish; proper Spanish could have been Ranchos del Rio or Los Ranchos del Rio Grande; the community is located northwest of Albuquerque, where it began a few years after WWII as vacant lots on a dry, windswept mesa seemingly out in the middle of nowhere, sold sight unseen to trusting people in states mostly along the East Coast; eventually an East Coast developer did build a town that remains the core of the city, now on national lists as one of the most desirable retirement communities in the nation, one of the safest towns in New Mexico and the third largest city in the state, surpassing even Santa Fe, 45 minutes away by car.

San Antonio: the Spanish name for the Catholic's St. Anthony, and the name of more than one New Mexico village in various stages of existence today.

San Ysidro literal: St. Isidore, *the farmer*, one of Spain's five Catholic saints; name of an old Spanish village near Jemez Pueblo.

Sandía literal: watermelon: the name Spanish explorers gave the mountain range that towers over Albuquerque on its northeast side, because of the colors the mountain's rocky western slopes often reflect at sunset.

Santuario de Guadalupe literal: Sanctuary of (the Blessed Virgin of) Guadalupe; name of a church in Santa Fe commemorating the reported miraculous visitation of Mary, the mother of Jesus, to Mexican peasant Juan Diego in 1531; the Spanish word *guad* is based on the Arabic word *wadi*, which means water source in a dry area.

Trinidad literal: (Holy) Trinity; name of town in southern Colorado near the New Mexico border founded by Anglos in the 19th century.

Spanish Words of Native American Origin

Abiquiú: Indian word Spanish used to name a town located on the Río Chama that was the starting point of the original Santa Fe Trail, begun there in 1829.

avocado: the Spanish spelling and pronunciation of the Aztec word *ahuacatl*, meaning testical.

chile: correct Spanish spelling of the Indian word that often is misspelled in Spanish and English as *chili*; New Mexico varieties have become famous worldwide.

Chimayó: originally an Indian village north of Santa Fe—when taken over by the Spanish, they kept the Indian name; also name of some heritage varieties of New Mexico chile peppers grown in the Chimayó area that many New Mexican gourmands consider the best in the state, especially the red peppers.

coyote: the Spanish spelling and pronunciation of the Aztec word *coyotl.*

New Mexico: the name *México* is the Spanish word derived from *Mexica,* the Nahuatl-speaking peoples who founded the Aztec Empire and gave what now is Mexico City its name; in naming New Mexico, a much bigger region than the present state, the Spanish had hoped Nuevo (new) Mexico would be a source of treasure rivalling that of Mexico City; some modern researchers, especially linguists, believe the Aztecs are native to New Mexico, and whether that is true or not, the Spanish spoken in New Mexico has many Aztec-derived words; everyone seems to agree the Aztecs migrated to the Valley of Mexico from northwestern Mexico or the American Southwest.

Sapelló: the Spanish kept the original Indian name of this small community between Las Vegas and Mora.

Tesuque: the Spanish spelling and pronunciation of the Tewa Indian name, *Te Tesugeh Oweengeh,* meaning the village of the narrow place of the cottonwood trees, and the name of both the Indian pueblo and the village founded by the Spanish north of Santa Fe.

New Mexico Cuisine

biscochito: small sugar cookie made with cinnamon, anise and red wine especially popular at Christmas among New Mexico Hispanics, among whom the recipe apparently originated; also spelled *bizcochito.*

chiles rellenos literal: stuffed chile peppers; a staple dish in New Mexico cuisine.

Christmas: customers at local restaurants usually are asked if they want red chile or green chile when ordering New Mexico cuisine; the customers may say red, green, or *Christmas,* meaning both red and green.

Dos Equis literal: double letter *x,* as in *xx;* name of a brand of beer made in Mexico since the 19th century.

guacamole: served as a dip or a salad, it is made with fresh mashed raw avocado and various other ingredients, and every family cook, and every restaurant, has its own version—no two taste exactly alike.

margarita literal: dear Margaret, *dear* used here as a term of endearment, as in *my dear*; name of popular tequila-based cocktail.

piñon: Spanish name for a New Mexico conifer that is the New Mexico state tree and source of the tree's famed aromatic firewood that perfumes the state on cold nights when fireplaces are burning; its pine nuts are a New Mexico delicacy, commonly referred to among most New Mexicans as piñon nuts.

salsa literal: sauce; a tomato and chile-based sauce made with fresh raw ingredients, served with tortilla chips as an appetizer and eaten as a dip; commercial cooked versions have become big sellers in the last few decades, bottled and shipped everywhere.

tortillas literal: little cakes; a type of bread the Spanish learned to make from the Indians in the Americas after introducing wheat to the New World.

ReaDers Guide

Proloque and Chapter 1

1. Using the process of free association, does the word Jemez in the Jemez River name bring to mind anything in relation to the Catholic Church?

2. Does the introduction to Father Marquez make him seem evil or saintly, neither or both? Why?

3. Does Father Marquez seem to be connected to the mysterious event in the middle of the night on the bridge? Does La Llorona, the ghostly witch whom he feels haunts him?

4. How does Father Marquez seem to fall into stereotypes of Catholic priests, or does he? If not, why not?

5. Try to imagine what explorers looking for the lush Florida coast would have thought and felt when they ended up on the Texas coast near present-day Galveston.

6. Then continue trying to identify with those early explorers as they worked their way up to what now is New Mexico through southeast, central and west Texas, lost, having no idea where they were, probably continuing to look for Florida, hoping against hope to find it.

7. What would they have eaten on the long trek from Galveston's coastal fishing to New Mexico's desert wildlife? Where would they have found water after they left central Texas?

8. What state of mind would the Spanish have had by the time they arrived in what is now southern New Mexico? How would their loyalty to their Catholic faith have sustained them psychologically and spiritually? And what if it didn't, at least for some?

9. Do witches play much of a role historically and traditionally in Catholicism, the way saints, miracles and Mother Mary do, along with the Devil and evil spirits that must be exorcised?

10. Is Zorro a supernatural figure in American culture, or a fictional one created through literature, television and film? Could Mrs. Shaw have been seeing the ghost of an actual Zorro who lived on earth, or only someone dressed in a Zorro costume like an actor or a Halloween trick or treater would?

Chapter 2

1. Is La Llorona a supernatural figure in Hispanic culture internationally, or merely a mythological one?

2. Either way, what would a healthy maternal reaction be to a son who liked to emulate La Llorona?

3. How would a mother know he was emulating La Llorona if he didn't tell her, since the costume he would probably create for himself also would closely resemble a Halloween witch, complete with wig but minus the hat?

4. How did his childhood friends know he was emulating her, or did they assume he was?

5. Did the Mora priest's childhood friends over-react to his behavior as a child, giving him a reputation that was not deserved?

6. Did his mother under-react to his behavior?

7. Should Connie be judged for not coming out as a lesbian while her grandmother was alive and her children were young?

8. Or should Connie be commended for saving her grandmother from possible trauma?

9. Was Connie right to assume her grandmother would not have understood?

10. Imagine that Connie had told her grandmother, and not only did the old woman understand, but even confided some of her own longings for, and love of, women when she was young.

11. Did Connie miss an opportunity for a deeper level of connection with her beloved grandmother by not being truthful with her in the name of being protective?

12 Should Connie have taken the risk of telling her grandmother?

Chapter 3

1. Are men who choose to go into the priesthood different in this era than they were even 100 years ago?

2. What could the priesthood have provided men who didn't fit into traditional culture in earlier eras?

3. What could the priesthood provide contemporary men who don't fit into modern culture comfortably?

4. Do the differences between then and now appear glaring, or only minor?

5. Is cross-dressing a harmless leisure pursuit, or indicative of something more sinister?

6. Does it seem logical that choosing a profession that requires men to wear long robes, which some consider dressing like women, is a way for those who have conflicts about their gender identity as well as their sexuality to perhaps find a way to live more comfortably with themselves?

7. Does any of this have anything to do with pedophilia? In what ways, if any?

8. Men and women who are actors, be it on stage or on film, or both, often enjoy dressing dramatically when not working in specific roles. They like being flamboyant in their personal fashion style. Does that make them cross-dressers, transvestites, gays or pedophiles? Or simply artistic and creative?

9. Is it appropriate for the retired detective to assume a child who dresses up like a mythological woman considered to be evil is defective?

10. And why would that make it possible if not probable that he became a pedophile and a murderer?

11. Is the detective jumping to conclusions, or simply using common sense within the context of his childhood and professional culture?

12. During the Salem Witch Trial era, many people became caught up in a mass frenzy that ended in the conviction of young women for the practice of witchcraft. Is it possible all the sightings people claim to be of La Llorona in Santa Fe and other parts of New Mexico, as well as much of the world where Hispanic culture is strong, are the result of a mass delusion and/or hysteria—a crowd mentality in some sense of that label?

13. Does the fact these sightings have been reported for centuries and aren't happening all at once, like they did in Salem, which was over a relatively short period of time among a specific community group, make them more valid?

14. Does a priest known to have the gift of a seer, a psychic, seem strange, even shocking, or something one would expect of many priests?

15. Is Father Marquez therefore more unusual among his fellow priests, or probably more normal?

Chapter 4

1. Does Father Sanchez act like he is guilty of either murder?

2. Does his behavior lead the reader to think he should be the main suspect, at least so far? Why or why not?

3. Does his apparent transparency about his childhood—dressing like a woman, a dead one, and a ghost, at that—make him more human and his denial of guilt more credible, or less?

4. Does he come across as a smooth liar, or a sincere man falsely suspected the first time and now, most likely, this time?

5. Is it easy or challenging to have compassion for him?

6. As an adult priest, does his matter-of-fact attitude toward La Llorona seem realistic for the community he serves?

7. Does Sister Rosalie seem to be the real thing—an old, mean nun, the kind children have hated for centuries? Or is she making herself into a caricature of the traditional cold, even cruel, Catholic sister, to hide her true self behind that persona?

8. If so, what might her true self be—a bad person capable of doing bad deeds, or someone driven out of extreme loyalty to protect the Church and everyone associated with it, especially Father Sanchez because she works so closely with him, and her brother, Father Marquez?

9. Dolly thinks she is being stonewalled by Father Marquez and Sister Rosalie, but is she? Isn't their behavior in the interviews what one would expect from people in their positions within the Church? So why would Dolly draw her conclusion?

10. Dolly isn't Catholic nor Hispanic. Might this cause her to misread the priest and the nun, or allow her to be more objective?

Chapter 5

1. Is it possible for La Llorona, as Father Marquez perceives her, to serve as a symbol of the worldwide troubles unleashed from the Jemez Mountains that he describes in his reminiscing of what began there in the 1940s?

2. If she is some sort of symbol, in what way, given her personal mythology? Can it intersect somehow with the historical reality of the atom bomb and untreatable pedophile priests?

3. Could this explain why Father Marquez sees her as both a good spirit and a bad one? She killed children and provides omens for the deaths of others, but she also cares for children?

4. Could a ghostly spirit like La Llorona be working out her own redemption for her wicked deeds against her own children, assuming she is real, since Father Marquez obviously believes she is?

5. Could his experiences with her simply be a sign of his own lifelong mental illness? If so, why, and if not, why not?

6. La Llorona's children were not twins, only siblings close in age. Could the Manhattan Project and the retreat center for priests at Jemez Springs be symbolized by her children, and if so, in what ways?

7. How has La Llorona's children's murder caused her story and theirs to diverge from the narratives presented by the atom bomb and the retreat center in Jemez Springs?

8. If the children's murder meant the end of their story, how can the myth around them and their mother that has lived on for an unknown and undocumented amount of time still be so alive in Hispanic culture worldwide today?

9. Is her story somehow integrated with the Evil Twins of the Jemez Mountains, as Father Marquez labels them?

10. Has she perhaps chosen to intertwine her story with them?

11. Or is the integration coincidental or even non-existent except in Father Marquez's psyche?

Chapter 6

1. The Sun Belt, which could be described as an overlay onto the traditional and historical Bible Belt, is said to have begun growing dramatically in population with the advent of air conditioning. Try to imagine the shock to Dolly's mother when she was taken as a bride from the temperate climate of the San Juan Valley in the Farmington area to the flat hot Great Plains of Lubbock in late June. With no air conditioning and no previous visits to prepare her for what it would be like.

2. Imagine how those early Spaniards must have felt when they traveled north from Mexico, often through Texas, into New Mexico on horseback, with horse-drawn and ox-drawn carts, and on foot. Does it make their eventual choice of the Santa Fe area as the state capital make more sense, knowing from whence they had traveled and the hardships and discomfort they had faced in order to get to northern New Mexico?

3. Did Dolly have an hallucination, or did her imagination merely go a bit wild when the owl hooted and then, apparently, whished by her?

4. Is the manner in which she experienced the owl, or as she believes, La Llorona, relatively normal in certain cultures worldwide, including Native American?

5. Could it be a normal expectation of a Catholic priest to have supernatural experiences, given the Church's long history of miracles, saints, exorcisms and demons?

6. So why has Father Marquez apparently felt the need to keep his experiences secret, and for his sister, a nun, to question his very sanity?

7. Is it possible the Santa Fe police force is unlike any other in the United States, given its eccentric and diverse community, the many ghost legends and apparent real-life experiences with at least some of those ghosts, and UFO stories and experiences?

8. Dolly and Father Marquez are not young, although he is quite a bit older than she. His experiences with La Llorona began when he was a child, he says, and Dolly's with ghosts when she was in her mid 20s. Does this give more credence to anything along these lines they might experience in the present and future, since they have had lifelong experience with this sort of thing?

9. Many older people with dementia claim to have similar experiences, who apparently did not before the dementia. Schizophrenics often claim to have such experiences when young, and if properly medicated, those disappear as they get older and more balanced through modern medicine. What makes Dolly and Father Marquez different from schizophrenic young people and demented older people, or are they?

Chapter 7

1. The laws and ethics protecting confessions to a priest always have been controversial in American Protestant-dominated culture, and remain so today. Why?

2. How does the confessional experience compare to patient-therapist confidentiality in the secular world? Is it right that they both seem to have the same legal protections, or do they?

3. What are some of the foods and condiments the early European explorers found in the New World and brought back to Europe that Father Marquez did not mention in his list? It is important to remember the Spanish settled Florida and the American Southwest about the same time when making such a list.

4. Make three lists giving reasons why the murderer could or could not be Father Marquez, Sister Rosalie or Father Sanchez.

5. Father Marquez thinks his sister is a bit crazy, and she thinks he is. Who seems to be correct at this point? Either or neither? Or are they both?

6. Is it possible Sister Rosalie is making up the stories she tells her brother about Father Sanchez dressing the boys in girls' clothing?

7. If she is telling the truth about the incidents, what do they reveal about Father Sanchez? Legally, spiritually, emotionally, psychologically?

8. If neither the two priests nor Sister Rosalie are the killers, who might be?

9. And if those three are not lying to each other about the murders, what motive could drive such a killer?

10. Should Father Marquez and Sister Rosalie confront Father Sanchez about the incidents she witnessed?

11. What repercussions could be created if one or the other, or both of them, do confront him?

12. Did she break any laws, Catholic policies or codes of ethics by not reporting the incidents to anyone? Why are she and her brother not discussing this aspect of the situation?

Chapter 9

1. Do the La Llorona connections to the case, as Dolly and Connie summarize them over lunch, seem like coincidences or a form of synchronicity? Does the answer depend on whether or not one believes in otherworldly beings and their involvement with humans?

2. If all the otherworldly aspects of the story are removed, what hard facts remain for the police to use?

3. Is Dolly's role helpful so far, or is she taking the investigation in superfluous and ineffective directions and if so, why?

4. How many plants grown in Santa Fe, for personal or business reasons, including the massive amount of herbs cultivated there, could be considered poisonous for humans and/or animals? Name some. Does this mean Sister Rosalie's greenhouse collection is not especially unusual?

Chapter 10

1. What can be expected from a tour of the basilica when it is closed to the public at night? What answers may be found, and how, where?